Ransom for a Holiday

By Fred Hunter

The Jeremy Ransom/Emily Charters series:

Presence of Mind
Ransom for Our Sins
Ransom for an Angel
Ransom for a Holiday

The Alex Reynolds series:

Government Gay

St. Martin's Press
New York

Ransom for a Holiday

Holiday

Fred Hunter

Design by Bryanna Millis

Library of Congress Cataloging-in-Publication Data

Hunter, Fred.
    Ransom for a holiday: a Jeremy Ransom/Emily Char-
ters mystery /
    Fred Hunter.
        p. cm.
    ISBN 0-312-16976-0
    1. Charters, Emily (Fictitious character)—Fiction.
I. Title.
    PS3558.U476R29   1997
    813'.54—dc21   97-25226
                                         CIP

First Edition: December 1997

10 9 8 7 6 5 4 3 2 1

For Barbara Hopper

Ransom for a Holiday

Prologue

Nathan Bartlett hadn't thought of boots, or gloves, or even his coat, though the temperature was below twenty, and the snow was almost a foot deep, and the barn was over two hundred yards from the house. He hadn't even thought to bring the flashlight, though he realized it would have done little more than illuminate the falling snow. As he'd stolen out into the night, all he'd been able to think about was the welfare of his sister.

He bent forward into the strong wind that blew the wet, heavy snow into his face, stinging his eyes and blinding him further. After trudging on in this fashion for a few minutes, he stopped and turned his back to the wind in an effort to quell the rising confusion caused by the driving storm that buffeted him. The thought of the recent discovery he'd made performed the same service on him mentally. He hoped that all his questions would be cleared up when he reached the barn. He hoped the situation was not as dire as he believed.

Looking back in the direction from which he'd come, the house was barely visible. They had no guests this weekend, so the two-story building stood like a darkened mass looming in the background, further obscured by the gauzelike curtain of snow. The only light visible was a dim glow from the front parlor reflecting off the snow. His sister was probably still sitting in there reading. Nathan hadn't told her where he was going or even that he was going out at all. He had slipped, as quietly as possible, out the back door. As he watched, a gust of wind swept across the light, causing a momentary rift in the sheet of white. Nathan blinked at the gravel driveway that ran along the side of the house. Though the parlor light didn't provide enough illumination to be sure of anything, he could have sworn that there was only one car in the drive when there should have been two. He sighed and thought, with some dismay, that the person that he was meeting must be late, and that he'd be forced to wait in the cold barn, which was something he hadn't counted on.

Nathan took a deep breath and turned back into the wind, throwing his left arm across his brow in an effort to shield his eyes. There was nothing to guide him: no lights coming from the barn itself, and no lights in the apartment above it, leaving the barn discernible only as a slight interruption in the snowfall. The wind whipped around the sides of the building, causing the snow to swirl sideways around it and making the huge wooden structure look like little more than an eddy in the eye of a storm.

It wasn't until he was upon it that the building itself became apparent. The bright red paint looked black in the night. He stopped for a moment, hugging himself against the cold before retreating into the barn, and listened for signs of life. He couldn't hear any human movement, only the steady howl of the wind and the occasional creak of wood as the barn protested against its treatment. Finally, Nathan shivered and grabbed the handle of the door. With one strong pull, he slid the door open.

He stood in the doorway for a moment. The stillness within the barn made the darkness seem even more deep, and he spared himself a nervous laugh at the idea of different shades of dark. He reached for the switch mounted just to the right of the door and flipped it, but the expected light failed to materialize. He repeated the motion several times, but nothing happened. He thought for a moment that perhaps they'd had a power failure during his short trek from the house to the barn. He glanced back toward the house, but the snow was falling so thickly now that it was a wasted effort. Even if the light was still on, he'd be unable to see it.

He turned back to the interior of the barn and took a tentative step inside.

"Hello? Are you here?" he called into the blackness.

His voice rang in the emptiness like the last vibrations from a muffled bell. He waited for a moment, then called again, "Hello? Are you here?"

He was met with a silence so defiant that Nathan almost jumped out of his skin when, after a lengthy pause, a voice returned from the darkness, "I'm here."

"The lights have gone out."

"Only in here."

Nathan could feel his brow furrowing. He looked from left to right, peering into the darkness and trying to discern from which direction the voice was coming. After a long pause, during which he wasn't quite sure what they were waiting for, Nathan said, "Well?"

"You were the one who wanted to see me." The voice stopped, then after a moment added with a slight laugh, "I don't know why you couldn't have waited for better weather."

"I don't expect you to still be around when the weather's better," Nathan replied. He paused for a moment, then put his right hand on his hip, and said, "I know who you are."

"I figured that much."

"And I want to know what you're doing here."

"Did you tell your sister you were meeting me?"

Nathan sighed. "I didn't tell Sara anything about anything."

"You didn't tell her who I am?"

"I didn't want to tell her until I found out what the hell you're doing here. I don't want her to be hurt."

"I don't want to hurt Sara."

"But that's exactly what you're going to do, isn't it? That's the only reason I can think of that you would come here. If you weren't up to something, then why the hell pretend to be somebody you're not? Why didn't you just tell us who you were to begin with?"

"That wouldn't have served my purpose."

There was a slight movement in the darkness, as if the person to whom the voice belonged was shifting to a more comfortable position.

Nathan breathed deeply. "And what would your purpose be?"

No response came from the darkness.

"Answer me!"

Nathan could hear movement again: the sound of shoes crunching on the ground, and a small *tink,* as if a can of some sort had been set down. After a brief pause, there was a click, and Nathan was instantly blinded by the bright light of a high-powered flashlight. He threw his hands up over his eyes.

"Jesus! Switch that damn thing off or get it out of my eyes!"

"You want to know what I'm up to?" the voice demanded with a sneer.

Nathan was angry now. He had discovered the identity of the masquerader on his own, and, despite the cold and wet and the dazzling light, he knew he had the upper hand in the situation and took exception to the tone of voice with which he was being addressed.

"I know what you want," Nathan said, his voice dripping with disdain. "It's the money, isn't it? Of course. You're after my sister's money."

There was a loud "Huh," from behind the light, as if the owner of the voice was greatly amused. The slightest beat went by before the reply came.

"No. I'm after yours. Catch!"

Without warning the light came hurtling toward Nathan, just above his head. Instinctively his hands flew up to catch it. As the light swirled around the room, the figure advanced on the unsuspecting brother, appearing to come forward in quick jerks like a dancer in a strobe light. Nathan caught the flashlight and fumbled to swing it around, sweeping the light across the tines of a pitchfork just before they plunged into his chest.

His scream was abbreviated by the suddenness of the attack and the deadly accuracy with which one of the tines was driven through his heart. Whatever was left of the sound he made was smothered by the blanket of snow that continued to fall unabated, as if its only purpose was to deaden the end of a life.

"The arrangements have all been made," said Lynn Francis as she came into the kitchen. She was carrying a sturdy Samsonite suitcase, light blue in color, which belonged to Emily Charters, the elderly mistress of the house. "Sara has made arrangements for Emily to have a room on the ground floor, so she won't be climbing up and down stairs. And you'll have one of the usual guest rooms on the second floor."

Jeremy Ransom was sitting with his elbows resting on top of the small kitchen table. His blond hair, which he'd cut very short for the summer, had now grown out to a businesslike length, which had the unfortunate side effect of making the increasing gray more prominent. On occasion, when he spent a little too much time scrutinizing it in the mirror, he'd hear a creaking, ancient voice in the back of his mind singing the phrase, "silver threads among the gold." He could only shake the words out of his head and dispel any misgivings by reminding himself that he was still just on the brink forty. He rose when Lynn entered the room.

"I'll take that."

"She'll still be a couple of minutes," Lynn replied, motioning for him to sit back down. She went to the sink and started to fill it to wash the breakfast dishes. "You know, she protests about the whole thing, but she really is excited about going away, I think."

Ransom smiled. In the short time he'd known Emily, he'd come to greatly admire her. She was sharp as a tack, with a keen eye and a shrewd mind that could put information together with an alacrity that Ransom found almost astonishing. She had demonstrated this time and time again over the past year, proving instrumental in solving one case of murder and offering insights into others as Ransom plied his chosen profession as a homicide detective for the Chicago Police Department. But even though she was never reluctant to share her views on the professional matters at hand, she still maintained a natural reticence when it came to personal matters that Ransom found very appealing. As a confirmed loner, Ransom regarded with abhorrence the idea of anyone intruding into the sanctuary his life had become, and, as a result, he had kept his life private from everyone. One of the main reasons that a filial warmth had developed between Ransom and Emily, and that he'd unofficially adopted her as his grandmother, was the tacit agreement between the pair that love existed but was never to be spoken of.

"Do you think I'm doing the right thing, taking her away?" said Ransom with an uncharacteristic touch of self-doubt.

Lynn glanced at him and smiled. She found it agreeable but somehow a little disheartening to find the normally overconfident detective a bit unsure of himself.

"A change of scene might be good for her," she said, flipping her tawny hair back off her shoulder by way of punctuation. Then she added with only a hint of coyness, "It's good for everyone."

"She's doing too much."

"How much is too much?"

"It's only been a couple of months since her bypass. She should be resting."

"Emily's not the type of person to take life lying down."

Ransom's expression displayed the fact that he wasn't pleased. He'd been shaken by Emily's near miss with death, not only at the thought of losing her but at the thought that, after all of his years of independence, he'd allowed someone into his life only to find his foundation deeply shaken. And the fact that he was now capable of being so shaken, shook him even further.

"That doesn't mean she doesn't have to take care of herself," he said at last.

Lynn glanced at him again. She pursed one side of her mouth and said, "I know it doesn't. And you're probably right. But you know Emily."

"Yes," Ransom replied wryly, "she's not going to rest unless I get her off by herself."

"Is that so?" said Emily with a twinkle in her eye. She'd appeared so quietly in the doorway that Lynn almost dropped the dish she'd been wiping. Ransom immediately rose and gave Emily his seat, holding her hand as she lowered herself onto the chair.

Lynn cocked her head sideways at the old woman and smiled. "You know it's true. Your friend here has me come in to clean for you twice a week, and still I find you've been doing housework when I'm not around."

"Things have to be done."

Lynn folded her arms across her chest. "I could take it as an insult, you know. Don't you think I do a good enough job?"

Emily's forehead, already wrinkled with age, creased with concern. "Of course you do, my dear. And I appreciate the two of you wanting to take care of me, but dust does settle all the time and one does need a reason to live."

Ransom laughed. "Emily, if dust is giving you a reason to live then I can't get you out of town soon enough."

Emily sighed wistfully. "I wasn't meant to be idle. I *enjoy* doing things."

"I know you do," Ransom replied more seriously, "and you

can do as much as you want once you've fully recovered. But as long as you're here at home I can't get you to do that, so maybe a little holiday, somewhere where you'll be waited on, will help."

Emily's shoulders elevated slightly in what, for her, passed for a shrug. Despite her protests, there was a gleam in her eye that showed Ransom she was looking forward to the trip. Maybe a little more than he thought was healthy for her. He shook his head again at his own folly. In his present state of anxiety, Emily couldn't win: If she was reluctant to go, he was worried, and if she was anxious to go, he was worried. He tried to put these thoughts aside.

"You'll have a wonderful time, Emily," said Lynn as she resumed washing the dishes. "My friend Sara has a nice room for you on the main floor of her bed-and-breakfast, so you'll only have to go up an incline to get into the place. And, even though they usually only serve breakfast, she's also planned to serve all your meals so you don't have to worry about going out for them."

"She sounds very accommodating."

"She's a really nice woman, and a good friend."

"How do you know her?"

"She used to work for the same company that I did, before I started doing for the likes of you," Lynn replied, giving a playful flip of the dishcloth in Emily's direction. Lynn Francis had once been the right-hand woman to the CEO of Harris Assurance, and had given up her exalted position to become what she cheerfully referred to as "charwoman to the rich and famous." She had chosen this path because it made her, to a great extent, master of her own time. Time had become one of the most important things in Lynn's life since her lover had become terminally ill. The freedom her chosen profession afforded her allowed her to take care of her lover at home. "Sara's mother died a while back and she used her inheritance to do what she'd always wanted to do, buy a B and B. I guess the two of us were just nice, simple girls at heart who happened to get snagged up in the corporate world. It was a great relief to get out."

Emily smiled knowingly at the young woman. "I believe there's a lot more to it than that."

"So, anyway," said Lynn, shying away from the hint of praise, "everything is taken care of and there's nothing for you to worry about—your room, your meals, everything. I'll be stopping in here every day for the week and checking on Tam, just as I promised."

As if in response to her name, the large, bottom-heavy calico shifted in her basket beside the stove, raising a pair of sleepy green eyes to her mistress. Tam was completely white except for a perfect circle on the top of her head that was half orange and half black. She'd been named for this circle, which made her look as if she were wearing a small hat.

"Well," said Emily with a dramatically resigned sigh, "I feel as if I'm being commandeered."

"Don't think you aren't," said Ransom.

"You'll love it," said Lynn with casual enthusiasm, "LeFavre is a pretty little town, and there's hardly anyone around at this time of year."

"But are you sure we won't be inconveniencing your friend? Most people like to spend Christmas alone with their families."

"I think Sara will be happy to have the company. Both her parents are gone."

"She was an only child?" Emily asked, raising an eyebrow.

Lynn glanced at Ransom. "Um . . . no, she had a brother. She lost him two years ago."

Emily clucked her tongue. "That's a shame."

"She hasn't had the house open to guests since that, so this'll be good for her, too. The two of you will be sort of a maiden voyage for her, getting her back in the swing of things. It'll do her good."

"It sounds to me," said Emily with a renewed twinkle in her eyes, "that you may have missed your calling."

Lynn stopped in her tracks and blushed attractively. "I don't know what you mean."

Emily smiled at her benignantly, and replied, "Of course you do!"

"It's time for us to be on our way," said Ransom with a glance at his watch.

He picked up Emily's suitcase as Lynn helped her on with her navy blue coat, lined with wool for extra warmth during the winter. Emily then covered her voluminous gray hair, that she kept piled in a bun at the back of her head, with a light blue knit hat. Ransom could never resist mentally noting thankfully that Emily's hat was devoid of the shiny little plastic dangles that he believed to be in favor with elderly women.

Emily and Lynn waited on the front porch while Ransom ran down to the car and stowed her suitcase in the trunk alongside his. During his brief absence, Emily turned to Lynn, and said, "Will you be all right over Christmas?"

"Sure I will," said Lynn, "Maggie's out of the hospital and back home, even though it may not be for long."

"She's home? My goodness! I thought she had tuberculosis."

Lynn wrinkled her nose. "So did her doctors. But it was a false positive. That happens too often with people with AIDS." Lynn stopped for a moment and sighed, as if remembering the relief she'd felt on first hearing the news. "We know something will get her one of these days, but at least it looks like we'll have another Christmas."

Emily's fingers gently tightened on Lynn's arm. Lynn smiled in return.

"So, I'll be fine," Lynn said brightly, "you just go and have a good time."

"I do appreciate you making the arrangements for us. Like most people my age, I don't go away very often. I don't really like to."

Lynn shot her a curious glance. "Then why are you doing it now? Did we really push you that much?"

"Oh, no, not at all," said the old woman. "No. But Jeremy has been very distressed, and I really think he needs a rest. It'll be good for him."

Lynn's eyes opened wide. "You mean you're going away for a week because *he* needs a rest?"

Emily leaned toward her, and said confidentially, "Well, you know, my dear, I don't think he's ever had one."

Ransom returned and offered Emily his arm, carefully leading her down the steps and along the walk. The air was crisp and fresh, and there'd been enough new snow overnight to at least temporarily cover the grimy slush that is a staple of Chicago winters. Once Emily was safely secured in the seat belt on the passenger side, Ransom climbed behind the wheel.

Tam had silently stolen onto the porch and brushed up against Lynn's leg. Lynn reached down and picked up the cat, which then rested in her arms as she watched Ransom and Emily drive away. Tam even suffered her right paw to be waved in the direction of her retreating mistress, though the look she gave Lynn afterward clearly indicated she doubted the sanity of the woman in whose care she'd been left.

Ransom turned on the radio, which he kept tuned to one of the two local classical stations, but found to his dismay that they were devoting an hour to Mozart. He could never understand why so many people found Mozart so soothing while the frenetic nature of his works only served to jangle Ransom's nerves. He felt sure that a steady diet of Mozart while he was behind the wheel would eventually cause an accident. He quickly switched to the second station.

They'd left late enough in the morning to miss the brunt of the rush hour, but traffic was still heavy enough that it took over forty-five minutes for them to pass the Loop, reach the Skyway, and get beyond city limits. As they passed through the center of the city, Ransom marveled anew at how, even with a layer of clean snow, as well as clear skies and a bright sun, Chicago could still manage to look dingy. But even that dinginess was somehow endearing. The city had formed his hearth and home for almost four decades now, and though he had, on occasion, vacationed away from it, he had never gone away without a pang of regret.

As they approached the city's border he found himself already entertaining the yearnings of a frequent traveler who longs for the comforts of home the minute he's away. He tightened his grip on the steering wheel, reminding himself of the importance he felt this trip had to Emily's health. A quick glance at her showed him that he'd been right in his estimation. Merely being outward bound seemed to have added more spark to her weary countenance.

Emily sat quietly by his side, her eyes moving back and forth, taking in her surroundings as if she were seeing them for the first time. Ransom had long since ceased to be surprised that Emily could find so much of interest at a time of life when he would have thought she'd seen it all. But Emily had once told him that her philosophy of life could be summed up very simply: only dull people find the world dull.

They descended the Skyway onto I-94, leaving Chicago behind for the brief stint through Indiana before reaching Michigan. The chaos of the city gave way to rolling drifts of snow, which, after a while, lulled Emily to sleep. It wasn't long before Ransom realized that, rather than relaxing in this serene setting, his grip had tightened on the steering wheel. He could feel the tension in his shoulders radiating up his neck and down his back. He took a deep breath, released it slowly, and found to his amazement that his jaw was beginning to unclench. He wasn't surprised by the action so much as by the fact that he hadn't known he'd been clenching it, and wondered if he'd been holding it that way only for a matter of hours, or if it had been that way for years. He smiled at himself.

He settled back against the seat and flexed his hands a couple of times on the steering wheel, making a brave attempt to get in the spirit of things. A calm, rational voice inside his head told him that he'd become too set in his ways, that if the prospect of a few days away from home would cause him further anxiety, then it had been much too long since he'd been away. But the conscious part of his mind wondered just how hard a week of peace and quiet would be on his nerves.

Sara Bartlett sat distractedly over a mug of coffee at the table that occupied one corner of the kitchen. The table was made of oak with the legs painted white and the surface dark green, which apparently was all that was needed for it to be certified a "country table" in the catalogue from which she'd purchased it. She'd had the kitchen completely redone with modern appliances, large and dependable enough to provide for the needs of ten guests, the maximum for whom Hawthorne House could provide at any given time. She'd retained the latticework cabinets that hung at eye level across two entire walls, although she'd had them stripped, sanded, and painted white. Yellow curtains with white lace trim covered the windows over the sink and on the two doors, one to the backyard and the other to the driveway.

Though Sara was barely thirty years old, the cares of the past two years had taken their toll: tiny, downward-sloping lines marked the corners of her mouth, making her look as if she were slightly frowning when she was displaying no particular emotion at all. Likewise, the corners of her eyes were marked by barely visible crow's feet which, at a short distance, looked almost like tears. She had dark, wavy, shoulder-length hair, and light blue eyes that would have been considered lovely had they not been dulled by circumstance.

Millie Havers, the middle-aged woman who worked mornings for Sara preparing home-made muffins for the guests and performing the general cleaning duties, stood at the sink finishing the last of the breakfast dishes. Though the kitchen appliances included a good-sized dishwasher, without guests there were hardly ever enough dishes to warrant using it. Sara had kept Millie on while the house was closed to guests more out of a need for company than a need for help. She'd recognized very early on that, left to herself in the large, isolated house, she would have gone mad. And there was always enough work to be done in a place the size of Hawthorne House. Millie never openly questioned Sara's decision to keep her on, hoping that the young woman, of whom she'd grown quite fond, would eventually be able to reopen the house and move on with her life. She was more than pleased that that day seemed to have arrived.

"It'll be nice for you to have a tree up again," said Millie, thinking it best to rescue Sara from her thoughts with some everyday conversation.

"I guess," Sara replied, lifting the mug to her lips and taking a sip.

"It's best," Millie pursued in her matter-of-fact way, "best to get things back to normal. It's been a long time."

"I've been planning to reopen for some time," Sara said halfheartedly, "I just never got around to it."

"Oh, I know that. It's good you're doing it now."

Sara laughed ruefully. "I don't think I'd be doing it now if my friend Lynn hadn't been so insistent. She asked me to have them—at the going rate, of course—because they need to get away. The elderly woman has been ill and can't travel very far."

"That's not all I meant, though," said Millie. "It's best to get back to recognizing the seasons and letting everything kind of . . . I don't know, kind of go on the way it should."

Sara didn't look at the woman. She liked Millie and saw her as something of a mother figure, more from Millie's matronly manner than from the fifteen-year difference in their ages. But although Millie was pretty wise and was usually right, Sara didn't believe that anyone could understand what she'd gone through.

"Well . . ." Sara said slowly, setting the mug on the table but keeping her hands around it as if needing the warmth, "well, you know that Nathan was . . . Nathan died just before Christmas."

"Two years ago," Millie assented quickly, trying to hurry Sara past this.

"That first Christmas I was just in shock. I don't think I even knew . . . that I was aware of the day. Then last Christmas . . . the second . . . was worse—because I wasn't in shock anymore."

"I know."

Sara sighed and smiled at the woman. "So now you might get your wish."

Millie frowned and brushed a stray strand of gray back from her forehead. "What do you mean?"

"This year I can feel life going on, I think. I don't like it, but I know it's happening. And you're right, it's probably for the best."

Millie's face slowly broke into a warm smile. "That's good, Sara. That's real good. It'll get better. You'll see."

"I'm still not sure I can face the tree, though."

"Then why have one? You don't need to."

"Of course I do. I'm having guests for the holiday and they'll be expecting the place to be decorated. After all, this is a business."

Millie shook her head. "Mmm, I don't know that I'd like spending the holidays with strangers." The moment it was out of her mouth she quickly turned her head away and muttered "Damn" at herself.

Sara swiftly alleviated her embarrassment. "They're friends of friends, and Lynn said it's important for them to get away. Anyway, Christmas is supposed to be a time of giving, isn't it? Let's just say I'm finally getting back into the swing of the holiday by giving the one way I know how."

Their conversation was interrupted by the sound of wet rubber boots smacking on the tile floor as Hansen Crane thudded into the kitchen. Hansen was in his early sixties and looked as if he were purposely trying to earn the label of a "character." He was somewhere over six feet tall and heavy-set, made to look heavier by the plaid wool coat that covered him from shoulder to thigh. He had frizzy hair, the color and consistency of steel wool, that ran down the back of his neck and a matching beard so scruffy it looked almost as if a tumbleweed had lodged on his chin.

"Welp," he said in his booming bass voice, "the tree's up and ready."

"Thank you, Hansen," Sara replied. "Would you like some coffee?"

"Warm you up," Millie added.

"No, thanks. You got anything else you want me to do now?"

Sara hesitated a moment, looking down into her mug as if the future might reveal itself to her in the brown liquid. "Yes. There's some boxes in the basement I'd like you to bring up and put in the parlor by the tree."

Hansen blinked. "What kind of boxes?"

"Ornament boxes. They're in the southeast corner of the basement. There's three of them. They're large and red with leaves of holly printed on them in green. You can't miss them."

"Doesn't sound like it," Hansen replied as he headed out the back door and down the basement steps.

"Honestly, that man can't do anything without making a commotion out of it," said Millie without rancor.

Sara smiled and shrugged. "He's big. Big men make noise."

"I 'spose," said Millie with a laugh as she retrieved a towel and began drying the dishes. "My Herbert's a big man, and you should hear him coming up the back stairs! He sounds like a herd of buffalo! I wouldn't trade him for a quiet man, though. I like always knowing where he is in the house. I wouldn't like having one of those husbands that pop up on you unexpected and scare the life out of you."

Sara laughed. "That's one thing you never have to worry about when you grow up in a city. There's usually so much noise that I don't think you can ever be surprised by something like that. That took some getting used to out here . . . the quiet. You can be . . ." Her voice trailed off and she seemed to sink again into reverie. It still amazed her how many things could bring back so vividly the loss of her brother. She'd been about to say that you could be startled quite easily in the country, when suddenly the last time she'd been truly startled flew back into her mind with such graphic clarity that her stomach did a slight lurch.

"You can be what?" Millie asked.

Sara came back to attention and shook her head. "Oh, nothing."

Before Millie could pursue this further, Hansen's distinct, heavy tread could be heard starting up the wooden steps from the basement.

Millie smirked and shook her head. "Just like in that movie—the scary one about the dinosaurs."

Hansen appeared in the back doorway carrying three large, identical boxes, each piled on top of the other.

"These the ones you were talking about?"

"Yes, thank you. Would you put them in the parlor?"

"Sure."

He trod loudly through the kitchen, sending the glassware in the cabinets rattling in protest.

The two women fell silent for a moment, Millie cheerfully drying the last of the dishes and Sara trying not to think of anything while finishing her coffee. After a moment, Johnnie Larkin came into the kitchen. Johnnie was about twenty-five years old and had managed to pass through the gangliness of youth without any negative residual effects. He was fairly poised for his age, with straight brown hair, bright brown eyes, and an ingratiating smile that some of the townspeople found a little too ready.

Johnnie had moved to LeFavre a little over three years earlier and had taken a cheap room in the apartments over the town's one drugstore. He'd quickly made friends with most of the year-round residents in his age group, and it became generally known not long after his arrival that he'd "run away from home to live life the way he'd always wanted to," namely by living in a resort community where he could work more or less on his own, and spend his plentiful free time at the beach. He made a good enough living doing odd jobs for the locals, from pruning trees and bushes to cutting up felled trees for firewood and mucking out barns. He'd been an increasing presence at Hawthorne House since Nathan's death, partly from Sara's need for help with heavy work, and partly because (as Millie often told her husband in the evenings) Johnnie had a rather obvious crush on Sara.

"I brought the little dresser down and cleaned it up," he said to Sara, "and I moved the bed frame down and put it together."

Sara smiled at him. "Thanks, Johnnie."

"I'll bring the mattresses down, but I'm afraid I'm going to need some help for that. They aren't too heavy, but they're awkward, you know what I mean?"

"Hansen will help you."

Johnnie's face clouded slightly. "Is he here?"

"In the parlor. Hansen?" She called his name and waited. After a moment he clomped into the kitchen. "Would you help Johnnie bring a mattress and box spring down to the den?"

"Sure." He looked at Johnnie and the mass of hair on his face formed into something resembling a smile. "Come on, young man." With this he left the kitchen. Johnnie followed with a hint of reluctance. After a couple of seconds, they were heard ascending the stairs.

Sara rose from the table, went to the sink, and rinsed out the mug, giving it a cursory wipe with the dishrag. She handed it to Millie, who dried it and placed it in the dish drainer.

Sara sighed heavily. "I guess I'm going to have to face it sometime."

She headed for the parlor. Millie followed her, wiping her hands on her apron as she went.

Sara stopped in the archway that separated the parlor from the hallway, laying her hand against one side of it as if she needed to prop herself up. The seven-foot pine stood tall and dark in the center of the front picture window, blocking out a good deal of the morning light and making the atmosphere in the room seem more than a little gloomy. To Sara, the tree seemed like a shadowy, unwelcome stranger, casting a cloud over her mood that she didn't believe would lift until the tree was removed and the holidays were over.

"Well, there it is," said Sara.

"Don't worry. It'll look better after we get it decorated," Millie said with forced cheer. "Just like old times."

Sara glanced at her over her shoulder. "I haven't owned the place long enough to have old times."

Millie pursed her lips and thought a second, then said, "Well, just like not-so-recent times, then. In you go."

They went into the room and Sara steeled herself for a moment before removing the lid on the top ornament box. Inside was a tangled mess of green wire and Italian lights in a variety of colors.

Sara sighed ruefully. "Nathan always put these away and he never took the time to store them properly. Honestly, we go . . . we went through this every year."

Millie looked over her shoulder. "Don't worry, I'll straighten them out."

She picked up the box and took it to a wing chair in one corner of the room. She sat down, laid the box at her feet, and began to carefully pull out the strands, twisting and turning them around and through each other, as if she were playing cat's cradle with barbed wire.

Sara placed the second box on the love seat in the center of the room and sat down beside it. She removed the lid tentatively as if she thought something might leap out of the box at her, then laid the lid aside and began to take out the ornaments one at a time, gingerly unwrapping them from their tissue paper and considering each item in turn.

Millie managed to get the end of one strand of lights separated and draped over her shoulder and was in the process of trying to locate the opposite end when she heard a single choking gasp from Sara. She stopped what she was doing and looked up to find Sara staring down into her palm, tears streaming down her cheeks.

"What is it? What's wrong?"

Sara sniffed a couple of times and sat still a moment, then slid two fingers between a tiny thread and held up the ornament she'd found for Millie to see. It was a tiny unicorn. The body was of clear glass, and the horn was tinted pink.

"It was a gift from Nathan. He bought this for me our first year here."

Millie's forehead creased with concern. "I know it's hard, sweetie, but you knew you'd have to go through these things someday."

"Yes, I know." Sara retrieved a piece of wrapping tissue and used it to dab her eyes.

It was then that they heard the sound of a car coming up the gravel driveway beside the house.

"Oh, damn! Don't tell me they're here already!" She finished wiping her eyes quickly and stuffed the used tissue in the pocket of her skirt. Then she got up from the love seat and went to the side window that overlooked the drive. The moment she looked out the window, her back stiffened, her normally pale skin reddening.

"Who is it?" Millie asked distractedly as she fought with the mass of wire.

"Jeffrey. Jeff Fields."

Millie stopped and looked up. "Really?"

"Um hm."

With more resolution than she'd yet demonstrated that morning, Sara strode from the parlor to the front door. It was near enough that Millie could hear what was said.

Sara opened the door before Jeff had climbed the last step to the porch. He was around Sara's age but had a solid, sturdy build that made him look a little older than he was. He had broad shoulders and a straight back that looked perfectly at home in his sheriff's uniform. His long, sandy hair was perpetually falling into his eyes, which were approximately the same shade of blue as Sara's. When he saw Sara, he smiled uncertainly, as if he knew it was the right thing to do but didn't know how it would be received. Sara didn't return the gesture.

"Hi, Sara. How're you doing?"

"Fine, Jeff. How are you?"

"I'm all right."

They stood staring at each other in the attitude of former lovers who come upon each other unexpectedly and don't know how to proceed. It was clear that Sara wasn't willing to give him any encouragement, and it was equally clear that Jeff wasn't going to allow himself to be cowed so easily. He continued to smile at her as if almost defying her to resume the conversation. She didn't.

"Aren't you going to ask me why I'm here?" he asked.

She shrugged. "I figured you'd tell me."

He glanced down at the wooden floor of the open porch and appeared to be lost in thought. If Sara could have read his mind, she would have seen that he was mentally kicking himself for his manner of approach, as if her very posture were telling him that he'd already blown it.

Finally he looked up into her eyes, and said, "I just thought . . . with Christmas coming I wanted to come out and make sure you were all right . . . and invite you over if you didn't have anyplace else to go. I don't like to think of you being alone at Christmas."

Sara folded her arms just below her breasts. "You don't have to worry about that. I have company coming."

"Company?"

"Guests."

"Paying guests," Jeff said, wishing he'd been able to make it sound less disdainful.

"This is a business, Jeff."

"I understand that." There was a slight beat before he added, "I just wanted to make sure you were all right." He turned and started back toward the steps, and added, "That's all."

Sara hesitated for a moment, caught in a confusing morass of emotions. She didn't want to give him any reassurance, but she couldn't stand the thought of being impolite to him, either.

"Jeff," she said a little too eagerly once she'd found her voice.

He stopped and turned to face her.

"Thanks for stopping by."

Jeff put two fingers to his forehead by way of salute, and said, "Any time." He continued down the stairs and across the paving stones that formed a path along a flower bed to the driveway. As Sara went back into the house, she heard him start the car and pull hastily out into the road.

Sara stood with her back against the door for a while before rejoining Millie. From where she stood, she was looking directly into the dining room. Though the sideboard was empty, in her mind she could see it piled with muffins, plates of butter, the coffee urn, and the tea kettle. She pictured the warm summer breezes stirring the tan chiffon curtains over the windows, and the guests as they came down alone or in pairs, impressed by the spread and happily helping themselves to food, then finding places at the table. She had successfully created a family atmosphere among disparate strangers.

Then there was her real family. Her brother, Nathan, helping her with whatever needed to be done around the house, particularly the books and the bills, and handling the rare complaint that came their way with a sense of tact that one would have expected in a much older man. It had been her dream, and that dream had come true, until one day when in the blink of an eye the dream was destroyed. What she was left with, these two years later, was not a nightmare, but something more like a trance. A static deadness that threatened never to go away.

She was startled from these thoughts by the sudden appearance of Hansen Crane thudding into the dining room from the den, followed closely and more quietly by Johnnie Larkin. Hansen continued into the kitchen and out the back door while Johnnie came into the dining room, apparently looking for Sara.

"Was that Sheriff Jeff?" he asked, his tone not-so-gently mocking.

"Yes."

"What did he want?"

"Nothing."

Johnnie looked at her for a moment, then said, "Well, is there anything else that needs doing before I go?"

"Um . . . yes. Hansen cut some firewood yesterday. He piled it in the barn. Could you bring some in?"

"Sure thing," Johnnie replied. He sounded as if he were anxious to be particularly ingratiating. He started out of the room but paused and turned back to her. "Sara, is everything all right?"

"Yes, of course. Go on, now."

Johnnie hesitated for just a second before heading out to get the wood.

Sara went back into the parlor without a word, sat on the love seat, and resumed the business of unwrapping ornaments. Millie was staring at the archway when she entered as if she'd been frozen in that position ever since Sara had gone to answer the door.

After a few moments, Millie said, "When are you going to forgive that young man?"

"Who?"

"You know who I'm talking about. Jeff."

Sara didn't look up. She merely scrutinized the glass country church she'd just removed from a piece of red tissue. When she realized that Millie was still looking at her, and not likely to stop until she'd received an answer, Sara set the ornament aside and pulled another from the box as she said simply, "There's nothing to forgive."

Emily awoke after a nap of over an hour, refreshed and with only a slight feeling of disorientation, which passed quickly.

"You shouldn't have let me sleep," she said with a little cough.

"It seemed like you needed it. And besides, you're supposed to relax, remember?" Ransom replied.

"Did I miss anything important?"

Ransom smiled and shrugged. "It's an interstate. Only miles and miles of 'amber waves of white.' "

Emily returned his smile, a playful twinkle in her eye. "If they were indeed amber, then you should have woken me."

With only one stop to have a light lunch and refresh themselves, it was just over three hours after beginning their trip that they came to the exit for LeFavre. Ransom pulled from his pocket the small hand-drawn map that Lynn had given him. At the end of the exit ramp, he turned left and drove for about a mile, where he came to a crossroad marked 130th Street.

"I wonder where the other hundred and twenty-nine are," he said wryly.

At the stop sign, there was a sign for LeFavre with an arrow pointing west, indicating that a left turn was called for. Ransom turned right.

"Shouldn't we be going the other way?" Emily asked, wrinkling her forehead.

"Not according to the map. Hawthorne House is actually about five miles outside the town proper, but it's still considered part of the town's jurisdiction."

"I see."

They had driven for a few more minutes when their destination came into view on the left side of the road. Though Lynn had told them that the place was big, they were not prepared for the actual size of the house. It was a huge two-story wood-framed building painted a pleasant, muted yellow, with ornamental shutters, porch railings, and all the woodwork painted white. Situated as it was atop a small snow-covered hill, Hawthorne House looked like a decoration perched on the uppermost tier of a cake.

Emily said "Good heavens!" as Ransom steered the car up the incline of the gravel driveway.

"Indeed," said Ransom.

He climbed out of the car, feeling the stiffness and weariness that comes with driving for so long. He stretched for a moment, then walked around to the passenger side and opened the door for Emily, carefully handing her out of the car. Sara was on the porch to greet them even before Emily was fully upright.

"Hullo!" she called to them. "I'm Sara Bartlett."

Emily gripped Ransom's arm as he led her across the paving stones, which had been swept free of snow.

"Hello," he replied, "I'm Jeremy Ransom. This is Emily Charters."

"Of course," Sara said with as much cheerfulness as she could muster. She came down the stairs to meet them. "Miss Charters, do you think you can manage the steps? If not, there's a ramp at the side door."

"Oh, no, no. There's only four steps. I'm sure I can manage."

Emily took hold of the railing with one hand while Sara took her other hand.

"Ah," said Ransom. "Well, if you're all right, then I'll get the suitcases from the car."

"I'll be fine, Jeremy," Emily replied lightly.

Sara led Emily into the front hall, and Emily stopped there for a moment to get her bearings.

"My goodness, this is lovely," said Emily. "Is the house Victorian?"

"Hmmm . . . maybe a little later than that. But it still shows signs of the period," Sara replied. She hesitated for a few seconds, then said, "Would you like me to show you the house, or would you like to rest for a while?"

"Oh, no, my dear, I like to see my surroundings before I bed down in them."

"Should we wait for Mr. Ransom?"

A knowing smile spread across the old woman's face. "No, I think we should probably go ahead. He might be a while."

Sara's dark eyebrows knit closer together. "But he was just going to get your luggage."

"So he said," Emily replied with a great deal of amusement, "but I suspect he's going to smoke, also."

Sara smiled. "Really?"

"It's one of his few vices. I don't approve of it so he doesn't do it in my presence. But I daresay that three hours in the car was quite trying for him."

"Ah," said Sara, her smile becoming a bit more conspiratorial, "then maybe I'd better start by showing you the parlor."

Sara gave her arm to Emily and led her around the corner into the aforementioned room. With the help of Millie Havers and Johnnie Larkin, Sara had managed to get the tree fully decorated. Now, with the lights glittering in the recesses of the branches, the tree no longer looked dark and foreboding, but instead was fulfilling its purpose as a colorful reminder of the season.

"That's a handsome tree," said Emily.

"Thank you," Sara replied absently.

"It's beautifully decorated. Did you do it yourself?"

"No. Millie Havers—she's the woman who helps me out here—she helped me, along with Johnnie Larkin. He helps out around here, too." Sara said all this a little hurriedly, as if trying to politely rush to another subject. The peculiar tone was not lost on Emily, who noted it without a word.

Sara directed Emily's attention to the fireplace in front of which stood two comfortable-looking wing chairs. Logs had been laid on the grate ready for the evening's fire, which Sara had thought would be a nice welcome to her holiday visitors. Then she led Emily to the side window.

"There's a view from here that I thought you'd be interested in," said Sara with a smile as she drew back the curtain.

This was the window that looked out onto the drive-way. There was Ransom, resting against the side of the car and smoking a small plastic-tipped cigar as if he was drawing his life from it.

"It is a nice view," said Emily, "and not exactly unexpected."

Sara showed her the rest of the first floor, which consisted of a large living room with bay windows that looked across the lawn into a wooded area, a dining room, and a large library just off the living room and next to the den. The library had floor-to-ceiling shelves, which were lined with musty volumes that showed signs of age and multiple readings. The only furniture consisted of two mock-leather chairs, beside which were small smoking tables.

"If you don't like the smell of smoke," said Sara, "you might not like this room."

"Oh, no," Emily replied as she gazed admiringly at the shelves, her ancient eyes conveying the closest thing to envy that Emily ever demonstrated, "this is splendid. There's something about the atmosphere of a library that lends itself to smoke. I always think libraries should be a bit close."

Sara smiled. "It probably lives up to that. It's been a while since anyone's been in here, except for when I come in to get a book. And that's only for a second. I like to read in the kitchen. I don't know why."

"I imagine it's a bit friendlier there," Emily said absently.

Sara found her mind wandering again as she considered this. She hadn't realized it before, but she didn't really like the library. Possibly because of the stuffiness, and partly because when the door was closed the room was so quiet and removed. And lonely. She needed nothing to accentuate the loneliness. She became so lost in her thoughts that she didn't hear Emily speak.

"Miss Bartlett?"

"Oh, I'm sorry," said Sara, regaining herself.

"I was just saying this house is very large. I thought Lynn mentioned that it had been a farmhouse at one time."

"Oh, only in a manner of speaking. It wasn't really a farm. It was built by a man called Zebediah Hawthorne, if you can believe such a name, who owned a vineyard. A lot of wine is produced in this area, you know. He built this house for his family, which was very large, but so was his business, so I guess he had the money to do it."

"What happened to the vineyards?"

"They're still there, just north of us—behind the house. Twenty years or so ago, Hawthorne's children . . . or grandchildren, I'm not sure which, sold the vineyards to a big company, which of course didn't need the house. So they sold it off with a generous plot of ground. It had two other owners before me."

Emily clucked her tongue. "I suppose that will always be the way. The children knew the value of the business that their father had built, but they didn't know the value of the family home."

Sara paused. The subject of family was one that would often catch her unawares and cause her pain, even when it wasn't in reference to her own. The mere mention of someone not valuing their family unexpectedly cut to her heart. She could feel tears beginning to well in her eyes.

Emily immediately noticed the change in the young woman's demeanor, and laid a hand gently on her arm. "My dear, is anything the matter?"

"No . . . I . . . no . . ."

"Hello!" Ransom called from the front door.

Sara almost sighed with relief at the interruption and exited the library without a word. Emily followed her. They found Ransom by the door holding Emily's suitcase, along with his own serviceable plaid cloth bag.

Sara closed the door behind him, and said, "Come right in. Oh, Miss Charters, I haven't shown you your room yet. It's right through here, next to the library."

She led them back through the living room and opened the door to the right of the library, then stood aside to allow her guests to precede her.

The room was fairly large and painted a very light shade of tan. There was a window facing east, looking out over the side lawn and wooded area, and another facing north with a view of the back of the property. The barn stood prominently in the near distance. The windows were covered with sheers of a darker tan than the walls, and there were white shades that could be pulled down for privacy.

The dresser that Johnnie had carried down earlier had been placed beside the east window, and directly across the room from it was a queen-sized pencil-post bed made of maple. The bed was covered with a huge, inviting comforter encased in a cover printed all over with tiny cornflowers. Beside the bed was a nightstand on which rested a boudoir lamp. In the corner of the room, between the windows, was a chair with a soft cushion and a straight back, perfect for reading in, and next to it was an antique floor lamp with a large, fringed shade.

"It's not as bright and cheery as I'd like, Miss Charters. . . ." said Sara as she pulled back the sheers.

"Please, call me Emily."

Sara smiled. "And please call me Sara."

Emily inclined her head by way of acknowledgment. "The room is lovely."

"Thank you. It was originally a bedroom. I used it as a den, or a reading room, as I like to call it, since it communicates with the library." She gestured to a door on the left side of the bed. "But we've made it a bedroom again in honor of your stay."

"Oh, I hope you haven't gone to too much bother."

"Don't be silly. It wasn't a problem. Lynn told me you needed to be on the first floor. She also gave me strict instructions that you were to be treated like the family jewels."

Emily's right hand went up to the neck of her dark blue wool dress. "That was very kind of her, I'm sure."

For the first time, Sara's smile took on a degree of warmth. "I knew if she said it, it had to be true. Lynn is a very hard person to win over. If she says you're a jewel, then I believe it."

"Thank you," said Emily primly, as if she thought it was faintly indecent to be praised so directly. But her eyes sparkled in a way that betrayed her pleasure.

"The door on the other side of the bed is the bathroom. I think it was the last owner who added a shower. It's not very big, but it's the best we have on this floor."

"I'm sure it will be fine."

Sara stopped for a moment and glanced around the room, then turned back to Emily, and said, "Now, is there anything I can get you?"

"I think I'd like to unpack my things. But afterward I might like a little tea."

"That would be fine. I'll show Mr. Ransom up to his room, and then have tea ready for you in the dining room in about twenty minutes?"

"The dining room?" said Emily hesitantly.

Sara glanced at Ransom, then back to Emily. "Yes. If that's all right. Would you rather have it in here? I'd be glad to bring it to you."

Emily smiled indulgently and shook her head. "There's really no need to be oversolicitous of me. No matter what Jeremy and Lynn may think, I'm not a bit of fine china. I'm not in imminent danger of shattering to pieces."

Sara smiled and brushed her hair back with her hand as her cheeks turned a slight pink.

Emily continued. "I was just thinking that . . . if it's just the three of us here for the holiday . . . we should probably stay a bit more informal. Would you mind if I had tea in the kitchen?"

"Oh!" said Sara with a laugh, "No, not at all. I'll have it for you there in just a little while."

"Thank you," said Emily as she turned to her suitcase, which Ransom had put on a stand at the foot of the bed.

Sara turned to Ransom, and said, "Now I'll show you your room, if you like."

"Thank you," he replied. Sara preceded him out of the room, and he paused in the doorway for just a moment. He looked back at Emily and said with a sly smile, "Don't kid yourself. You *are* a bit of fine china."

Once he'd left the room, Emily stood looking down at the contents of her suitcase. After a moment a sigh escaped her lips and she gently closed the case. She then crossed to the chair by the window. She reached down and pressed the cushion a couple of times with her hand, and once satisfied as to its firmness and height, she lowered herself onto it. Despite her claims to the contrary, she'd found the trip fatiguing, and found that fact a little distressing. As she sat there with her eyes closed, she assured herself that she would have found a three-hour drive a bit tiring even before having the operation for what she called her "little problem," the heart attack that had necessitated a quadruple bypass.

She took a few deep breaths to relax herself and sank back into the chair. She was surprised to find that cares and worries, of which she hadn't been consciously aware, seemed to be melting off her in the quiet of this room and the comfort of the chair. For the first time she realized that Jeremy might just have been right, that she had needed to get away from the normal routine of her life in order to properly relax, and it might not have just been Jeremy who needed a vacation.

Sara led Ransom to a large bedroom at the top of the stairs. It was furnished in much the same way as Emily's room, except for the addition of a large reproduction of an antique wardrobe.

"Hm," said Ransom as he opened the wardrobe and inspected the interior, "very nice."

"Very practical," Sara emended. "When they built a lot of these old houses they didn't think much of closet space. Now, the bathroom is just to the left of this room. With no other guests you'll have it pretty much to yourself. And there's a small room just down the hallway that you'll find particularly useful."

"Hm?"

"It's a smoking room. You're welcome to use it. There's an exhaust fan in the window that keeps the room, and the rest of the house, fairly clear."

Ransom raised his right eyebrow. "You seem to have thought of everything."

"We . . . I like my guests to be comfortable."

Ransom smiled and laid his suitcase on top of the dresser.

"Tell me, Mr. Ransom . . ."

"Most people just call me Ransom. Except Emily."

Sara gave a single nod of acknowledgment. "Tell me, exactly how is Emily? I mean, she says she doesn't need special care, but Lynn seemed to think she was quite weak."

Ransom sighed. "It's hard to tell with Emily. When I first met her, I mistook her for a frail old woman. She straightened me out on that point very quickly. As for today . . . to look at her you wouldn't think she'd had open-heart surgery just a couple of months ago. She's always been strong and she's not the type to give in to weakness or to like a fuss being made over her. That doesn't necessarily mean that it doesn't need to be made."

Sara stood looking at him, her head tilted to one side and a questioning expression on her face. "What does all that mean, though?"

Ransom shrugged. "It means if you're going to watch out for her you'd better not let her see you doing it."

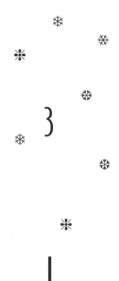

ohnnie Larkin strolled the aisles of Macklin's Supermarket, the largest of its kind in the area. Although there was a small grocery store in LeFavre, when the locals had any sizable purchases to make they usually drove the fifteen miles to the neighboring town of Mt. Morgan, in which Macklin's was located. Johnnie pushed his shopping cart along with two index fingers and whistled as if he didn't have a care in the world. He wore a blue plaid shirt and a pair of overalls with the shoulder straps unfastened and tied around his waist. The bib hung down below his waist like a denim loincloth.

"Hello, Mr. Crabtree," Johnnie called in his friendliest manner to an elderly man who stood with a hose spraying a fine mist over the vegetables.

Mr. Crabtree turned around slowly, his arthritis precluding any more rapid movement. His unblinking eyes stared dully at the young man.

"Hullo, Johnnie," he said with formal cordiality after a pause. His tone was unsure enough to make it sound as if he didn't particularly care for Johnnie, but couldn't remember the cause.

"You have any sweet potatoes?" Johnnie said, enjoying the old man's discomfiture.

"Uh-huh. Over there. Right in front of you."

"Thank you, sir," Johnnie replied, touching a finger to his forehead.

He selected several potatoes from the bin, eyeing them carefully as if he really knew how to tell a good one from a bad one, then tossed each in turn into his cart. He then selected some baking potatoes in the same manner, and retrieved two bags of fresh cranberries from a shelf above the bins.

"Looks like you're doing an awful lot of shopping," said Crabtree with feigned disinterest, his natural curiosity getting the better of his reticence. "You having people in for the holidays?"

"It's not for me, it's for Sara. Sara Bartlett," Johnnie replied happily, knowing that anything he told the old man would probably be common knowledge within the hour.

"She opening up Hawthorne House again? For the holidays?"

"Just for a few select people," said Johnnie. Implicit in his tone was the idea that he was one of the select.

"Well, I'll be," Crabtree said as he turned the hose on a bin of celery. Then he added, more to himself than for Johnnie's benefit, "Used to be people stayed home at Christmas."

"Sara tries to make Hawthorne House as much like home as possible," Johnnie said, giving the old man a gentle, friendly pat on the back. He could feel Crabtree stiffen at his touch.

Johnnie paused for a moment and withdrew his hand, wasting an indulgent smile on Crabtree as the old man walked away muttering, ". . . still nothing but a glorified hotel."

Johnnie tried not to begrudge Crabtree's coolness. He knew that although LeFavre, Mt. Morgan, and many of the surrounding towns catered heavily to the tourist trade, most of the locals jealously guarded their small-town spirit, entertaining a mild distrust of anyone who hadn't been born in the area, or lived there for several generations. They also regarded the tourists as a necessary evil, treating them like spoiled children who needed to be relieved of their excess money lest they spend it foolishly—somewhere else.

But, although he knew that the gentle snubbing wasn't reserved for him alone, Johnnie couldn't help feeling the injustice of it. He liked to think of himself as thick skinned but, in the arrogance of his youth, he believed he should be accepted at face value on the strength of the character he exhibited, rather than on his place of birth or the length of time he'd lived in the area. He shook his head in mild disgust at the thought.

With a sigh, Johnnie reached into his side pocket and withdrew the lengthy list with which Sara had provided him. After checking it over to make sure he'd gotten everything he needed from the produce section, he resumed his whistling and headed for another part of the store. He rounded the corner into the baking goods aisle and literally ran into Amy Shelton. He caught sight of her just in time and turned his cart aside at the last moment, just grazing the side of Amy's cart.

Amy Shelton was pretty if a little on the plain side. She had light blue eyes and long blond hair that she held in place with a pink headband. Her white blouse and navy blue skirt were both very clean and pressed, and a sweater that matched the color of her headband hung across her shoulders. Her winter coat, which was unstylish but serviceable, was stuffed in the child seat of her shopping cart. Though her appearance was decidedly starched, there was a softness about Amy that made most people treat her as if she were a porcelain doll.

"Oh! I'm sorry!" she exclaimed as the carts collided.

"My fault," said Johnnie.

When Amy realized who it was she'd bumped into, she blushed a deep red.

"Oh!" she said again. Her hand flew to her heart and fumbled with a button on her blouse as if she had just discovered she wasn't dressed. "Oh. Hello, Johnnie."

"Hi. Long time no see."

"Yes," she stammered. "Yes. How have you been?"

"I've been just great. How about you?"

"I'm fine. Just fine."

There was an extremely awkward silence during which Johnnie continued to look at Amy while she studied shelves lined with bags of sugar as if she were convinced that there really must be a difference between the brands.

"How's your mom and dad?" Johnnie asked in an attempt to break the silence.

"They're fine. The same as always."

Johnnie started to say something else, but Amy headed him off.

"We're having my brother and his family in for Christmas. We haven't seen them in a long time. It'll be nice. We're all looking forward to it."

"That's nice. Look, I just wanted to say—"

"I really can't stay and talk. I just ran in to get some things we need. Some last-minute things. I know there's still a few days till Christmas, but I don't want to have to be running back and forth to the store while my brother's here. Excuse me."

She pulled her cart back and started to push it around Johnnie, but he laid a hand on the side to stay it.

"Amy, I just wanted to say—"

"No!" she said loudly, then shot an embarrassed glance up and down the aisle to make sure she hadn't attracted anyone's attention. She then lowered her voice, and said, "There's no need to say anything. It's all right." She stopped and looked up into his eyes for the first time. "Please don't say anything."

Johnnie looked at her with a sad smile and removed his hand from her cart. Without another word she wheeled the cart away and disappeared around the corner.

It took him another half hour to finish his shopping. He paid for the groceries and was waiting for the cashier to finish bagging them when Jeff Fields came up and laid a handful of frozen dinners and a carton of Coke on the counter. In an apparent effort to ignore Johnnie, he turned his full attention to a rack of tabloids hanging next to the cash register.

Johnnie glanced down at Jeff's groceries and smiled. "Whoa! The staples of a bachelor's diet."

Jeff returned the smile reluctantly, more to conceal his emotions than from any desire to invite further conversation. "I guess."

"I hate when I have to buy frozen dinners," Johnnie pursued. "It makes me feel like such a stereotype."

"Well, there's some of us that don't care what people think."

"I suppose."

There was a momentary silence interrupted only by the sounds of the brown paper bags rattling as the cashier filled them. Jeff would have liked nothing better than for the silence to continue, but thought it best to take the initiative in directing the conversation rather than let Johnnie continue.

"You look like you're stocking up there," said Jeff, jutting a thumb in the direction of the rapidly filling bags.

"We're having people in for Christmas."

"We?"

"Up at the house," Johnnie explained with a smile that indicated he was choosing his words purposefully. "Oh, then of course, you know that. You stopped by earlier, didn't you?"

"I stopped by Hawthorne House," Jeff replied, the remnants of his smile freezing on his face.

The tone of this exchange wasn't lost on the cashier, who shot a glance at Jeff, catching his attention before she rolled her eyes.

"Sara's put up a tree this year. We decorated it this morning."

"Sounds like you're making yourself pretty useful."

"Yeah. Of course, Sara needs a man around the house since her brother died."

Jeff folded his arms across his chest and leaned against the counter. "Hm. Maybe she'll find one."

There was a slight glitch in Johnnie's ingratiating smile, something like the blink of a computer screen in response to a flash of lightning. But it was only fleeting. His smile returned full force as he said, "By the way, I don't guess there's been any breaks in finding out who killed her brother?"

"There's nothing new, no," Jeff said, trying with difficulty to stem the flow of blood to his face. Given the fact that he could feel the temperature of his skin rising, he knew he wasn't being successful.

Johnnie heaved a dramatic sigh. "I don't suppose there's much chance of finding out who did it . . . after all this time."

Without visibly changing his expression, Jeff's smile seemed to become more menacing.

"Well, you never know what may come up."

"Yeah, right," said Johnnie.

The cashier had finished packing the bags at this point and Johnnie tossed them into the cart and rolled it out the front door, whistling as he went. Once he was gone, the cashier leaned halfway over the counter and said to Jeff, "You know, if this was that Angela Lansbury program on TV, that guy would be dead before long."

Jeff's smile melted. "Well, we can always hope."

"Do you mind if I go on working while you have your tea?" Sara asked.

"Not at all," Emily replied with a smile as she took a sip. Although Sara had a large collection of mugs for the coffee that was the preference of most of her guests, she'd thought Emily would prefer a normal cup and saucer. Sara had also set out a plate of brightly decorated Christmas cookies in the center of the table.

"I could fix a sandwich for you if you'd like."

"Oh, no. We had lunch on the way. This is fine."

"I thought maybe a meat loaf would be all right for tonight. With lots of vegetables on the side. I didn't know whether or not you'd given up on meat," said Sara, wiping her hands on the brown-checkered towel that hung from the refrigerator handle.

"Not entirely," Emily said as she replaced the cup in its saucer. "Of course, doctors would have you give up anything pleasurable, but it's difficult to change a lifetime of eating habits, and at my time of life there hardly seems any point."

"Oh, don't say that."

Emily sighed. "None of us go on forever."

Sara smiled sadly and hesitated before opening the refrigerator door. "Yes, I know."

Emily watched Sara with a keen eye as she removed two packages of meat and placed them on the counter. Her movements were slow but precise, as if whatever had just clouded her thoughts made her afraid that she might forget something important.

"This is a very lovely house," Emily said, hoping to take Sara's mind off whatever was troubling her.

"Thank you," Sara replied with a gratified smile.

"It must be terribly difficult to keep it up."

Sara looked at her and blinked. "Not really," she said with forced matter-of-factness, "I'm financially very secure."

She'd laid the slightest stress on the word "financially." Emily was surprised that, although money didn't appear to be a problem for Sara, it would be the first concern to pop into her mind. Emily's eyes widened and her lips formed an apologetic frown. "Oh, my goodness! I'm sorry, I wasn't referring to money. You see, my own house is fairly small—little more than a bungalow, really—and I find it difficult to keep it properly on my own anymore." She stopped and smiled to herself, adding, "At least that's what Jeremy tells me. That's why he hired your friend Lynn to come in and clean for me."

"Oh!" said Sara with an embarrassed laugh, "I misunderstood you. Yes, this place really is a lot for . . . for one person, but I have plenty of help. Millie Havers comes in in the mornings. She prepares breakfast—usually fresh muffins. She's a terrific baker. And she helps me clean. You'll meet her tomorrow morning. And there's Hansen Crane. He lives out back in the apartment over the barn. He does work around the place, and I pay him a little and give him a place to live. He keeps the grass cut and does most of the gardening and whatever else I ask him to do. He's getting on in years, so I don't like him to do the real heavy work—but you know how some men are, he'll do it anyway. And I have a young man, Johnnie Larkin, who comes in whenever I need him to do the heavier things."

"Well, it sounds as if you're pretty much taken care of," said Emily as she lifted the cup to her lips again.

"Yes, I'm not . . . I have enough help."

Sara had put the meat into a large bowl and paused in the process of cracking a pair of eggs into the mixture. Her gaze traveled out the window over the sink. From there she could see the blanket of snow covering the yard, and the woods beyond it. The leafless trees stood crowded together, their branches straining upward like a riot of naked arms reaching to the sky for help.

"Is there anything the matter, Sara?" Emily asked gently.

"What? No. No . . ." She cracked the eggs into the bowl and dropped the empty shells into the garbage can. "I was just thinking how pretty this area looks during the summer. I don't know, somehow when everything's blooming it doesn't seem so . . . so . . ." Her voice trailed off.

"Lonely?" Emily offered.

"I was going to say isolated. Isn't that funny? We're exactly the same distance from town no matter what the season, but during the winter it seems more isolated."

Emily lightly laid her fingers on the sides of her cup and sat silently watching the young woman with concern. She was reluctant to bring up a painful subject, but at the same time felt that it was preying on Sara's mind and talking about it might help her.

Emily cleared her throat, and said, "Sara, Lynn told us that you lost your brother a couple of years ago. I'm very sorry."

"Thank you," Sara replied as if by rote. She paused for a beat in the process of mixing the contents of the bowl.

"Was his death very unexpected?"

"Very," said Sara, a touch of irony in her voice. Then she added before Emily could ask the next obvious question, "He was killed. Murdered."

"Oh, how awful," Emily said with feeling. But despite the

sympathy she felt, her interest was piqued. "Did the police apprehend whoever did it?"

"No. No, they didn't."

Emily's eyebrows elevated at this. "You mean they have no idea who did it?"

Sara shot an annoyed glance at her. "They have ideas, all right," she said with an edge. When she saw the surprised look on Emily's face, she immediately relented. She gave Emily a half-hearted smile, and said more softly, "They had ideas, but nothing panned out. Everything came to a dead end."

"I'm really very sorry," said Emily. "It must leave you feeling very much at loose ends."

Sara stopped and looked at Emily with mild surprise.

"Yes. Yes, it does," she said. Then, adopting a more professional tone as she wiped her hands on the towel again, she added, "Now, what kind of vegetables would you like with your dinner?

While the vegetable menu was being discussed inside the house, outside Johnnie steered his old but reliable hatchback up the wide driveway and parked next to Ransom's Nova. He switched off the ignition and jumped out of the car in a single motion, then strolled to the back of the car and popped the hatch. He was no longer whistling, but his satisfied smile served as an indication that he was still entertaining his own pleasant thoughts.

It was because of this that he didn't hear the approach of Hansen Crane until he was almost upon him.

"Hi, there, Johnnie boy," said Crane with a jocular tone that had just a touch of sarcasm about it.

Johnnie paused in the act of pulling the first grocery bag from the back of the car. He was glad that his face hadn't been in view when he first heard the voice, because it never would have done to give Crane the satisfaction of seeing the smile disappear, any more than it would have done for Crane to have seen it to begin with.

"Hello, Crane," Johnnie said with elaborate deference as he straightened up, bag in hand.

"You the one that messed up my woodpile?"

" 'Scuse me?" said Johnnie, feigning confusion. "How can you mess up a woodpile?"

"By pulling wood out willy-nilly, lettin' the stack fall all over the place, and not piling it back up where it belongs."

"Is that what I did? You sure it didn't just fall over on its own?"

"I don't know why, I see a mess and I just think you had something to do with it."

The smug look on Crane's face almost forced Johnnie into saying something he was sure he'd have been sorry for later. He had to remember his position, plus the fact that Sara, for reasons he could never understand, actually liked the old man. He heaved a sigh meant to let the older man know he was being indulged, and said, "I'll go restack them as soon as I get the groceries inside."

"That woodpile's been messed up since this morning," said Crane, laying a hand on the upraised hatch of the car.

Johnnie paused for a second, then said, "At least it can wait till I get these inside."

"It's plenty cold out here," said Crane, his smile remaining in place as if a testament to how cold it was, "the food'll keep."

"Look, Crane," Johnnie began, but one glance at the unmoving older man told him it was no use. Instead, with an attempt at grace that was visibly costing him a struggle, Johnnie said, "Oh, all right! I'll take care of it."

He dropped the bag back into the car and marched off toward the barn. Crane smiled after him as if he'd achieved some sort of victory.

It was almost twenty minutes before Johnnie brought the first load of groceries through the back door into the kitchen.

"My goodness!" said Sara as she took one of the bags from him and set it on the counter. "You took your time about coming in. I thought I heard you drive up ages ago."

"That was your Mr. Crane," Johnnie replied with an apologetic smile that didn't quite hide his annoyance, "Don't blame me if anything's defrosted!"

"I hardly think that's possible in this weather," said Sara, glancing into the second bag as she took it from him. "Oh, Johnnie, this is Emily Charters, one of my guests for the week."

Johnnie beamed his most ingratiating smile and doffed an imaginary hat at Emily. "Hello, I'm pleased to meet you, ma'am!"

"Good afternoon," Emily replied, her eyes fixed on Johnnie appraisingly.

"Now," said Sara, "what was this about Hansen?"

"Who knows?" said Johnnie. "He got a bee in his bonnet about the woodpile. He said I left it in a mess, as if there was such a thing as a neat woodpile."

Unnoticed by Johnnie, Emily nodded to herself as if her appraisal had been verified.

"Honestly," Johnnie continued, his tone taking on an amused exasperation, "that old man is nuts!"

"And did you mess it up?" Sara asked with a smile.

"Well, yeah," Johnnie replied sheepishly, "but cleaning it up could've waited until I had the groceries in, but no, he insisted I do it right away."

"Well, no harm done. And you know that Hansen likes to have things done a particular way."

"Yeah, I know," Johnnie replied with a knowledgeable nod. "I'll get the rest of the bags."

Sara gave a little laugh when he was out of earshot. "There's always been a little tension between Hansen and Johnnie. It's so typical. Hansen doesn't seem to think Johnnie knows anything because he's young, and Johnnie doesn't think Hansen knows anything because he's old."

"Oh, yes," said Emily, "quite understandable."

Sara began to unpack the groceries. "It's been worse the past couple of years because with . . . well, I've needed more help around here so I've had Johnnie around more, and that's caused more friction. To tell you the truth, I tend to be a little indulgent when it comes to Hansen. He can be a bit quirky, and he's set in his ways, but he does know what he's doing. I've been trying to get Johnnie to understand that since Hansen's old—" She stopped suddenly and glanced at Emily, her cheeks turning pink. "I mean, that he should . . ."

Emily smiled as she rescued Sara from the faux pas in which she'd become mired. "If you were going to say you've been trying to convince that young man that he should respect his elders, you'll get no argument from me. It's one of the ironies of life that by the time you learn to respect your elders, quite often you no longer have any elders left to respect."

Sara laughed genuinely for the first time. Emily couldn't help thinking how pleasant it sounded coming from her, and how sad it was that circumstances prevented her from doing it more often.

Johnnie returned with the remaining sacks of groceries and set about helping Sara to unpack them and put them away.

"You'll never guess who I ran into at Macklin's," he said.

"Who?"

"Jeff Fields, for one."

There was a beat before Sara said "Oh?" She removed some cans from a bag and put them on the shelf above the refrigerator.

"Yeah. He seems to be getting around today." Johnnie's face hardened as he added, "He should do less visiting and shopping and do more investigating."

Sara stopped. "You didn't say that to him."

"No," Johnnie replied slowly, "no, of course not."

Sara stared at him for a moment, then went back to unpacking.

Johnnie continued, "But . . . well, never mind. He wasn't the one I was surprised to see. Guess who else I saw."

"Tell me," said Sara, her tone intimating that she wasn't in the mood for guessing games.

"Amy Shelton."

Sara paused with her hand on top of the refrigerator. "Really?"

"Yeah."

"How was she doing?"

"She seemed to be doing okay. She said they're having family in for Christmas."

"That's nice." Sara retrieved a couple of more cans from the bag and slid them onto the shelf. With her back still turned to Johnnie she said, "What else did she have to say?"

"Nothing, really. She was in kind of a hurry . . . so she said. I . . . I got the feeling she didn't want to talk to me too badly."

Sara turned around and looked at Johnnie, her expression anything but pleased.

"Why would you think that?"

"Because she knows I work—" He stopped abruptly and cast a glance over his shoulder at her. His face paled a little, and he couldn't have looked more apologetic if he'd tried. "Well, you know how she is. She's always been kind of an odd one."

"No, she hasn't," Sara said firmly. "I remember her as being a very nice person."

"Okay, okay," he said resignedly, raising his palms as if to repel an invisible assailant, "but you know how some people are."

Sara didn't respond. Johnnie looked down at the floor for a moment, then back up at her. "I guess when she saw me there were just too many connections. I'm sorry."

Sara shook her head ruefully as she went back to the groceries. "I just hate to think of her not doing well, that's all."

"She's all right. She said she was looking forward to the holidays."

As he said this her gave Sara a light rub on the shoulder from which she didn't recoil. Emily watched this entire exchange silently with slightly raised eyebrows.

Johnnie placed one of the bags on the floor, dropped to a crouch, and began to transfer the baking potatoes and sweet potatoes into separate bins in the bottom drawer next to the sink.

"It looks like you're going to be making quite a spread," said Johnnie, trying not to sound too obviously as if he were changing the subject.

Sara glanced at Emily, and said, "Well, I have very special guests for Christmas."

"You're going to be really well taken care of," Johnnie said to Emily, "you should see all the food."

"I'm looking forward to it," Emily replied.

"Yeah," said Johnnie as he stood up and proceeded to fold the bag. "You really have something to look forward to. Sara's a great cook. Christmas dinner should be something really special."

Sara was not so far lost in her thoughts that she missed the none-too-subtle hints.

"Where are you going to have Christmas dinner, Johnnie?" she asked, casting an amused glance at Emily.

"Oh, I don't know," he replied with practiced nonchalance. "I suppose at my apartment. I can make something."

"Why don't you have Christmas dinner here?"

"Oh, that's all right. I appreciate it, but I don't mind being on my own. If I did, I never would've left home!"

Sara placed a hand on her hip, and said, "You can go on being polite just so long before I'll take you at your word."

Johnnie laughed, and said, "Okay, okay! I accept. Thank you very much! Oh, before I forget it, I should give you your change." He reached around toward his back pocket and his face suddenly went white.

"What's wrong?" Sara asked.

"My wallet's gone!"

"It's right there." She pointed to where his wallet was lying, on the floor by where he'd been crouching. Sara started to reach for it, but Johnnie quickly snatched it up off the floor as if he was afraid that one of the two ladies might want to abscond with what little he had.

"Damn!" he said with an embarrassed smile. "I've gotta stop doing that! I don't make enough to lose anything."

He gave Sara the change from the shopping and slipped the wallet into his back pocket, giving it an extra pat as if that would hold it in place. "Now, do you need me to do anything else? I don't have anything planned for the rest of the day. If you need me, I'm available."

"No, that's all right. Thank you."

"Oh. Okay." He sounded disappointed. "I'll be going, then. 'Bye, Miss Charters. Nice to meet you."

Emily smiled in response.

"He's a nice boy," said Sara once Johnnie had gone.

"He's hardly a boy," Emily replied as she took a sip of tea.

Sara laughed gently. "I suppose you're right. He's only about five years younger than me."

"He seems interested in you."

Sara glanced at Emily. The look on the young woman's face was a mixture of what Emily took to be admirably modest embarrassment tinged with something a bit darker. Though she had no way of knowing what the cause might be, Emily could have sworn that Sara found the idea of Johnnie's interest somehow distressing.

"I don't think . . . well, maybe he is. But I'm . . . I'm not really interested in anyone. Not now."

Emily looked at her quizzically for a moment, then set her cup back on its saucer. "I'm so sorry. I didn't mean to be so personal."

"Oh, no," said Sara, recovering herself and waving the matter off, "I just never think of Johnnie that way. He seems so young."

Emily nodded thoughtfully. "Yes, he does."

4

Ransom woke with the curious but not unpleasant sensation of being swathed in a floating cloud with an angel hovering somewhere overhead. It was a few minutes before he became fully cognizant of his surroundings. The cloud was nothing more than the combination of an extremely comfortable mattress and a soft, white comforter. The angel he'd sensed in his half-waking state was the slowly rotating ceiling fan meant to help keep the heat circulating.

Though Ransom had never been one to sleep late, as he lay there he thought how easy it would be to stay peacefully wrapped in the warmth of the bed, lolling in and out of sleep, for the better part of the day. But it wasn't long before he became aware of the inviting aroma of freshly brewed coffee and muffins apparently just coming out of the oven. With only a modicum of reluctance, he pushed back the covers and slid out of bed. He retrieved his black satin robe from the back of the chair over which it was draped and slipped into it. As he tied the sash, he went to the window.

The view was only partially obscured by a massive oak tree, denuded for the winter and spreading some of its more spindly branches across the window like a spider web. Through the branches he could see the front yard and the road. Far in the distance he could make out a farmhouse, which sat like the fixed point of a triangle from which the property on the opposite of the road spread out. There was something unreal about the scene, as if he were seeing a painting of farmland in winter rather than the farmland itself, and he experienced the same curious sensation one sometimes feels when looking at a painting, of wanting to be drawn into it. It was his first glimpse of how hypnotically seductive this type of tranquility could be, and he made a mental note of his need to resist it.

Though it was after eight in the morning, there was very little in the way of activity outdoors. There wasn't much in the way of traffic, either, which he attributed to the fact that this wasn't exactly a main thoroughfare. But as Ransom gazed languidly out the window, he saw a car appearing over a ridge in the distance on the left. He didn't find anything particularly surprising about this, or in the fact that as it came nearer, he could make out the sheriff's emblem on the passenger door. The car passed the house with the same steady pace with which it had approached, neither too fast nor too slow, and continued on at the same rate until it had disappeared. The driver's head hadn't turned as he passed.

Ransom marked the seemingly innocuous event with a simple "Hm."

After he'd showered, shaved, and dressed, he came downstairs to find Emily already seated in the dining room and eating a fresh muffin as she talked with Millie Havers.

"The blueberries are frozen, of course," Millie said. "You should taste them during the season. You can get beautiful blueberries at roadside stands in these parts."

Emily swallowed a bit of muffin, then said, "Oh, I'll bet they're wonderful. But these muffins are very, very good."

"They can't be half as good as I can do in the summer," said Millie. Despite her self-effacement, her beaming smile showed the pride she took in the praise. "Those frozen ones don't hold a candle to the real things. I guess we have to sacrifice a little taste to have them all year round."

"That's true," said Emily with a tinge of wistfulness, "but taste isn't the only thing we sacrifice, you know. We sacrifice all sense of time as well."

Millie paused in the process of wiping her hands on her apron and furrowed her brow. "What's that, miss?"

"Time. I remember when I was a little girl how we looked forward to 'strawberry time' and 'blueberry time' and so on. But these days we have to have everything all the time. We've lost the sense that there's a time for everything." She took another bit of muffin and chewed thoughtfully before adding, "Then of course, it *is* nice to have them."

"You're right there, Miss Charters."

"Am I late for the sermon?" said Ransom from the doorway, where he'd paused to listen during this exchange.

"Oh, Jeremy! Good morning. This is Millie Havers. She made these lovely muffins."

"Pleased to meet you," said Ransom.

"Help yourself," Millie said with a smile as she gestured to the covered basket in the center of the table.

"Miss Havers has been telling me about all the things to do in the area."

"We have a lot of nice little shops in town," said Millie, "and antique stores here and there. They're usually only open weekends off season, but 'most everything will be open this week. And the Presbyterian church on the north end of town has a Nativity play they're doing on Wednesday night and a carol service they do on Christmas eve. It's usually pretty good. Always gets me in the mood of the season."

"That all sounds very nice," said Ransom, "but remember, Emily, you're here for a rest."

"Oh, I remember," said Emily in such a perfect travesty of a little old lady that had she been any younger one would have thought she was doing an imitation of herself.

Millie laughed, and said to Ransom as she exited to the kitchen, "I'll get you some coffee."

"They're so nice and accommodating here," said Emily, "I can't believe that they normally wait on people like this."

"You just naturally bring out the domestic in people," Ransom replied as he spread butter on half a muffin.

As they finished breakfast they discussed their plans for the day. Emily said she thought she'd like to visit some of the shops, and Ransom agreed, with the proviso that they have lunch in town to avoid having to come all the way back to the house.

Sara appeared for the first time that morning as Ransom and Emily were preparing to leave. She looked a little more haggard than the day before. There were small, light gray crescents under her eyes serving as evidence of a poor night's sleep. She gave Ransom a map of the local antique stores, which were scattered around the area. Ransom transferred a doubtful glance from Emily to the map before folding it and sticking it in his pocket. He thanked Sara and told her they wouldn't be there for lunch.

"I worry about that young woman," said Emily as she and Ransom headed toward LeFavre.

"How so?"

Emily gave him a gently reproving look as if she thought he might just be having her on. The right corner of her mouth slid up into a half smile. "Now, Jeremy, I'm sure you must've noticed that Sara seems to be troubled."

Ransom shrugged. "It hasn't been all that long since her brother died."

"It's been two years."

"That's still not that long."

Emily said "hmm" and sat silently for a few moments. "He was murdered, you know."

"Was he?"

"And the murderer was never caught."

"That could make it harder to get over the loss," said Ransom in a matter-of-fact tone that seemed to indicate that he wasn't interested in pursuing the topic.

"Yes, that's true, I'm sure. . . ." Emily said musingly as she turned away from him, letting her gaze travel to the landscape. "But I can't help believing there's more to it than that."

The town of LeFavre sat in a semicircle around a small bay fed by Lake Michigan. It was accessible by a two-lane street off the main highway. The street inclined downward into the town then continued along the waterfront. The last turn before reaching the water was Main Street, onto which Ransom steered the car. He parked in one of the many empty spaces and they sat there for a few moments taking in their surroundings.

There were rows of shops in a variety of styles and sizes, all of them old, on each side of the street. The absence of newer architecture made it look as if, at some point in the past, the townspeople had decided that any further progress would upset the ambiance of the place and had simply stopped. What they were left with was a Main Street that was unself-consciously quaint.

The sidewalks were lined with trees spaced at regular intervals, carefully maintained and kept trimmed to approximately the same size. Each of them was decorated with hundreds of white Italian lights, which, although they couldn't be seen to their full effect at that time of day, even in the sunlight lent a pleasant, glittering effect to the scene.

Once out of the car, they made their way very slowly up one side of the street with Emily supported on Ransom's arm. The store windows displayed a variety of home-made wares, ranging from hand-dipped candles to oil paintings. They passed by shops selling clothing, candies, and pottery, and one that appeared to sell nothing but cotton throws on which detailed maps of the town had been printed in the customer's choice of colors. There was also an ice cream parlor called the Soda Shoppe, which was closed and shuttered for the winter. Despite his fondness for Emily, the pace was maddeningly slow for Ransom, who compensated by setting his jaw and concentrating on each step they took as if he were dissecting the components for further study. His efforts did not escape Emily's notice. At one point, she wordlessly patted his hand in acknowledgment of his effort.

The first store that they actually went into was a small wood-framed building that had obviously been converted from a house. The bulk of the front was made up of a large convex lattice window through which they caught glimpses of hand-made jewelry displayed on huge, rough rocks scattered about the floor.

When they entered, they found the proprietor—and artisan—of the store behind the counter by the cash register, working with some small bits of silver and beads. She was a very large woman who was probably in her fifties but looked a good deal older. She had very long, multitoned gray hair and leathery skin that bore signs of too much time spent in direct sunlight. She wore a faded cotton peasant dress and a strip of matching fabric tied around her forehead as a headband. There were rings on each of her fingers, oversized hoops from which small feathers dangled on her ears, and a necklace of large turquoise stones for which her ample breasts served as a display rack.

"Welcome to The Silver Eagle," the woman said, spreading her arms wide as if delivering a benediction.

"Hello," Emily said primly, hoping to stem any potential effusiveness.

"Feel free to look around."

Emily wandered to a glass case that held some of the simpler items: small silver crosses and geometric figures designed to be suspended from a chain around one's neck. A miniature metal tree on which gold and silver chains in various weights and lengths had been hung sat at one end of the case.

"I didn't know you liked jewelry," Ransom said quietly, as if there were some chance that the proprietor wouldn't hear any conversation being held in this tiny store.

"Oh, I don't really, other than my earrings," Emily replied, absently giving the small pearl in her left lobe a tug, "but I was thinking of getting Lynn some token to thank her for taking care of things for me while we're away."

"Here?"

"Not necessarily. We've just started."

"Hm," Ransom replied. He left her scrutinizing the things in the case while he wandered around looking at some of the trinkets arrayed on the rocks. On one he found a pair of onyx earrings in the shape of turtles, their heads stretching toward the sky. On another, there was a small, unpainted bit of clay cleverly shaped to look like an adobe hut with a ring through its chimney to allow for a chain.

"There's a price tag on everything," said the proprietor, "but if you got any questions, all you have to do is ask."

"Thank you," Emily replied. "Do you make all of these things yourself?"

"Sure do," said the woman, joining Emily by the case. "With my own two little hands. Well, maybe not so little!"

She thrust her hands out to show Emily. They were, indeed, very large, the skin was dried and cracked and the nails bitten down to stubs.

"You do some very delicate work," said Emily with a note of surprise in her voice that wasn't lost on the woman.

"Don't seem possible, does it?" she said, rubbing her palms against the sides of her dress. "But if you're delicate here"—she thumped her chest with her index finger—"it comes out in your work."

"Well, I must say that these things are very lovely."

"Thanks," said the woman proudly. There was a slight pause, then she asked with the interest of someone who spends a great deal of time alone, "You folks just in for the day, or in for the holidays?"

"We'll be here through Christmas."

"Ah. You got relatives around here?"

"No, we just came to the area for a little vacation."

"Really? Where're you staying?"

"Hawthorne House."

The woman didn't exactly recoil, but the change in her attitude was apparent. It was as if she had retreated behind an invisible iron door, promptly and defiantly slammed shut. Though neither Ransom nor Emily had been facing her when it happened, the abrupt shift in the atmosphere was so acute that they both turned, almost in unison, and looked at the woman.

"Is anything the matter?" said Emily, her thin gray brows knitting together.

"No. No, 'course not," said the woman, brushing her hands on her dress again as if she were having trouble getting something off them.

"Are you quite sure?"

" 'Course I am," said the woman. She crossed back to the counter at which she'd been working when they'd come in.

"Forgive me," Emily pressed on with a glance at Ransom, "it just seemed to me that the mention of Hawthorne House had some effect on you."

"No," said the woman, making an attempt to recover the warmth she'd shown them earlier. "When you said it, it just reminded me about . . . well, no, I don't tell tales out of school." When she added this last she looked from Emily to Ransom and back again, her expression giving them both the idea that not only did she tell tales out of school, she probably told them everywhere else, as well.

There was a slight pause before Emily said, "We *know* about the murder."

"You do?" The woman eyed Emily with something resembling wariness, as if she thought it highly suspicious that someone would stay in a place where they knew a murder had been committed. "Okay. You know. Well, all I was going to say was when you mentioned that place it reminded me of the murder. I didn't mean anything against anybody."

Emily's eyes narrowed and her mouth formed a smile that on anyone else would have been called wicked. "I'm sure you didn't."

"It's just that we don't have that kinda thing happen here often. It don't bring back to mind pleasant thoughts. . . ." She stopped and glanced down at the materials with which she'd been working, then muttered, ". . . past or present."

"They investigated the murder, didn't they?" Ransom cut in, "And they didn't find anything."

"No, *they* didn't find anything." The woman's emphasis of the word "they" dripped with acid, and a smug smile spread across her face. Ransom thought that if he could have done it with impunity, he would have lifted one of the heavy rocks and hurled it at her.

They let the matter drop and spent a few more uncomfortable minutes looking at the jewelry before leaving the store, Emily having decided that she didn't think anything there would quite do.

Once outside, Emily said, "Well, that was certainly curious. Whatever could've made her act so strangely?"

"Do you mean when we came in or later?"

"You know very well what I mean. Why, she seemed almost angry."

"Hm."

Emily remained lost in thought as they continued down the street, barely giving her attention to any of the windows they passed. They reached the first corner at which they found an establishment aptly named The Corner Drug Store. It was a two-story red-brick building, the only one on the street that actually looked as if it had been meant to be a store. The second floor was a row of nondescript apartments.

As Ransom and Emily paused in front of the store, a door to their right, which led up to the second floor, was carelessly thrust open and out came Johnnie Larkin. He barely seemed to give them a glance as he went by, but suddenly stopped in his tracks when he recognized Emily. He wheeled around.

"Hello! Hello, Miss Charters!"

"Hello," said Emily with the formality she reserved for people she found a bit too boisterous. "I don't believe you've met my friend, Mr. Ransom."

"No, I didn't." Johnnie stuck out his hand and shook Ransom's vigorously. "Please to meet you." He turned back to Emily, and said, "So, you made it into town today!"

"Yes."

"Well, I'm gonna be out to the house later. I got some work to do at the Darcy farm, but Sara usually has stuff for me to do, too, so I'll probably see you later!"

Without waiting for any reply, he hurried off down the street and around the corner, leaving Emily and Ransom staring after him.

"A very energetic young man," said Emily.

"Humph," was Ransom's reply. "Do you want to go in the drugstore for anything?"

Emily peered in through the window, and after a few moments her interest seemed to be caught by something. "I think so. I think I should like some postcards."

Ransom held the door open for her, then followed her in. They stopped just inside the door, and Emily said quietly, "I think it would be better if I did this myself."

Ransom gazed at her with a puzzled look. He glanced from the counter and back at Emily, raised his right eyebrow, and smiled. "I'll look around."

Ransom paused at the end of the aisle where they'd been standing and watched her. To his trained eye, he thought he could see her growing more frail as she approached the counter. He disappeared down the aisle.

A tall carousel of postcards stood on one end of the counter, and behind the counter an elderly man sat on a stool reading a book. He was wearing old black jeans, a white shirt, and a bolo tie clipped at the neck with a small silver moose head. Inured as he was by years of exposure to casual browsers, he gave no sign of noticing Emily's approach.

Emily turned the carousel slowly, occasionally exclaiming at the beauty of the cards. There were pictures of the bay, the beach, Main Street, and some of the historic or more distinctive houses in the area.

"You have some very beautiful cards here."

"Um hm," said the old man without looking up.

Emily continued to turn the rack, letting out a sporadic, disappointed "Oh, dear." When she still hadn't managed to wrest the man's full attention, she took a faltering step backward and put her right hand to her cheek. She said absently, "I was hoping . . . oh, dear."

The old man sighed and set his book aside. "Help you find something?"

Emily gave him a relieved smile, and said, "Well, I don't know. I noticed that you have postcards here of some of the local houses. And I was hoping to find the one at which I'm staying—I have a friend, you see, who likes postcards and is always nice enough to show some interest in what I'm doing. It's always nice for someone to show interest in what you're doing, don't you think? But as I was saying, I don't see a picture of it here. I don't suppose you have any cards that aren't on display."

"Not really," he said, not unkindly but not apologetically, either. "Sometimes we run out of a particular card and have to re-order. We might have it coming in later. What house are you staying at?"

"Hawthorne House."

"Hawthorne House?" the man echoed blankly. "No, we never did carry one of that."

"Really?" said Emily with feigned surprise. "I understood it to be a very old house—it's certainly very well maintained—and from what I've heard, it's had quite a history."

The old man nodded his head, and replied, "It has a history, all right."

Emily's eyes widened and her voice took on a quaver. "What do you mean?"

He returned a condescending smile that Emily took as a sign that he enjoyed making timid women uncomfortable. "I don't mean anything. Just that some people might be afraid to stay there."

"Afraid?" said Emily, her eyes growing even wider. "Do you mean that the house is . . . is *haunted?*" Her voice became low and hollow as she spoke the last word, as if she thought that merely saying it might draw the spirits of the dead from the very floor around her.

"Pah!" said the old man, "I don't think there's nothing to worry about from the dead. It's the living you have to worry about."

"What do you mean?" Emily asked, clutching her purse more tightly.

The man leaned toward her, cocked his head sideways, and lowered his voice so that he sounded just as if he were telling a ghost story to a group of children around a campfire. "That woman that owns the place—Sara Bartlett—her brother was murdered two years ago. Pitchfork was driven right through his chest. And they never *did* find who did it!"

"Oh, my!"

The old man sat back on his stool and folded his arms across his chest, his satisfied smile indicating he was pleased with the re-action he'd elicited.

"Of course, some of us have our own ideas on that score."

"I don't understand."

He counted off each reason on his fingers as he said, "Only one person had any interest in his death, only one person gained by it, only one person really *knew* the boy well enough to kill him."

Emily put a hand to her heart and looked as though she might give in to a faint. "You don't mean Sara? That nice young woman? Why would she kill her own brother?"

"Who knows?" said the old man with a shrug. "But I'm not the only person 'round here that thinks Sara Bartlett might've got away with murder."

I'm sure you're not, thought Emily sharply as she struggled to maintain her timid visage.

Ransom collected her not long after that and led her out of the store. A degree of her frailty seemed to disappear once they were out on the sidewalk.

"Are you feeling better?" Ransom said, a sly smile playing about his lips.

"I beg your pardon?"

Ransom shot a glance at the drugstore window. "I thought for a minute in there that you'd gone a little weak."

"Well, you know, Jeremy, there is a certain type of person who likes to play on the credulity of others. . . ."

"Are you referring to him or to you?"

She smiled but didn't comment. ". . . and it is sometimes possible to use that to your own advantage."

"And was he one of those people?"

"Oh, yes," Emily said with a tinge of sadness, "he was rather of a type. I wouldn't be surprised to learn that he spent his youth setting fire to cats."

"Good Lord, Emily!" Ransom laughed. "Did you learn whatever it was you wanted to know?"

Emily frowned. "Local sentiment appears to be that Sara killed her brother."

Ransom's eyes narrowed. "Why?"

"Apparently for no other reason than she knew him better than anyone else."

Ransom grunted in response to this.

They spent a few more minutes browsing the windows of the shops before deciding it was time for lunch. They stopped at the Red Lion, a pseudo-English restaurant in which the ambiance and the food were equally pleasant. It was also one of the few restaurants open year-round. Still insistent on Emily's complete rest and relaxation, Ransom made it a point to stay off the subject of the unsolved murder. For her part, Emily shied away from the topic for fear that her continued interest would increase Ransom's anxiety on her behalf. She chose instead to ruminate on the matter to herself. The end result of this concerted effort to avoid the subject was that, despite the light conversation in which they engaged over their Caesar salads and trifle, the murder was the foremost thought in both their minds. *Rather like trying not to think of spotted elephants,* Emily thought as she spooned the last bit of the dessert into her mouth.

After lunch, they spent a little more time sight-seeing, then, though they hadn't completed their circuit of even one side of the street, decided to put off doing any more until the next day.

When they returned to Hawthorne House, Emily retired to her room for an afternoon nap, and Ransom retrieved an ancient, dog-eared book and his cigars from his room and went to the smoking room. He switched on the exhaust fan and settled into one of the Naugahyde chairs, then he extracted a cigar from the pack, stuck the plastic tip between his lips, and lit it.

He closed his eyes as he drew in the smoke, then slowly released it. He hadn't been aware of how much tension he was experiencing until he felt it dissipating with the smoke into the air. He took another drag, feeling his shoulders relax and his muscles loosen as he released another stream of smoke. After a few more puffs in the self-imposed darkness, his eyes slid open and he looked out the window. The snow spread out across the landscape like a blank page on which nothing would ever be written. Accustomed as he was to the excess sensory stimulation provided by the crowded view from his Chicago high-rise apartment, the relative nothingness of his new surroundings left his nerves hungry. He smiled to himself at the thought of his disquiet being caused by all this peace.

Ransom was interrupted in this reverie by the sound of the door opening. He started to rise when he saw it was Sara, but she quickly motioned for him not to bother. She looked less haggard than she had that morning, and Ransom suspected she had napped while they were gone. But the circles were still under her eyes and her face was ashen. Even if she'd been able to get some rest, it hadn't helped her very much.

"I didn't see you when you got back from town. I just wanted to make sure everything was all right."

"Everything was fine," he said, trying his best to sound more congenial that was his norm.

"Did Emily do all right?"

"She got along fine. We tried not to overdo it."

"Good."

A silence fell between them. Ransom took a puff of his cigar and scrutinized the young woman, who still stood hesitating in the doorway, looking at the floor. From her intense, frustrated expression, Ransom decided that she desperately wanted to ask him something more, but either didn't think she should or didn't know how to proceed.

After a moment, he said, "Miss Bartlett, you're letting the smoke out of the room."

"Oh," she exclaimed, looking up. She smiled at him and stepped inside, closing the door but not letting it latch. She stood with her hand on the doorknob, as if she still wanted very much to talk to him but didn't want him to think she was going to be a bother.

"Well, what did you think of our little town?"

Ransom continued to eye her for a beat before answering. He had a feeling he knew what it was she wanted to know, and he was trying to decide on how to relay the information without causing her embarrassment.

"The town was very nice," he said, then narrowing his incisive eyes at her added, "I can't say that I find the people overly friendly."

The anxiety on Sara's face increased noticeably. "Did anyone say . . . was anyone rude to you?"

"No. Just reserved." Ransom paused for a moment, then without sounding the least bit as if he were trying to draw her out said, "We chalked it up to the usual small-town bias. That's all it is, don't you think?"

Sara looked for a moment as if she were going to confide in him, but instead she cast her eyes back to the floor. The sadness in them made it abundantly clear that she knew the real cause of any reticence that might have been shown her guests. "Yes, I'm sure that's all it is."

Ransom sighed inwardly. She was certainly making it difficult.

"I imagine you experienced much the same thing when you first moved here. But that must've changed by now."

Sara's cheeks flushed and her hand tightened on the doorknob. "It takes people a long time to forget," she said softly.

"Forget? . . ." Ransom replied, raising an eyebrow.

She looked up at him and her voice quavered when she said, "To forget . . . that you're new. That's all I meant. You can't get lost here the way you can in Chicago. There's not enough people. And the ones that're here don't have a lot of other things to think about." She glanced at her watch, then back at him, and said, "It's getting late. I've got to get dinner started." She opened the door and paused just long enough to add, "I'm glad you had a good time in town."

With this she disappeared, closing the door behind her.

Ransom sat for a few minutes taking thoughtful puffs from his cigar and considering Sara's plight. After a while he shrugged and turned to his book.

He'd brought with him a volume of Dickens's Christmas books that included *The Haunted Man,* which he intended to reread over the holiday. It was one of his favorites: the story of Redlaw, a man haunted by painful memories of his past. Redlaw encounters a ghost who is "the awful image of himself," and pleads with the apparition to erase his painful memories so that he might have some peace. The ghost complies, but the blessing turns into a curse when Redlaw discovers that it's the painful events and memories in our lives that give us compassion and humanity.

As Ransom opened the well-worn book and settled back into the comfortable chair, the sorrowful expression on Sara's face still uppermost in his mind, he wondered if perhaps Dickens, for once, had been wrong.

Emily woke in the middle of the night with the sudden alertness of someone whose sound sleep has been interrupted by an unexpected noise. She lay there for a minute, listening intently for a recurrence of the sound, but there was nothing but the crackling silence of the still night air.

She slowly turned her head and looked at the luminous dial of the travel alarm she'd placed on the bedside table. It was a few minutes after two. She rested her head back on the pillow and stared at the ceiling for a few moments, but she heard nothing, not even the settling noises so common to older houses.

Emily closed her eyes and sighed. She was just about to drift back off to sleep when she heard it again, a sob so muffled it might have come to her from another world rather than somewhere in the house. She pushed back the comforter and shifted her legs over the side of the bed, pulling herself up into a sitting position at the same time. She slipped her feet into a pair of soft house slippers, and pulled on the cream-colored cotton robe she'd laid across the foot of the bed. With a little effort she stood up and stayed there for a moment trying to decide from which direction the sob had originated. It occurred to her that it had been so faint it might have come from the library. She went to the commuting door and pressed her ear against it. Hearing nothing, she turned the knob and pulled the door open as quietly as possible.

The moon cast enough reflected light through the library window for Emily to see at a glance that the room was unoccupied. She went through the library and opened the door to the living room, still trying not to make any noise. She stood in the doorway for a moment and was just about to step out into the room when she heard another choking sob, still muffled but this time clearly audible and coming, she thought, from the kitchen. She rounded the corner and looked in.

Sara was sitting in the darkness on the chair at the far end of the table. She had one leg drawn up under her floral flannel nightgown, her right arm was hanging over the back of the chair and she was covering her mouth with her left hand. The tears on her cheeks glistened in the moonlight.

Emily was standing very still in the archway trying to decide whether to advance or retreat when Sara chanced to look in her direction.

"Oh! Miss Charters!" she said, jumping up from her chair and wiping her eyes with the sleeve of her nightgown. She remained by the chair. "I didn't see you there. I'm sorry, did I wake you?"

"No," said Emily. She thought for a second about what might be the best way to proceed, then said, "No, I was having a little trouble sleeping. That happens sometimes. I'm afraid it's one of those things that comes with age. I didn't know you were up—but I was wondering, would it be much trouble if I had some tea?"

There was a pause during which Sara looked quite confused, as if she thought she might not have understood Emily correctly. Then she said, "Sure, it's no problem."

She switched on a small light over the stove, which illuminated the room just enough to see but not enough to be startling, then set about heating the water for tea.

Emily took a seat on the opposite side of the table. She hadn't really wanted any tea, but she thought the best thing for Sara at that moment might be to keep busy.

"You'll have to forgive me," said Sara, making an effort to regain her composure. "I don't usually . . . I'm not usually up in the middle of the night. I don't usually fall apart like this."

"Sometimes it helps," said Emily quietly as she watched Sara.

"I've just been . . . there've been a lot of things lately."

"My dear, I know it's none of my business, but don't you have someone you can talk to about your troubles? Lynn told us that both of your parents were deceased, but surely there must be someone. . . ."

Sara shot her a surprised glance. "I don't know that both of them are dead. My mother died about six years ago, but she and my father divorced when I was very young, and I never saw him again." She paused for a moment, then as if in answer to an unasked question added, "It was a very acrimonious divorce."

"But surely you have someone—"

"I have some friends, I suppose," Sara replied with an awkward shrug, "but no relatives. Nobody like . . ." Her voice trailed off.

"I understand."

"Do you?" said Sara as she laid cups out. She then put a couple of tea bags in a ceramic teapot and set it in the center of the table.

"I think I do. I know that your brother was killed and that the murderer was never caught. And I was in town today. It's a small town, and in a small town, if you talk to people at all, you're bound to hear the local gossip."

"I know what they think," said Sara with feeling, "and I don't care about it."

"You don't?" Emily replied with some surprise.

"No, I don't. I realize I seem . . ." She stopped and thought for a moment, then shook her head dismissively. "No, I don't know how I seem. But I really don't care what a bunch of local busy-bodies think. I realize some of them say that I killed my brother, but I know I didn't. Their thinking it isn't going to change the facts."

"That's very sensible of you."

Though the kettle had not yet begun to whistle, the water was making enough noise to indicate it was ready. Sara switched off the burner as she removed the kettle. She filled the teapot on the table and replaced the kettle. Emily continued to watch her intently, waiting for her to continue.

"The thing that I can't . . . the thing I can't get beyond is that even though I didn't kill Nathan myself . . . I *know* I was responsible for his death."

With this she crumpled into her chair and buried her face in her hands. Emily's eyebrows slid upward, sending creases across her forehead. She reached into the cuff of her robe, pulled out a clean linen handkerchief, and handed it to Sara, who accepted it with a nod and dabbed her eyes.

"Forgive me," said Emily, "but I don't understand. If you didn't kill your brother, how could you be responsible for his death?"

Sara gestured limply around the room. "Because of this."

"Yes?"

"This was my dream. *My* dream, you see? It was me who wanted to own this place . . . to have a place like this. If it wasn't for me and my stupid dream, we never would have been here and Nathan never would've been killed."

"But you don't know that," Emily remonstrated softly.

"Yes, I do!" Sara said. Her tears were flowing more freely now, and she kept Emily's handkerchief pressed against her nose. "It doesn't matter who killed him, really. Whether he was killed by one of the locals for some reason, or if he was killed by somebody who was just passing through, any way you look at it, he was killed because he was *here!* And he was here because of me."

"Sara," said Emily gently but firmly, "I understand how you might feel that way, but I really do believe that, without knowing why your brother was killed, you cannot know for sure that it had anything to do with his being here."

Sara's watery eyes blinked at Emily over the top of the wadded-up handkerchief. "What else could it have been?"

"Oh, I don't know. Any number of things, I suppose. But when we don't have all the facts it's very easy to jump at the most obvious conjecture as being gospel truth. But I can tell you that the older you get, the more you find the obvious can be very deceptive."

Sara hazarded something of a smile. "You know, Lynn warned me about you. She said you could be pretty deceptive yourself."

"I beg your pardon?" said Emily, though there was a twinkle in her eye.

"She said that you pretend to be a little old lady, when you're really as sharp as Solomon and straight as a die."

"Well, I don't know about that," said Emily, her pleased smile betraying the pleasure she took in the secondhand compliment.

A silence fell between them, during which Sara lifted the pot and poured out the tea. She put a spoonful of sugar in her cup and stirred it pensively. After a moment, she said, "It doesn't really matter, you know . . . I mean, why Nathan was killed."

"But of course it does," said Emily.

"No, I mean it won't change things. No matter why he was killed, when Nathan died, my dream died with him. Nothing will ever be the same."

"Well, if I may ask a question, under the circumstances don't you think it might be better if you didn't stay here? Why not sell Hawthorne House and start fresh somewhere else?"

"Because it wouldn't make a difference." Sara put her hands around her cup as if to warm them and straightened herself in her chair. "You see, when Nathan was killed and nothing . . . nobody was found, my life was sort of thrown into . . . a void, I guess you'd call it—one that just never goes away. I wander around and around as if I'm only half-awake, looking for a way out, but nothing has ever seemed right since Nathan was killed. And I don't think that void will be closed until there's . . . some solution. Do you have any idea what I mean?"

"Of course. I would think it's the most natural way to feel under the circumstances. There is a rather large mystery there, and the human mind wants all mysteries to be solved. But sometimes the world has other ideas."

"What do you mean?"

"Only that not all mysteries *can* be solved, at least not in this life. And sometimes the only way to go on is to shut the door on that void on your own."

"I wish I could," Sara replied sadly. "I really wish I could."

They sat in silence for a moment, with Sara staring disconsolately into her teacup as Emily watched her, a compassionate smile spreading across her face. "On the other hand," she said at last, "perhaps the best thing for us to do would be to solve the mystery."

"Jeff did all he could," Sara replied, her voice ringing hollow.

"Well, I happen to know someone who is rather adept at solving puzzles."

"You do?" said Sara, sounding as if she were afraid to entertain any hope.

"You know him, too: Mr. Ransom is a homicide detective. He might be persuaded to look into this for you."

Sara hesitated. "Oh . . . I couldn't ask it. He's supposed to be enjoying himself."

"That's true," said Emily, her smile becoming more mischievous, "but I don't think he is."

Sara looked stricken, and before she could say anything Emily continued quickly, "Oh, no, Sara, you mustn't think it's because of you. You've provided a perfectly lovely place for us. I'm afraid that Jeremy is used to a great deal of mental activity. He's not the type of man who can rest easily." She lifted the cup to her lips, and added, "Yes . . . a little puzzle might be the best thing for him."

5

The following morning, Millie had pots of coffee and tea waiting on the dining table for Ransom and Emily when they came to breakfast. Piles of scrambled eggs lay ready in a food warmer on the sideboard, and Millie told them she was just about to pull some country biscuits out of the oven for them.

"What makes them 'country' biscuits?" Ransom asked.

"I'm making them in the country," Millie replied over her shoulder as she bustled out to the kitchen.

Ransom prepared a plate of eggs for himself and for Emily, put them at their places on the table, and took his seat. Once he was situated, Emily said, "Jeremy, there's a little matter I'd like to discuss with you."

"Yes?" he said distractedly as he scooped a forkful of eggs into his mouth.

"There's something I'd very much like you to do for me."

"What's that?"

"I'd like you to look into Nathan Bartlett's murder."

Ransom stopped abruptly in the act of taking a drink of coffee. He set the mug on the table with a light thud, sat back in his chair, folded his arms, and raised an eyebrow. "Whatever for?"

Emily's eyes became more incisive as she leaned in toward

him. "Because that young woman, Sara, needs to know what happened to him. She's living under a very dark cloud—you noticed that as well as I did yesterday when we were in town. And the only way to dispel that cloud is to find out once and for all who killed her brother."

Ransom gazed at her for a moment before answering. "I'm sure the local authorities looked into it when it happened. I'm also sure they're very capable people."

"That may be, but they didn't *solve* it, and in this case it's the results that matter rather than the effort. Because it wasn't solved, Sara lives under constant suspicion. In a town such as this, if the matter is never resolved then the suspicions will always be with her. People may be polite to her, they may treat her courteously, even kindly, but there will always be that wariness and doubt toward her."

"There may be that, anyway. That's the way it is with gossip."

"But that's just the thing," Emily replied earnestly. "You know, Jeremy, gossip is very often true. That's why when the gossip is false, it's so damaging."

"Which leaves me to wonder," said Ransom, "if Sara didn't kill her brother, why are people so willing to believe she did?"

"Because people are poison," said Millie hotly as she banged into the room through the kitchen door. She was carrying a small basket full of biscuits over which she'd laid a cloth napkin to hold in the warmth. " 'Scuse me. I'm sorry, I didn't mean to listen in. I just heard the tail end of what you were saying. Anyone with an ounce of sense in their heads would know Sara would never kill anybody, let alone her brother! And anybody that says different is just spreading poison. And I tell you something else, too: Jeff Fields did his job, no matter what anybody tells you!"

"I beg your pardon," said Emily, the shine in her eyes showing the admiration she felt at the woman's defense of her employer, "but who is Jeff Fields?"

Millie set the basket in the center of the table and brushed her hands on her apron. "Jeff's the sheriff. And he *did* investigate that murder, he just didn't find anything. That's all there is to it, no matter who tells you different."

"Why would anyone tell us 'different'?" Ransom asked, apostrophizing the idiom wryly. Emily shot him a glance.

Millie looked at the palms of her hands, then their backs, as if checking for traces of whatever she'd been trying to brush off. She faltered when she answered him as if she thought she might be betraying someone. "Well, because Jeff and Sara, they were going together when it happened. They were . . . well, I would've said they were in love. But then Nathan had to go get murdered and Jeff had to investigate, and when nothing came of it . . ." She shrugged as her voice trailed off.

"When he didn't bring anyone in," Ransom said, narrowing his eyes, "the local people thought maybe he didn't exactly do his job."

"That's right!" said Millie, nodding angrily.

"And if he didn't do his job it was because Sara was the guilty party, and he was in love with her."

"But he wouldn't do that," Millie protested. "He's a good man. And the fact that he was the one . . . well, I don't think Sara ever got over it. I don't know that she'll ever forgive him."

Millie's eyes began to tear up, and rather than stand there and cry in front of them, she said "Oh, hell!" and fled to the kitchen.

"A rather convincing testimonial," said Ransom.

"Jeremy, you're not to be cynical," Emily said, coming as close to severity as she ever had with him. She folded her hands on the table. "I *know* that Sara didn't kill her brother."

"How do you know that?"

"Because she thinks she's responsible."

He smiled at her. "Emily, you're going to have to explain that."

She related to him the entire midnight conversation she'd had with Sara. When she finished, she added, "You see, Jeremy, it's bad enough that the people of this area blame Sara for Nathan's death, but if this case remains unsolved, Sara will go on blaming herself for it, too, simply because she was the reason he was here in this town."

Ransom sat back in his chair and considered this soberly, never taking his eyes off Emily's. After a few moments he said very pointedly, "You realize, of course, that in all probability—I'd almost go so far as to say in all possibility—she's right. Whether he was killed by someone from the area or whether he was killed by someone who was just passing through, whatever the motive, it's most likely her brother would be alive today if they hadn't moved here. You may be asking me to prove that Sara's fears are true."

Emily sighed. "That's a chance we'll just have to take. I believe that for Sara the uncertainty is worse. Maybe in time she'd be able to come to terms with it, if you're right. But if you can solve the case, at least some of her questions would be answered."

"A two-year-old trail is likely to be very, very cold."

"I have the utmost faith in your abilities."

"Even *I* need something to work with."

Though she might have been discouraged by his mild protest, the degree of interest in his voice told Emily she was on the right track.

"Well, Jeremy, if nothing else you can prove that the solution is simply unattainable."

"I suspect, my dear Emily, that you've been taking lessons on the sly from Sergeant Frank Newman."

"Whatever do you mean?" said Emily with elaborate innocence.

Ransom eyed her for a few moments, absently tapping his index finger on the tablecloth. At last he sighed, and said, "Well, perhaps I can ask a few questions."

He said this with as much reluctance as he could possibly muster and still be thought gracious. But it didn't escape Emily's notice that, for the first time since they'd arrived in town, he didn't seem bored.

"Thank you," she said with so little emphasis one would've thought she'd asked him nothing more than to pass the biscuits.

"Miss Bartlett, at Emily's request, I thought I'd do a little checking into the death of your brother."

Sara nodded her head silently as she took a seat. Ransom had sought her out directly after he and Emily finished their breakfast. He ushered her into the smoking room, closing the door behind them. He pulled a chair up and sat facing her.

"I'm not sure that's a good thing," Sara said, giving a nervous tug to the hem of her skirt, which immediately slid back up over her knee. "I'm not sure it's very wise to stir it all up again."

"It would seem that it's never completely settled down for you."

Sara averted her eyes from him, appearing to be intently studying something just beyond his right shoulder. "Well, that may be . . . maybe it's just my imagination. . . ."

Ransom gently drummed his fingers on the arm of his chair, a sure sign that his professional impatience was returning. "Do you really believe that?"

She brought her eyes back to his, and after a beat she quietly said "No."

Ransom gave her his most ingratiating smile. "Then why don't you tell me what happened the night your brother was killed?"

It was, of course, a very painful topic for Sara, but there was something so reassuringly direct in Ransom's manner that she felt as if she'd been asked to relate the story to a disinterested third party.

She started slowly. "There was a very bad storm that night. A blizzard. I was . . . I spent the evening . . . the late evening . . . in the parlor. That's the front room, where we have the Christmas tree. Nathan had gone up to his room . . ."

"When was that?"

"Um . . . about nine o'clock, I think. He said he was going to watch TV or something. When I went up to bed . . ." Ransom looked as if he were about to inject another question, but she beat him to it. "That was about eleven. I went up to bed. I stopped by his room on my way and he wasn't there."

"Why did you do that?"

"What?" said Sara, looking almost startled.

"Why did you go into his room? Did you usually do that?"

She shifted in her chair. "Well, yes. I usually stopped in to say good night if his light was still on."

"And was it?"

"No. But his door was slightly open, and that wasn't usual. So I went in, and he wasn't there. I called to him, but he didn't answer, and I started to look all over the house . . . and then I started to get scared. I'm not . . . I don't usually get scared like that, but there was the storm and everything, and I couldn't imagine where he'd gone."

"It was perfectly natural," said Ransom kindly.

Sara gave him an abbreviated, self-deprecating smile, which seemed to be the best she could manage. "It was like he had just . . . vanished from the house . . . like he'd been spirited away."

"Hmm . . ." said Ransom. He continued to study her face intently, and from her vacant expression, he felt it was apparent that she didn't realize the irony of her choice of words. "What did you do then?"

She absently twined a strand of her dark hair around her index finger as she answered. "Well . . . I knew he hadn't driven anywhere—the storm was so bad, I didn't think he could've if he'd wanted to—but I knew he hadn't because the driveway is right by the side window to the parlor. I would've heard a car. But I knew he wasn't in the house, and the only other building near here is the barn. I thought he might've gone back there to talk to Hansen about something. Hansen Crane, our handyman, lives over the barn."

"You didn't hear him go out?"

She shook her head. "No, I didn't."

"Wouldn't you ordinarily?"

She hesitated for a moment, looking as if this were the first time she'd ever thought of this. "Yes . . ." she said slowly. "Yes, I suppose I would. But the wind was making a lot of noise, so if he went out the back door, I might not have heard him . . . if . . ."

Ransom completed this for her. "If he was being quiet. What happened next?"

As she continued, she unwound the strand of hair from her finger and re-coiled it in the opposite direction. "I went to the back door and looked out. I couldn't really see the barn at all through the blizzard. I couldn't tell if the lights in Hansen's apartment were on. But I still thought that was the only place Nathan could've gone, so I put on my coat and took the flashlight we keep by the back door, and went to the barn. When I was just about there, I could see that Hansen's lights were out, so I went into the barn itself to check there. And I found him. . . ." She let go of her hair and her hand dropped into her lap. She was staring at the floor next to Ransom's chair, looking as if she were seeing it all again. Her eyes began to well with tears as she continued with some difficulty. "He was there . . . in the center of the floor . . . lying on his back . . . with that thing . . . that pitchfork . . . sticking out of his chest." She stopped and flicked the tears off her cheeks with her fingers. "I'm sorry."

"That's perfectly all right."

"I screamed when I saw him . . . and ran out of the barn and up the side stairs to Hansen's apartment and banged on his door. He let me in and we went back to the house and called the sheriff." She shrugged sadly as she said this last to indicate that was all there was to her story.

Ransom stared at her a moment through narrowed eyes, holding the tip of his right index finger to his lips. At last he laid his hand back on the arm of his chair, and said, "Did it take him long to answer the door?"

"What?" said Sara, once again as if he'd startled her.

"Hansen Crane. Did it take him long to answer the door?"

"Oh," she said, her expression clearing, "yes, it seemed like it took him forever. But I was . . . so upset, I can't be sure. But yes, I think it took him a long time. Why?"

"I was just wondering if you had to wake him."

"Oh, yes. I think so."

Ransom considered this for a moment, then recrossed his legs and said, "Did you see anything on your way to the barn?"

"Anything? No. I could barely see anything at all for the storm. Anything like what?"

"Footprints."

"Footprints? No, I didn't see any footprints."

Ransom raised an eyebrow. "Not even your brother's?"

Sara shook her head slowly. "No. Not even his."

Ransom sat completely still for a few moments, processing the information. At last he cocked his head, leaned in toward her, and said, "One last thing, Miss Bartlett. Do *you* have any idea who killed your brother?"

Sara raised her eyes from the floor and met Ransom's. "My brother was the kindest man alive. He didn't have any enemies."

"What about friends?"

"He had lots of friends."

"Anyone special?"

Sara averted her eyes again and shifted in her chair. "I don't know what you mean."

"Of course you do," Ransom countered without emotion. "Miss Bartlett, if you really want this matter resolved, it's important that you're completely honest with me."

Sara's cheeks flushed as she replied, "I have been." She stopped and adjusted her skirt, which apparently hadn't come along with her the last time she'd moved. With the fidgeting and the redness of her face, she couldn't have looked more uncomfortable if she'd tried. "Well, Nathan had a girlfriend. They were very close. Her name is Amy. Amy Shelton."

"She lives in town?"

"Yes," Sara said, looking almost as if she thought she'd just betrayed her best friend to the Gestapo. She added quickly, "Amy couldn't possibly have had anything to do with Nathan's death. She loved him. She couldn't have killed him."

"Then who did, Miss Bartlett?"

Sara threw her hands up in frustration. "I don't know! I haven't got a clue!"

When Ransom had finished with Sara, he found Emily in the parlor standing by the Christmas tree, admiring the ornaments from close range.

"There are so many beautiful things on the tree," she said. "Some of them are like ones I remember from my childhood." She lovingly fingered a delicate German glass ornament that looked worn enough to be an original. "Some of these must be family heirlooms."

"Very nice," said Ransom, his mind obviously on something else.

"Did you have your talk with Sara?"

"Yes, and it was quite interesting." He filled her in on what Sara had said. "If she's giving me an accurate account of what happened that night, I can almost see why popular opinion is against her. The whole of the story rests on her version of it alone. Nobody else was on hand."

"Hansen Crane was," Emily reminded him.

"Apparently he was asleep."

"Apparently?" Emily echoed with an amused smile, enjoying his dogged refusal to accept any statement at face value.

Ransom replied, "Somehow I can't imagine that being killed with a pitchfork is a very quiet business."

"That's true," said Emily thoughtfully, "and as he was stabbed in the chest, one would think he would've seen it coming and cried out."

"Or even if he hadn't seen it coming, he'd probably cry out on impact. People rarely 'go gently,' unless they do it at home in their beds."

Emily nodded. "And sometimes not even then."

They fell silent, both of them lost in their thoughts. Finally Emily said, "Well, how do you propose to proceed?"

Ransom sighed. "Would it be all right if we postponed our second junket into town? Do you mind being left here?"

"Oh, no," said Emily, "I shall be quite all right. I've brought *King Lear* along to keep me company."

Ransom gazed at her in disbelief. "You brought *Lear* to read on a Christmas trip?"

" 'A sad tale's best for winter,' " Emily quoted with a smile.

"That's not from *Lear.*"

"Very good, Jeremy. You're correct. But it was appropriate to the moment, none-the-less."

Ransom laughed. "Then if you don't mind staying here, I'll go to the sheriff's office and have a talk with him. Maybe he'd be willing to tell me what he found when he investigated."

"Oh, I'm sure he will," said Emily with elderly gusto, "I'm sure he'd do 'most anything to see this matter settled."

"Why do you say that?"

"Because," said Emily with a twinkle in her eye, "he was in love with her."

Emily watched from the parlor window as Ransom drove away, pleased not only that he was looking into Nathan Bartlett's murder, but also with the expected side effect: he hadn't been over-solicitous of her all morning.

Once his car was out of sight, Emily left the parlor and went to the kitchen, where she found Millie giving the pots and pans a hearty scrubbing. Though it was a chore that most would probably find tedious, Millie seemed to be enjoying herself.

"Hello, miss," said Millie. She wiped the back of her hand across her forehead and gestured to the sink full of water. "Even with guests, to my mind there just doesn't seem enough dishes to bother with that electric thing."

"Yes," said Emily wistfully, "and there's something about cleaning that's very satisfying to one's soul, don't you think?"

Millie laughed. "There's some wouldn't say so."

"Do you mind if I join you for a little while?"

"Suit yourself. I'd be glad for the company."

Emily took a seat at the kitchen table. "I always think that the kitchen is the most inviting part of any house."

"It's the heart of the home. That's what they say."

Millie was silent for a moment while she scrubbed out the pan she'd used to scramble the eggs. Then she said, "I thought I heard Mr. Ransom drive off. Didn't you want to go into town with him?"

"He had something he wanted to do on his own."

Millie paused in the act of rinsing off the pan and turned to Emily. "Is he really going to look into Nathan's murder?"

"Yes," Emily replied, "he's already started."

"Well, thank God for that," said Millie, resuming her tasks, "and good luck to 'im."

Emily cleared her throat. "You know, you might be of some help to us in that respect."

Millie shrugged. "Don't see how. I wasn't out here that night. Truth is, I'm almost never out here at night."

"It's not necessarily that night that I'm interested in. It's difficult to believe that Nathan could've been killed without something leading up to it."

"I don't find it hard to believe at all."

"Really?" said Emily, emitting an aura of innocent interest in the woman's opinion.

"Sure. I don't think it's all that mysterious. I just think he was killed by a tramp. No other explanation for it. Nobody didn't like Nathan. There must've been some tramp out there, taking refuge—like they say—in the barn—just a place to sleep for the night. Nathan caught him, and the tramp killed him." Millie shrugged with her palms up, as if she truly believed she'd explained everything.

"Yes, but *why* would Nathan have gone out to the barn in the middle of a storm?"

"Who knows? Maybe he just remembered something he forgot to do."

Emily pressed on, trying to gently direct Millie away from what Emily felt was a rather shaky theory in an attempt to elicit some more pertinent information. "And why would a tramp have killed him? Surely Nathan, if he was as nice as everyone says he was, wouldn't have been a threat to him."

Millie hesitated, casting a doubtful glance at her hands. "Well, I don't know about that. But who's to say what some vagrant will do if you come on him unexpected."

"That's very true," said Emily, "but suppose . . . well, let's suppose for a moment that there was some other reason for the murder. Tell me, what was going on back then?"

"How d'ya mean?"

Emily adjusted herself in her seat, an unconscious sign that she was getting down to business. "What I mean is, can you give me the lay of the land?"

Millie rested her hands on the sink and pursed her lips, lost in thought. "Well, the place had been open to the public . . . three years then. Everything was going pretty well. There's never a lack of business around here during the summertime. And Sara has a knack for this sort of thing. Um, she hired me on right off the bat, and about a year later, Hansen showed up and she hired him, though I don't think Nathan was too happy with that at first."

"Really?"

"Oh, that's nothing to think of!" said Millie. "Nathan was from the city and I don't think he ever heard of such a thing as a drifter before. He asked all kinds of questions about him. Even to me. He asked me if I knew anything about him or about his past or where he'd come from. But I didn't know anything. He's just a typical drifter. I'm surprised he's stayed here this long."

"That's very interesting," Emily said. "And did this happen just before Nathan died?"

"Oh, no!" said Millie, waving her hand in the air as if the idea was a gnat that needed to be brushed away. "It couldn't have anything to do with this. That was way back almost two years before Nathan was killed."

"I see," said Emily. "And when did Johnnie Larkin appear?"

"Um . . . around about the same time as Hansen, maybe a little later."

"Did Nathan have any objection to Johnnie?"

"Oh, no," said Millie, her face breaking into a smile. She seemed to find the thought of Johnnie amusing. "Johnnie's young. You don't expect young people to be as settled as somebody Hansen's age. And you gotta remember that Johnnie works for a lot of people. Hansen was moving here onto the property."

"That's true," said Emily thoughtfully. "Now, what about Sara's and Nathan's social life?"

"Well," Millie said a bit reluctantly, "well, they were both pretty busy with running the place."

"Surely they wouldn't have been as busy off season?" said Emily coaxingly.

Millie smiled. "Oh, okay! Just about everyone seemed to like Sara back then. But she was seeing Jeff Fields, especially. He came out to welcome her and check to see that everything was all right out here after she got her license to open the place. I think they hit it off right away. They started going together and got pretty serious . . . at one point. They were quite a pair."

"And Nathan?"

"He didn't socialize much, so people didn't know him as well as they knew Sara. But them that knew him liked him, especially Amy Shelton."

"Amy Shelton?"

A fond smile spread across Millie's face. "He was sweet on her. And she was sweet on him, too. They probably would've ended up married if it hadn't happened."

"Can you tell me if anything unusual was happening back then?"

"Like what?"

"Well, was Nathan acting completely normal before the murder? Did anything seem to be on his mind?"

Millie pursed her lips as she cast her mind back over the expanse of two years. "I don't know . . . I suppose he might've been a little preoccupied."

"In what way?"

"Oh, I don't know," said Millie, frowning with consternation at her own inability to articulate what she was thinking, "I'm just saying it. Don't know that I ever thought it before. I can't say I know why I thought of it."

"So it was nothing specific that you could put your finger on," Emily offered, her gaze intensifying.

"Nope. Like I said."

"He didn't say or do anything that was out of the ordinary?"

"Not that I can think of," Millie replied, setting about washing a baking sheet.

Emily folded her hands on the table, let out a frustrated sigh, and lost herself in thought. After a few moments, she said, "Millie, if Nathan wasn't killed by Sara, and he wasn't killed by a tramp, that leaves someone else . . . presumably from the area. Don't you have any idea of anyone who might've wanted to kill him?"

Millie pursed her lips again, and said, "Well, there's many around here who'd cut you with a word, or kill you with a look, but I don't know if anybody'd take a pitchfork to you."

"And yet, someone did," said Emily pointedly.

Millie paused and glanced at her. "Yeah, that's right." She went back to her washing. "If it hadn't happened, it wouldn't seem possible."

Emily nodded her head, though she didn't appear to be paying attention to her.

"I wonder . . ." she said reflectively.

"What's that?" asked Millie.

"I wonder why they didn't get married."

Millie stared at her for a moment as if she thought Emily

might just have slipped a cog. "Well, Miss Charters, they didn't get married because Nathan was killed."

"Oh, no," said Emily, "I didn't mean Nathan and Amy, I meant Sara and the sheriff."

Millie's expression transformed into a deep frown. "I don't know for sure, but it's a damn shame. That murder seems to have soured everything."

"Yes," said Emily, "it did."

6

The county sheriff's office was on the main highway, halfway between LeFavre and Mt. Morgan. It was a small building of pale yellow brick with a disproportionately large parking lot. As Ransom pulled into a space near the front door, he couldn't help thinking that the place looked more like a rest stop on the interstate than a sheriff's office.

The interior was no more prepossessing than the exterior. There was a long, cheap counter spanning almost the entire length of the room. Behind it were three desks, none of which were in use at the moment. The floor was covered in wide tiles that had been white at one time, but were yellow with age and heavily scuffed with usage. Several hard, straight wooden chairs sat in a line against the wall. They were so thickly varnished that they didn't just look wet, they looked as if they would ripple if anyone sat on them. On the right-hand wall behind the counter was an office door with a glass window etched in an intricate enough pattern to keep the interior of the office obscured.

Standing behind the counter was a young blond man who Ransom took to be a deputy. He was dressed in a khaki uniform which, in his case, was an unfortunate choice of colors, since, with his Aryan looks, the uniform made him look uncomfortably reminiscent of Nazi youths. Then again, Ransom thought, that might have been the point.

"I'd like to see Jeff Fields," said Ransom.

"Is there anything *I* can help you with?" replied the deputy without so much as a hint that he was willing to comply with Ransom's request.

"It's a personal matter," Ransom said without emotion.

"That right? You a friend of Jeff's? I don't remember ever seeing you."

Ransom closed his eyes and sighed. When he opened them again, he said, "Is he here?"

The deputy smiled broadly, apparently feeling he'd achieved the desired effect, and called out, "Jeff! Gentleman here to see you!"

There was movement in the office on the right. Ransom could see a blob of color approaching through the etched window. As it neared, it increased in size, fragmented into jagged pieces, and splayed apart like a cubist painting come to life. When the door opened with a loud groan, the shards of color congealed into the person of Jeff Fields.

Ransom had tried on occasion to subdue his penchant for making snap judgments about people he was going to question for fear that these impressions, if too steadfastly adhered to, might cause him to disregard or miss important information. However, his failure to stem the flow of first impressions was mitigated by the fact that his initial assessments were, more often than not, highly accurate. So it was with dismay that he realized that his first glance at Jeff Fields yielded absolutely nothing. He might as well have been looking at a wall. It might have been from being on vacation, or from his unofficial standing in this community, the closeness of the holiday, or any of a hundred other things. He preferred to believe that it was because Fields really was a wall.

Fields stared at Ransom for a moment with such practiced inscrutability that Ransom couldn't help but admire the technique.

It gave him a minor glimpse into what it must be like to be on the other end of one of his own investigations.

"You wanted to see me?"

Ransom gave a single nod. "On a private matter."

Two creases cut wide swaths across Fields's smooth forehead.

"A private matter? I don't know you."

"Yes, I know. My name is Ransom," he said with a coy smile, "I'm staying at Hawthorne House. . . ." He let his voice trail off suggestively.

If he'd been hoping for some sort of reaction on the part of the sheriff, he was disappointed. There wasn't so much as a twitch. But Ransom could sense a change in the atmosphere of the room, not so much from the sheriff as from his deputy, who paused in the act of shuffling some papers on the counter and looked first at Ransom, then at Fields. Fields didn't budge for a moment, then pushed his door open and said "Come on in." There was no warmth in the invitation.

The inner office was as unimpressive as the rest of the place: the same drab yellow walls and the same overzealously varnished furniture. As Ransom took a seat in front of the desk, he thought the impression of his posterior would probably remain there until someone else's reformed it.

"So you're staying at Hawthorne House," said Fields without preamble. "So what's the problem?"

"I've been asked to—unofficially, of course—look into the murder of Nathan Bartlett."

Although Fields could not have been described as being animated, this news seemed to turn him to stone. "Sara asked you to do that?"

"The request came from her, yes," said Ransom, seeing no reason to bring Emily into it.

"You a detective?"

"I'm a homicide detective, from Chicago."

"And Sara brought you in to find out who killed her brother, huh?"

Ransom rested his elbows on the arms of the chair and pressed his fingers together. "As a matter of fact, I'm one of her guests for the week. She was told I was a detective and I agreed to look into this for her. The matter seems to be causing Miss Bartlett a great deal of distress."

"She doesn't think I did everything I could?" There was no hint of recrimination in his tone, nor did he appear to be hurt by the prospect. But Ransom thought his choice of words might indicate a measure of remorse felt by the sheriff.

"She didn't mention it," said Ransom with a smile he hoped might widen the chink in the sheriff's armor. "However, *I'm* sure you did everything you could. I have no desire to interfere with an ongoing investigation, but I'm assuming that after two years, the investigation is . . . not ongoing."

Fields looked at him for a moment, then replied, "There's nothing to investigate, Mr. Ransom."

Ransom cocked his head sideways, and said, "I don't want to get in your way. I know what I would think if someone came barging into my area and stepping on my toes."

Fields folded his arms across his massive chest. "What would you think?"

Ransom smiled. "I would think they were barging in and stepping on my toes. But that's not what I'm trying to do here. The only thing I'm trying to do is help that young woman, if I can."

"You think you can do better than I did?"

Ransom sighed and sat back, resting his arms on the chair's. "It's been suggested that you might have had an interest in not solving the case."

Fields's face began to flush, then almost as if he'd become aware of betraying some emotion, the redness quickly ebbed as though he'd recalled the blood from his face.

"When did you get to town?" he asked.

"The day before yesterday."

Fields whistled. "You've been busy already, haven't you?"

Ransom put his palms up and shrugged eloquently. "Just sight-seeing."

"Damn sight more than that." Fields heaved a deep sigh before continuing. "Look, I know what the people around here say, because, even though none of 'em have had the balls to say it to my face, it still gets back to me. I know they say Sara did it and I let her get away with it. I'm sure you've heard I was going with Sara. Hell, I'll go even further than that—I loved her. Still do. But I'm a good cop, first and foremost. If I could've proved that Sara killed Nathan, it might've killed me to do it, but I would've brought her in." Here he stopped, dropped his head down and added half under his breath, "Damn near killed me as it was." He drew his head back up and faced Ransom. "What most people don't know is that it's not enough to think somebody did it. It's not even enough to know in your heart that they did it. If there isn't any hard evidence, as far as the law's concerned, they *didn't* do it. You know that."

Ransom nodded. He did know that, and there wasn't a cop in the country who didn't have to grit his teeth when he thought of it. But he thought he knew something else, too. From the vehemence with which Fields had delivered this declaration, Ransom felt there was something really troubling to the sheriff about this case—something that went beyond merely not having it solved.

"So you didn't have any hard evidence?"

"We didn't have any evidence at all," Fields replied.

"Would you mind telling me what you did have?" Ransom asked, rejoining his fingers.

Fields didn't reply right away, choosing instead to stare stone-faced at the detective for a moment, looking, Ransom thought, not unlike someone had pulled his plug. Ransom leaned in toward him. "Sheriff, it might surprise you to know that you're not the first person to tell me since I arrived in town that you're a good cop."

Fields looked as if he would have liked to brighten, but restrained himself.

"And no, it wasn't Sara who told me that. I have no reason to believe otherwise. I know that any law enforcement agent worth his salt, whether sheriff, cop, or desk clerk, wants to see a murderer apprehended"—he paused for effect, and added pointedly—"by any means necessary. Perhaps in my unofficial capacity I can find out things that you couldn't in your official one. But either way, I have to believe you want the murderer found."

Fields looked uncertain for the first time, though that uncertainty flickered across his features for barely a second.

"Yes, I do," he said at last.

"Then will you tell me what you had back then?"

"All we had was Sara's statement—that she didn't know Nathan had gone out, that she went to look for him and found him dead in the barn, and that she went up, got Hansen, and called me."

"She called you personally?"

"I don't see anything surprising about that. I was on duty that night anyway. She knew that."

"Sara *knew* you were on duty that night?"

Fields paused. " 'Course she did. If I wasn't, we would've been together. So?"

"Nothing, I just wanted to make sure I understood you. You questioned Hansen Crane, of course."

"Of course," Fields echoed. "Said he was asleep and didn't hear anything until Sara came pounding at the door."

"There wasn't any reason to think Hansen might've killed Nathan?"

Fields shook his head. "Only because he was on the premises. But Hansen didn't have anything against Nathan that anybody knew of, and so far's we know, he'd never seen or heard of him before he came here."

"Hansen just showed up one day? That would've been about a year after Nathan and Sara moved here."

"Yeah. But there's nothing in that, either. People drift into town here and there, stay a while, and go. It happens in places like Chicago, too, Mr. Ransom, except you got so many people there you don't notice them."

"So he just showed up on the Bartletts' doorstep one day and asked for a job?"

"Yeah, but that wasn't the first place he went. He stopped by several places asking for work before that. I'm sure half the people knew he was looking for work before he ever made it out to Hawthorne House. Just happened they were looking for help."

Ransom thought about this for a moment, then said, "So it would appear that he wasn't specifically seeking out Sara and Nathan."

Fields paused, then said broadly, "Well, he could've been stopping other places first just to give that impression, but we have no reason to believe he's anything more than what he appears to be."

Ransom narrowed his eyes, and said, "If someone other than Sara Bartlett killed her brother, then *somebody* in this town is not what he appears to be."

What little there was of a smile on Fields's face disappeared. He clearly didn't enjoy being bested.

"Hansen's like Sara, there's no hard evidence against him," said Fields soberly, "but unlike Sara, he didn't have any known motive."

"What would Sara's motive have been?"

"She got her brother's money."

"Did she need it?"

"She not only didn't need it, if she'd wanted it, he would've given it to her. That's how close they were."

"That's not much of a motive," said Ransom, looking off in the distance as he ruminated. "And there was no other evidence?"

"Nope," said Fields with an abbreviated shrug. "The storm was so bad that there wasn't even any footprints by the time I got out there."

In a way, this verified what Sara had told him.

"And there weren't any fingerprints on the pitchfork," Fields added.

"Not surprising."

"No, it wasn't. If there *had* been, I might've had to bring Sara in, but the fact of the matter is, her fingerprints wouldn't have proved anything, because they *should've* been on it, 'cause she's used it once or twice. So's Hansen. But it was wiped. And there was no reason for either of them to do that."

The two lawmen sat and stared at each other, both aware that there was one reason that either Sara or Hansen, if they'd been clever enough to think of it, might have wiped the handle of the pitchfork: so the sheriff would reach the exact conclusion that he had. But that still left them with no evidence, so whatever their motive might have been, it had the desired result.

At last Fields said, "So you can see what I mean. We have no evidence, and no other suspects."

"What about Amy Shelton?"

"Amy!" Fields exclaimed with a deprecating laugh. "You ever seen Amy?"

Ransom shook his head.

"She could barely wield a table fork, let alone a pitchfork. She's a weak little thing."

"Hmm," said Ransom with elaborate consideration, "I understood she was in love with Nathan."

"So?"

"Sooo," Ransom said slowly, "love, hate, they both can lead to murder for one reason or another."

Fields sighed heavily. "Look, Mr. Ransom, no matter what you think, I did do my job. Just because I don't think Amy could do it doesn't mean I didn't follow her up. As it happens, she was supposed to have had a date with Nathan, but they called it off because the weather was so bad. She has an alibi. She stayed in all evening and all night, verified by both her mother and father."

Ransom raised an eyebrow. "I would hardly expect her parents to do anything other than back her up."

"Neither would I," said Fields, his mouth turning down at the corners, "but I have no reason not to believe them, either. Hell, the weather was so bad, *nobody* went out that night unless they had to. Why do you think people are so dead set on Sara as the killer?"

Ransom paused for a second, then replied, "For the same reason you are."

A silence fell between them during which they continued to stare at each other across the sheriff's desk, both of their expressions nearly unreadable.

Finally Ransom said, "Sara told me that she knew Nathan hadn't driven anywhere that night because she would've heard the car."

"Yeah?"

Ransom smiled. "So I assume that means she would've heard someone else's car as well—if someone had driven out there."

"That's right," said Fields with a nod to show that he already knew all this.

"Is there any other way out there—some way that somebody could get to the barn without driving up to the house?"

"There's an access road to the vineyards about two hundred yards behind the barn."

"Were there any tracks there that night? Any sign of a car?"

Fields heaved a bored sigh. "Mr. Ransom, you don't know what it's like to live in the country. Out here, when we have a storm like that it isn't just tracks that disappear, it's the whole damn road."

"So there was nothing there?"

"Not that was still there by the time we got out there."

"Hm. Then it doesn't look good for Sara, does it?" he said with a smile.

"And at the same time," Fields replied with a superior smile, "that's why Sara wasn't arrested. Someone else *could've* gone out there. But whether or not that's likely . . ."

He let his voice trail off and they fell silent once more.

"Well," said Ransom, suddenly rising from his seat. The bottom of his pants hesitated a second before following him. "I appreciate your time. Thank you very much."

"Mr. Ransom," said Fields as he rose from his desk. Ransom stopped and faced him. "No case is closed in this county until I say it is, whether or not the investigation is active. If you find out anything, I expect to hear about it."

Ransom smiled. "Certainly." He crossed to the door, opened it, and paused in the doorway, looking back at Fields. "By the way, Sheriff, I was wondering if you were . . . for some reason . . . expecting more trouble out at Hawthorne House."

The deep furrows returned over Fields's brow. "Why would you ask that?"

"Because I could have sworn I saw you drive by there yesterday morning. It seemed to me that you . . . just might have been keeping the place under surveillance."

Fields allowed a flat smile to spread across his face. "Just cruisin' the area, Mr. Ransom. Just doing my job."

After a beat Ransom returned a much broader smile, and said, "Of course."

Well, Gerald, thought Ransom as he started his car. He stopped before putting it in drive, brought up short by the fact that this was the first time in two years he'd headed into an investigation without the aid of his full-time partner and part-time Boswell, Gerald White. Ransom had always found White able and unassuming, and more importantly, unlike others with whom he'd been partnered over the years, White didn't get in the way. He readily accepted the position of second banana, doing a lot of the leg work and allowing himself to be used as a sounding board for Ransom's deliberations, while not shrinking from offering his own ideas. It wasn't until this moment, when Ransom was ready to let the ideas fly, that he realized just how important a position his partner held. It was a role that Ransom knew Emily could never fill, not because she was incapable of being a sounding board, but because, despite Ransom's faith in his own abilities, he harbored the notion that she just might be even more clever than he was. With all these thoughts in mind, as well as the information imparted by Jeff Fields, Ransom pulled a plastic-tipped cigar from the pack in his pocket, lit it, and headed back to Hawthorne House.

He found Emily quietly reading *King Lear* in the parlor.

"You look like you haven't budged since I left," he said.

"Oh, no," said Emily as she laid the book aside, "I've only just come back here. I've been doing a little investigating on my own."

"Have you?" said Ransom, taking a seat beside her.

"I had a little talk with Millie Havers." She told him what she'd learned.

"So basically," said Ransom with a sigh, "everything was fine between everybody, and the murder came completely out of the blue."

Emily nodded. "The only thing at all out of the ordinary was that Nathan seemed a little preoccupied, but Millie was quite unspecific about that."

"Well, that could have been anything. He could have been worried about business, or he could have been thinking of proposing to Amy."

Emily considered this for a moment, then said, "Now, tell me, what did Jeffrey Fields have to say?"

When Ransom had finished telling her, Emily sat back in her chair and gazed at him, her eyes alive with interest.

"It seems very significant to me that it was known that Jeffrey Fields would be on duty that night."

"It did to me, too. It meant that he would almost certainly be the one to get the call about the murder . . . assuming that it was discovered that night."

"Oh, it meant much more than that, it meant that most likely it was generally known he wouldn't be *here* that night."

"That's true," said Ransom, "and with the weather as bad as it was, the murderer could also be fairly certain there wouldn't be any casual visitors here."

They fell silent. Ransom stared into the unlit fireplace, while Emily's gaze was fixed on the Christmas tree as if she thought she might divine some insight from amidst its branches.

"The problem, as I see it," said Emily at last, "is *why* would someone want to kill Nathan Bartlett? Everything seems to have been innocuous enough. I don't see any sense in it at all."

Ransom smiled ruefully. "I think that's why people are so willing to believe that Sara did it. With the lack of any motive anywhere else, her money motive is the most obvious. And barring that, she's the most likely person to have had a motive nobody knew about."

Emily straightened herself in her chair, folded her hands, and adopted the schoolmarmish attitude she so often displayed when taking matters in hand.

"Jeremy, I really believe that Sara wants this case solved. I can't imagine her doing that, or agreeing to let you look into it, if she was the murderer. Now, how do you think we should proceed?"

Ransom sighed heavily and fingered the pocket that held his cigars. "Well, I think we have to proceed on the assumption that Sara is telling the truth. And, if she is, then there are some other assumptions we can make."

"Yes?" said Emily.

"Sara told me one thing that I think was very important: she didn't hear Nathan leave—and ordinarily she would have—and this was after telling her that he was going to his room. This tells me that he didn't want her to know where he was going."

"And that he was going to meet somebody, and didn't want her to know about it."

"Exactly. Also, I think we can assume that Nathan was killed not long after he left."

"How do we know that?"

"Footprints," Ransom replied simply.

"I beg your pardon?"

"When Sara went out to the barn, there were no footprints

in the snow—they'd been wiped away by the wind and the storm. That had to have taken some time. The last time she saw Nathan was around nine, she went looking for him shortly after eleven. I think he was killed shortly after nine."

"That's very interesting," said Emily slowly, her eyes narrowing. "You know, it occurs to me, Jeremy, that the most likely person for him to be going to meet was Hansen Crane."

"Possibly," said Ransom, tapping his upper lip with his index finger, "except why wouldn't he have told his sister that he was going to talk to Hansen? After all, he talked to Hansen all the time. Sara wouldn't have thought anything of it. Why would their meeting have to be clandestine?"

Emily considered this for a moment. "You know, I think it's very interesting that Nathan asked so many questions about Hansen Crane."

"Yes," said Ransom with a thoughtful nod, "but I have to agree with Millie about one thing. It seems to have taken place much too long before the murder to have anything to do with it."

"Perhaps . . . but there's always the possibility that Hansen Crane found out about Nathan's interest much later. And he was on the premises that night."

"Hm," said Ransom. "But according to Jeff Fields, there was no reason to believe Crane killed Nathan."

"When it comes to that," said Emily, "we have no reason to believe *anyone* killed Nathan, except that he's dead."

Ransom laughed. "Well, you have me there, Emily." His expression grew more sober. "This is the problem with taking up two-year-old threads—they fall apart so easily."

Ransom stared into the fireplace for a few moments. "You know, I got the uncomfortable feeling that Jeff Fields doesn't want this case solved."

"Really?" Emily replied with genuine surprise, "Why?"

"I can think of a couple of reasons. No matter what he says to the contrary, he really does think that Sara did it, and he doesn't want to put her away."

"I suppose that's possible," said Emily rather doubtfully.

"The other possibility is worse. Jeff Fields could be the murderer."

"The *sheriff?*" said Emily, her expression absolutely scandalized.

"Why not? If they were, as we've been told, on the road to being married, then maybe he was the one that wanted all the money and not her."

"But Jeremy, they didn't end up getting married."

Ransom shrugged. "He didn't count on the effect Nathan's death and the investigation would have on Sara. It wouldn't be the first time that someone committed murder for gain and ended up with nothing. *And* it would explain why he didn't 'solve' the murder, and why he's not happy with having me look into it."

Emily's eyebrows slid upward, her expression one of mild amusement. "That all may be true and, I admit, it's quite plausible, but I can think of another, less sinister, reason for not wanting your intrusion."

"What's that?" he asked, his tone slightly irritated at being referred to as an intrusion, especially by the person who'd asked him to intrude.

She leaned forward a little in her chair. "Because he wants to be the one who solves it."

Ransom stared at her for a moment, letting this sink in. Although he'd told Fields that any lawman would want a murderer apprehended, no matter what the means, Ransom had to admit—if only to himself—that he would prefer to be the one who did it. It hadn't even entered his mind that the sheriff might feel the same way.

He replied reluctantly, "I suppose he could feel the same way about it as I do."

"Oh, no, that's not what I mean at all, Jeremy. I mean he might want to do it *for Sara.*"

"*For her,*" said Ransom slowly rolling the words around in his mouth.

"So," said Emily, "what will we do next?"

Ransom sighed. Despite Emily's faith in him, he couldn't get past the feeling that they were chasing the wind. Though they'd questioned three of the people involved with Nathan, they'd turned up nothing more than Jeff Fields had at the time, and he didn't exactly share Emily's confidence that they would ever find more. The one thing that made Ransom want to pursue the case was the renewed enthusiasm he saw in Emily's eyes. This was the first time since her operation that she was really showing signs of returning to her old self. Ransom felt it incumbent upon himself to encourage this.

"Well," he said, "no matter how little he appears to figure into it, we keep coming back to Hansen Crane, so I should talk to him. If nothing else, he can confirm what we've learned so far."

"Hmm . . ." said Emily, looking down at the floor reflectively and pursing her lips. "You know, people keep referring to him as a typical drifter with one exception. Millie Havers pointed out that she was surprised that he's stayed around so long."

"Maybe I'll ask him about that," Ransom replied with a smile.

"And there's one other person it would be very important to talk to."

"Amy Shelton."

"Exactly!" said Emily. "If Nathan was, indeed, preoccupied before he died, she might be able to tell us why."

1

The laundry room was a small, square space, not much bigger than a pantry, located just off the kitchen. Sara was in the process of transferring a load of linens from the washer to the drier when Millie came down from the second floor.

"Well," said Millie, brushing a stray strand of gray hair back over her right ear, "I got the beds made and the bedrooms clean, though there was hardly any more to do but dust. Miss Charters is neat as a pin and that Mr. Ransom is maybe the cleanest man I've ever seen in my life."

Sara glanced at her over her shoulder and managed a weak smile. "Thank you, Millie."

"So, I guess I'll be getting along." She grabbed her coat from the peg by the back door and slipped it on. She hadn't taken her eyes off Sara. She paused in the doorway, looking as if she wasn't quite sure whether to go or stay. "Sure is nice having guests again, isn't it?"

"Yes, it is." Sara set the timer on the drier and pushed the start button. Millie stepped out of the way so she could pass back into the kitchen.

"And you couldn't hope for a better way to start up again than with those two. They seem to be as nice as they can be."

"That's true." Sara retrieved a handful of potatoes from the bin below the sink. She placed them on the counter and looked at them for a moment as if she couldn't remember what she'd intended to do with them.

"Sara," said Millie gently, "you all right?"

"Yes. Yes, of course. It's just . . ." She turned her plaintive eyes to her older friend. "Do you think I've done the right thing?"

Millie's brow furrowed, sending across her forehead a web of creases that seemed to spread out in all directions. "What do you mean, honey?"

"In letting Mr. Ransom open up this can of worms again."

Millie shrugged, an action she hoped would convey that the situation wasn't as bleak as Sara seemed to think it. "Don't know. He might be able to help. And he couldn't hurt."

"If only I could be sure of that."

Millie frowned, causing a further set of wrinkles to shoot away from the corners of her mouth like drooping fireworks. "Sara, do you know something about all this that you never said?"

Sara looked at her for a moment, her expression blank. "No. Of course not." She stopped and frowned, trying to think of how to put what she was feeling. Millie, who had always been rather direct, continued to watch her unflinchingly, which only added to Sara's discomfort. At last Sara sighed, looked back up at Millie, and said, "Do you know what foreboding is?"

"Yeah."

Sara slowly shook her head as she said, "I just have this feeling something terrible's going to happen."

Millie smiled warmly. It was a gesture that erased all the creases from her face except those time had put there. She crossed to Sara and laid a matronly hand on her shoulder. "That's just jitters," she said in her usual matter-of-fact tone. "Probably all that'll happen is nothin'!"

There was a sudden loud knock at the back door that so

startled both the women that Millie dropped her hand to her side and spun around to look, and Sara let out an involuntary "Oh!"

The door popped open and Johnnie Larkin stuck his head in and said, "Sara? You there?"

Sara and Millie heaved relieved sighs. Millie said, "Johnnie, you just about scared us out of our shirts!"

"Oh. I'm sorry," he said, coming in and up the stairs. "I didn't mean to."

Sara laughed, feeling the tension in her body ebb a little. "It's all right. We were just talking and you startled us."

"Sorry," said Johnnie with a smile so puckish that he looked exactly like a schoolboy who'd just stuck a frog in the face of a little girl and made her scream. "I just came out to see if you had any work today."

"No, I'm sorry. Nothing that I can think of."

"Okay."

"You didn't have to drive all the way out here. You could've just called."

"Oh. Well . . ." He looked down at the floor and ran a hand through his long, dark hair. "It's okay. I was driving by this way, anyway, so I just thought I'd stop in and ask."

"What brought you out this way?" said Millie with a mischievous grin.

"Huh?"

"You said you were out this way."

"Oh. Yeah. I just had some work this morning."

"Where at?" said Millie as conversationally as she could.

"Um . . ." He glanced from Millie to Sara. "At the Darcy farm."

"The Darcy farm?" said Sara, recounting the potatoes as if for some reason she were having trouble retaining the total. "That's way on the other side of the highway."

Johnnie's normally ruddy cheeks grew redder and his eyes went back to the floor. "I didn't mean I was going right past here. But I was out in the car and thought I might as well stop by instead of going all the way home and maybe having to come back, you know?"

Millie's smile broadened and she thought it best to beat a hasty retreat before Johnnie noticed the look on her face. She was sure it would have told him how transparent he was, and though she didn't mind teasing him a little, being a basically kindhearted woman she wanted to spare him any real embarrassment. She tied her plaid scarf around her neck, and said, "Well, I better get going," then trundled down the back steps as they called good-bye to her.

Sara watched Millie go with feelings that were a mixture of amusement and abandonment. She turned a smile to Johnnie. "Well, as long as you're here, would you like a little lunch? I've got some ham."

"Oh, I don't want to impose," he replied, though the way his eyes had lit up at the invitation his eagerness to accept it was obvious.

"You're not imposing. I wouldn't have asked."

"Oh. Okay then."

Sara took a fresh loaf of bread from the bread box and some leftover ham from the refrigerator. She unwrapped the ham, set it on a cutting board and started to cut off a few thick slices. Johnnie watched her for a moment, then eager to be helpful retrieved a couple of plates from the cabinet and set them on the table.

"So, how's it going, having guests again?"

Sara shrugged. "Not as bad as I thought it might be."

"Good. Then do you think you're gonna reopen permanently?"

"Maybe. We'll see."

Johnnie opened the refrigerator and peered inside. "So . . . if you're going to reopen, maybe you'll need more help around here."

With her back to him, Sara allowed herself to smile. "That's about it. 'If' and 'maybe.' "

Johnnie located a jar of mustard, straightened up, and closed the refrigerator. "Well, that's good, 'cause I'm always available."

"I know," said Sara lightly.

He put the mustard on the table and went to the drawer by the sink to get a knife. Instead of going back to the table, he leaned against the sink and watched Sara, his eyes full of anxious expectation.

"Sara . . ." he began tentatively.

She quickly handed him the loaf of bread, and said, "Would you put this on the table for me?"

She silently cursed her own good nature as she arranged the ham slices on a plate. She knew she should never have asked Johnnie to stay for lunch, but, even though he'd driven out to the house of his own accord, it wasn't in her nature to let someone go away completely emptyhanded. And Johnnie was one of those men who looked as if he would never have a proper meal if left to himself.

Although Sara had been in a mental fog for a long time, she hadn't been completely oblivious to Johnnie's attention, though she'd hoped it was something that would remain unspoken. Johnnie's rather obvious crush was just another cause of mental confusion. In her rare moments of clarity she couldn't see any reason for not returning his affections: after all, there was nothing inherently wrong with him. In fact, he had many good qualities. He was helpful, he was eager (maybe a little too eager), he was dependable, and he was something of an outsider in the community, like herself. Unlike most of the people in the area, Johnnie seemed to have absolute faith in her innocence of any wrongdoing. She might go so far as to say that he wore his faith in her like a badge of honor. She chalked it up to the natural perversity of human nature that it was his unwavering faith that made her uncomfortable. It reminded her of religious zealots who cling blindly to their beliefs as if entertaining any doubts will cause the object of their admiration to shatter.

She shook her head as she rewrapped the rest of the ham. If she were completely honest with herself, any discomfort she felt around Johnnie was not being caused by him, but was coming from within herself. It was because of Jeff Fields, who stood as another issue from her past that might never be resolved. For the first time since Ransom had agreed to investigate she realized that she was holding out hope not only that she'd be able to close the door on Nathan's murder, but that she'd be able to close it on her relationship with Jeff as well. The problem was that she didn't know on which side of that door she wanted to end up. She let out an involuntary shudder.

"Is anything wrong?" said Johnnie, his voice rising with worry.

"Oh, no, I just had a little chill," Sara replied as she replaced the ham in the refrigerator. She then transferred the plate of ham slices from the counter to the table and took a seat.

"My God!" said Johnnie with a laugh. "You never do anything by half, do you?"

"What do you mean?"

He pointed to the plate on which the ham was tastefully arranged, the slices overlapping in a circle.

"Force of habit, I guess," she said with a rueful laugh. "I always feel like I'm preparing for the guests."

Johnnie grinned. "Well, I'm not company, I'm family."

Sara tried to return the smile. "Yeah, you are."

Johnnie slapped a couple of slices of ham on a slice of bread, spread mustard on another slice and closed the sandwich while Sara nibbled at a piece of ham. He was lifting the sandwich to his mouth when his gaze traveled over Sara's shoulder. He stopped with the sandwich in midair, his eyes widening.

"What in the hell is he doing?"

"Who?" Sara turned around to see what Johnnie was looking at. Through the window in the back door they could see Ransom, bundled up in a down coat and long black scarf, trudging through the snow toward the barn.

"Oh," said Sara, "Ransom. Mr. Ransom. He's probably going out to talk to Hansen. He's a detective. He's looking into Nathan's murder."

Johnnie gaped at her in astonishment. "You've got to be kidding!"

"No."

"I thought he was a guest! You mean, you actually hired a detective?"

She shook her head. "No, he really is a guest. But he's a homicide detective and he offered to see if he could find out anything. I should've mentioned it to you, I guess. I don't know whether or not he'll want to talk to you."

"To me?" Johnnie's face did a quick transformation from disbelief, to wariness, to perplexity, as if each new idea was flashing across his face like a slide show as he rapidly considered all the possible ramifications of this. Finally he screwed up his face in question, and asked, "Do you think that's a good idea?"

Sara gave her characteristic shrug. "It couldn't hurt."

He tapped his sandwich against his plate a couple of times as if he were trying to get its contents in order, then said, "You're right. It's probably a good thing." He took a bite of the sandwich and chewed it as if it were an idea he was mulling over with his teeth. "I never did think Jeff Fields had enough brains to take on something like that. I mean, sure, he's all right for giving out traffic tickets and maybe bringing in a drunk or two, but beyond that, I don't know." He paused and looked at Sara for a reaction, but she just continued to pick at the piece of ham, absently sticking bits of it in her mouth. Johnnie continued, "And I don't think I could ever forgive him for treating you like you had something to do with it. That's crazy. Just goes to show he doesn't have his whole brain working."

Sara dropped the ham on her plate and stared down at it. "He was just doing his job. And I was the obvious . . . I don't think he could avoid it."

Johnnie smacked his lips derisively, and said, "Oh, well, maybe it can all get settled now."

"Let's hope so."

Johnnie ate in silence for a few moments, glancing at Sara occasionally as if hoping to find some sign of acceptance. After a couple of minutes he said, "And you know, Sara, maybe once this is all behind us, you and me could—"

Sara suddenly glanced up at him, stopping him in midsentence. He found it disheartening that, rather than looking surprised or unaccepting, she just looked pained.

He sighed. "Well, maybe we could do something together some time. Go to a movie or something. Maybe get to know each other better."

The wild rush of emotions flooded in on her again. In the mass of conflicting thoughts, she remembered Emily's admonition that sometimes you had to fight your way out of the void on your own. With no faith in the outcome of the investigation, she thought just maybe it was time for her to pull herself up by her bootstraps and try going forward on her own. But the idea was still unappealing.

"I can't think about that now," she said out of the blue. She suddenly realized she'd said this aloud in answer to her own thoughts. She looked at Johnnie, whose face had fallen, apparently from having taken this as her answer to him.

Sara decided it was best not to correct this for the time being.

Ransom climbed the rough wooden staircase up the side of the barn to Hansen Crane's apartment. Though it wasn't very cold by the standard of a lifelong Chicagoan, it was still cold enough to slow his movements a bit. These days it seemed to him that the cold made his joints congeal. Ransom shook his head in disgust, taking this increased sensitivity to the temperature as just another sign that he was getting older. When he reached the top of the stairs, he knocked on the window of the cracked wooden door and waited. Across the inside of the window was a worn curtain, and as he waited he tried to decide if the barely visible pattern on it had been sun faded into obscurity or was just bleeding through the other side. He was about to knock again when the curtain twitched slightly, then was abruptly swept aside. The effect of the face appearing in the window was startling. Despite the general heartiness of Crane's face, there was something about the bushy beard and long, stiff gray hair that immediately brought to Ransom's mind the idea of Santa Claus in the last stages of dissolution. But even without the unsettling mental image of the patron saint of children in decay, the wariness in Crane's eyes would have been enough. Ransom didn't trust him.

Crane let out a muffled grunt at the sight of Ransom, then opened the door.

"You're that detective, aren't you?" he said, blocking the doorway.

"Yes."

"Sara told me you were snooping around. Can't say I like the idea."

Ransom raised his right eyebrow. "Sara said 'snooping'?"

The bush around Crane's mouth twitched. Ransom assumed he was smiling. "She said something nicer, but it boils down to the same thing, don't it?"

"Do you think I might talk to you?"

"I don't have anything to say I haven't said already, to the real police."

Though Ransom didn't change expression, he bridled inwardly. He was fully aware that he was operating outside of any official jurisdiction, but, up until now, nobody had questioned his authority. It was a blow to his pride to realize that people had been answering his questions more out of their love for Sara than out of any respect for him. But it was apparent that for someone like Hansen Crane, usually wary of strangers, whether or not he had any affection or loyalty to Sara he wouldn't relish being questioned by anyone. Ransom would have liked nothing more than to whip his badge out of his pocket, flash it at Crane, and proceed with all the authority that accompanied it, but that not being possible, he decided to take a different tack.

"I understand that Miss Bartlett has been very good to you."

"Do you?" said Crane, his ability to emit words apparently not depending on lip movement.

"She gave you a job when you needed one," said Ransom

with a shrug that implied that anyone should understand this, "and a decent place to live."

"What if she did?"

Ransom sighed. "Then I wouldn't think it would be asking too much for you to answer a few questions that might help her. What harm would that do?" Ransom paused for a moment, then narrowed his eyes slightly and added as simply as before, "Unless, of course, you have something to hide."

Crane seemed to harden in place, giving Ransom an inkling of how sudden and thorough a process it must have been when Lot's wife made her ill-fated mistake. Ransom was just beginning to think they'd reached a standoff when the handyman suddenly inhaled deeply, then slowly exhaled.

"That strikes me as being what they call a 'cheap shot.' "

Ransom smiled. "Did it work?"

The curve in the center of Crane's beard deepened. "The part about Sara did," he replied, stepping aside to let Ransom enter. "I guess I do owe her. Come on in."

Crane's flat delivery belied his words, making it clear to Ransom that he still didn't believe he owed anyone anything. Ransom stepped past the old man and into the apartment. It consisted of one medium-sized room, fairly dark due to the fact that there were only two small windows at either end of the room in addition to the one in the door. The ceiling sloped downward on both sides and the walls were bare wood and completely unadorned. A very small section of the far end of the room was partitioned off with paneling into what looked like a small shed, which Ransom assumed fit the description of a water-closet.

The room was completely devoid of personal items, except for a few bits of clothing hanging from a short makeshift rod jutting out from one wall and a can of tobacco and a pipe that lay on the table. The table was small with chrome legs and a blue plastic top, and had two matching padded chairs. The set looked as if it dated from the fifties. There was a tattered braided rug in the center of the floor, a twin bed pushed up against one wall, and a small, ancient refrigerator that chugged noisily in one corner. Next to the refrigerator was an electric stove so old it could have actually been the prototype. Everything looked like it had been hastily purchased at resale shops to accommodate someone whose tenure was unsure, although Ransom reminded himself that for all he knew these things really could have been sitting here since the fifties.

The meager heat was provided by a set of electric floorboard heaters that looked as if they'd been installed in the not-too-distant past.

"So, what do you want to ask me?" said Crane, dropping his bulk onto one of the chairs, which let out a loud squeak in protest.

He hadn't invited Ransom to sit down, which the detective chalked up to a lack of manners rather than a desire for him not to stay long. Ransom crossed to the table, pulled out the other chair and sat down as purposefully as he could. The bush around Crane's mouth formed a slight crescent, which Ransom found particularly irritating at the moment.

Crane slid a dirty fingernail under the lid of the tobacco can and popped it open. Since the can was almost full, a bit of tobacco sprayed onto the table, which Crane ignored. He stuffed some tobacco into the pipe, cramming it down tight with his thumb. He then stuck the pipe in his mouth, his teeth biting down on it with a pronounced click. He pulled a pack of matches from his side pocket and made a great show of lighting the pipe, puffing in and out rapidly several times and sending bursts of smoke upward as if he were signaling Indians. Ransom sat with his arms folded throughout this display, making it clear that he could wait until he had Crane's full attention before continuing.

"Well?" said Crane at last with some irritation.

"I just want to ask you a few questions. You've probably heard them all before."

Crane inclined his head, a gesture that told Ransom that the handyman was sure that was true.

"I've already been told that you were here when the murder took place."

"Uh-huh."

"Can you tell me what happened?"

Crane leaned a bulky elbow on the top of the table, and said, "Well, you oughtta know that already, too."

Ransom smiled. "Only one side of it. I'd like to hear . . ." He started to say "your version," but decided it might be best to use less confrontational terminology. "I'd like to know how it looked from your perspective."

Crane huffed. "Didn't look like nothin'. First thing I knew, Sara was pounding on the door and yelling out my name."

"What were you doing at the time?"

"Sleeping. Just like I told the sheriff. What else would I be doing that time of night?"

"Isn't that a little early for bed?"

"Maybe in the city," said Crane with a grunt, "not for hard-working folks."

"Hmm," said Ransom. "When did you go to bed?"

Crane blinked. "Huh?"

"It's a simple question. What time did you go to bed?"

"Well . . ." Crane hesitated. He stuck his thumb and fore-finger inside his beard and scratched at his chin. Ransom tried not to grimace. The motion made it look as if there might be something residing in Crane's beard that he was trying to pick out. Finally Crane gave an abbreviated shrug, and said, "Well, hell, that was two years ago! How the hell should I remember what time I went to bed?"

Ransom pursed his lips. "We might be able to make a rough estimate. Sara said that you took quite a while to answer the door. You must've been sleeping pretty soundly."

"Nothin's wrong with my conscience."

"I simply meant that that would mean you'd been asleep for some time. Could it've been two hours?"

"Don't know," said Crane with another shrug.

"Well, let's try it this way. Would it be common for you to go to bed before, say, nine o'clock?"

"It's common for me to go to bed whenever I get tired," Crane replied, his tone mocking Ransom's.

The detective stared fixedly at him for a moment, then said, "No matter, I'm sure the sheriff has it in his file."

Crane's eyes narrowed slightly and his bushy eyebrows slid toward each other. He looked as if he didn't like the idea of something he'd said being written down somewhere. "What's so important about when I went to bed, anyway?"

"You say you were asleep when Sara knocked."

"I was," Crane interjected a little testily.

"But Nathan was killed earlier. I suspect that he might have been killed a little after nine."

Ransom paused. He could have sworn the handyman had stiffened slightly, but he didn't give any visible signs of movement until a thick stream of smoke poured out of the side of his mouth. It was an action so calculated to be startling that Ransom almost laughed.

"So, I was wondering if maybe you heard anything unusual earlier . . . maybe a couple of hours before Sara came to your door."

Crane snorted. "Only thing I heard was the storm, and that wasn't unusual."

Ransom gazed at him for a moment, but the handyman's expression remained stoic.

"So," said Ransom at last, "what did you do when Sara came to the door?"

"She told me what she found. I took her back to the house and she called the sheriff."

Ransom's face became a picture of puzzlement. "You didn't look in the barn?"

"Why should I?"

"To check to see if Nathan was really dead."

Crane emitted a "Humph." "I had no reason to doubt Sara."

"You weren't curious at all?"

"I seen enough death."

Ransom cocked his head. "Have you?"

"I'm sixty-three years old. You haven't seen death by then, you haven't been living."

He made it sound as if death by pitchfork were a common occurrence. *Then again,* thought Ransom, *for all I know it might be out here.*

"And that was all there was to it?"

"That was it."

Ransom closed his eyes for a moment and sighed. "Do you have any idea who might've wanted to kill Nathan?"

Crane shrugged. Ransom was beginning to find the motion annoying. "Sorry."

"Did anyone dislike him?"

"Not that I know."

Ransom sat back in his chair and folded his arms. "What about you?"

"What about me?"

"Did you dislike Nathan?"

"Nothing to dislike. He was pretty much the same as everybody else."

"Hmm," said Ransom as if he were pondering this thoughtfully. "I suppose you would know. You've probably met a lot of people in your time."

"You're bound to if you live long enough."

"I mean in your travels. I understand you've been a sort of nomad."

"I get around."

"Have your travels ever taken you to Chicago?"

There was a slight hesitation before Crane responded. He took the bowl of his pipe in his finger, adjusted the stem between his teeth, and another cloud of smoke poured out of the corner of his mouth. Finally he said, "Can't say I remember."

The two men stared at each other for a few moments like two animals from different breeds of the same species, challenging each other for territory. After a while, Crane looked down at the tabletop, drummed his fingers on it once, then looked back up. "Why?"

"I was just wondering if perhaps you'd chanced to meet Nathan Bartlett sometime."

A broad smile made itself evident beneath Crane's beard. "Nope. I never set eyes on him before I came here." He announced this proudly, as if that one statement formed the bedrock of his honesty. Ransom wondered if it was the only absolute truth he'd spoken. After a pause Crane asked hesitantly, "Why d'you ask that?"

"Well . . ." Ransom replied with a coy smile, "people seem to think that Sara murdered her brother because she was the only one who knew him well enough. . . ."

Crane let out a disdainful snort, and said, "Well, sorry to tell you, but I didn't know him before I came here."

Ransom continued as if he hadn't been interrupted. ". . . And because she was the only one out here . . . beside you, of course. You have to understand it would be natural to suspect you since you were the only other person on the premises the night Nathan was killed." Ransom let that hang in the air between them for a few seconds before he added, "Weren't you?"

" 'Course I was," said Crane, "anybody else had come out here I would've seen 'em."

Ransom didn't allow his expression to change. He merely waited a bit, then said lightly, "But you were asleep."

The few inches of visible skin on Crane's face reddened, though he didn't avert his eyes from Ransom's. He forced a smile, and replied, "That's right. I was asleep."

A momentary silence fell between the two men, then with his characteristic abruptness, Ransom leapt from his chair as he said, "Well, thank you for your time, Mr. Crane. You've been very helpful."

Crane rose from his chair tentatively, like a balloon that hadn't been fully inflated. There was a puzzled look in his eyes that showed he dearly wanted to ask the detective how he'd been helpful, but he restrained himself. Ransom moved to open the door, but paused with his hand on the doorknob and looked back at Crane.

"You know, I find you very interesting."

"Why's that?" asked the handyman, almost as if responding to this was a compulsion.

"All those years you spent on the road, and suddenly you settle down here. I've never known a real drifter to do that before."

There was a pause before Crane responded. "You get used to comfort."

Ransom glanced around the room rather pointedly. "I guess that could be true. The *prospect* of comfort could be very enticing."

Crane froze in place. He looked as if he'd just been hit by a strong gust of wind against which he had had to steel himself.

Ransom smiled, popped open the door, and left Crane behind.

"He knows something," said Ransom as he looked out at the barn from the back window of Emily's room. The sky was overcast with dark blue-tinted clouds that threatened to shower the area with more snow.

Emily sat in the reading chair with her hands folded in the lap of her deep purple dress.

"Did he say something to make you think that?"

Ransom shook his head. "No, but it was the *way* he didn't say it. He was a bit too pleased to tell me he hadn't known Nathan before he came wandering onto the scene. It made me feel as if I hadn't asked the right question, and he was glad of it."

Emily's eyes were fixed on the bedpost nearest her as she considered this. At last she turned her incisive blue eyes back to Ransom, and said, "Was there anything else?"

Ransom sighed. "There was one thing I found very interesting. I reminded our Mr. Crane that he had been a suspect when the murder occurred. When I asked him if it was true that he and

Sara were the only ones out here that might, he said that if there'd been anyone else he would've seen them."

"That sounds very logical," said Emily, her puzzled expression showing that she wasn't quite sure why Ransom found this of interest.

"But when I reminded him that he'd been asleep, he said, 'Yes, I was'—but his face turned red when he said it. He looked like I'd caught him in something."

Emily's eyes widened and her eyebrows arched, forming two carets over her eyes. "But you hadn't."

Ransom nodded. "That's just the point."

Emily looked at him for a moment, then her face brightened with understanding. "Oh, I see. When you reminded him that he'd been asleep, he blushed because he mistakenly thought you'd tripped him up and caught him in a lie."

Ransom lowered himself on the edge of the bed. "And I suspect that means that he wasn't asleep, and that he either saw or heard something." He paused for a moment, then added pointedly, "And that would explain Millie's puzzle."

"I Im?"

"Millie's puzzle. Why would a drifter suddenly decide to settle down?"

Emily continued to gaze at him for a moment, her hands gently flexing into one another as she silently turned this over in her mind, trying to work it out. Suddenly it came to her, and the corners of her mouth turned downward. "Oh, dear."

Ransom nodded. "Exactly. He's stayed here and hasn't spoken out because he's blackmailing someone."

"Or he's waiting for something," said Emily reflectively, "but . . . oh, dear!" she said again, her frown deepening. "The implications of that are very distressing. The most obvious person from whom he could extort money would be Sara, *if* she was the one he saw. She's the only one we know of connected with this case who has any money. It would explain more than anything else why she's allowed him to stay." Emily wrung her hands in her lap in a display of frustration so utterly uncharacteristic of her that it worried her companion. She said, "Oh, I do hope that Sara didn't murder her brother. I would hate to think my own brush with death had so sorely affected my judgment of human character."

Ransom was still very much aware of his own fears, which had been fading, that Emily had been seriously altered by her heart attack and subsequent surgery. But those fears had all revolved around the resignation with which she seemed to approach her own death, they were not out of any belief that her unerring insightfulness had been damaged. But he also remembered how quickly she'd regained her vigor the moment she'd become interested in the case he'd been working on at the time, so he refused to accept that there'd been any lasting damage to her sense of perspective.

"Emily, I would still take your impressions over the facts. Even though the facts—or what we know of them—continue to point in Sara's direction."

Emily smiled on him benignly. "Thank you, Jeremy."

He rose from the bed and went back to the window, resting the tips of his fingers against the sash.

"And when it comes to Hansen Crane, there are some good arguments against it being Sara that he might have seen, or that he's blackmailing—if that's what he's actually doing."

"Oh?" said Emily with interest.

"Well, first of all, the apartment over the barn isn't exactly palatial. I would think if he was extorting money from Sara he could do a better job of it."

"Remembering, of course, that he isn't used to very much. It may seem palatial to him."

Ransom glanced at her over his shoulder. "I *hardly* think—" he began in the tone he usually reserved for one of Gerald White's musings. He stopped suddenly, remembering to whom he was speaking, and modulated his tone. "I don't think he could fail to notice the difference between his apartment and this house."

The change of tone wasn't lost on Emily, who couldn't hide the amusement in her eyes. "The point is well taken."

Ransom looked away from her and cleared his throat. "Yes, well . . . secondly, even if Sara was giving Crane a place to stay because he knows something, it still doesn't explain why he'd *want* to stay here. Sara already has all her and her brother's money. He could've gotten whatever he wanted out of her and been long gone, which would've been infinitely safer."

"Hmm," said Emily thoughtfully. She looked as if she'd like to accept this, but found it a bit doubtful. "But Sara is still the only one we know of who has any money."

"That's right. But we have to remember that this is still pure speculation." He stopped, curled his lip, and added wryly, "If only Gerald could hear me now I would never hear the end of it! I'm forever admonishing him about the dangers of speculation."

"I wouldn't think you could hope to solve any mystery without allowing yourself to entertain various possibilities."

"Agreed. But there's a difference between doing that and letting your imagination run wild without any basis in fact." He paused again, then heaved a deep sigh. "I'll tell you one thing I *believe* to be fact. If we could find out what it is Crane's waiting around here for, we'd probably have the whole thing sewn up."

Emily didn't respond right away, and Ransom turned around to find her pressing her thumbs together as if she were invoking some kind of spell, and her gaze had once again fixed on the bedpost. After a few moments, she said quietly, "Pure speculation . . ."

"Emily?"

"Maybe that's what it is . . . pure speculation . . ."

"Emily, are you all right?"

Emily suddenly wakened from her semitrance and looked at him. "Oh, yes. I'm sorry."

Ransom hesitated a moment, his look of concern giving way to a smile. "All right, what is it?"

"I'm not sure. It's just the phrase you used seemed to set something off in my mind." She shook her head with frustration. "I do wish I didn't feel as if my mind was in such a muddle."

"It seems perfectly fine to me."

As Ransom said this his eyes were drawn back out the window by a sudden movement in the distance.

"Hello, what do we have here?"

Hansen Crane had come out of his apartment and stood at the top of the stairs testing the air. He turned up the collar on his coat and descended the stairs.

"That's funny."

"What is it?" Emily asked.

"Maybe nothing," he replied, not taking his eyes away from the window, "but I barely left Crane five minutes ago and he looked like he was settled in for a while. Now suddenly it looks like he's going somewhere."

"Hm," said Emily with a thoughtful nod, "perhaps our speculations weren't very far off."

"How do you mean?"

"Maybe you lit a little fire under Mr. Crane."

Crane reached the bottom of the steps and with what Ransom took to be a rather determined step headed for the house.

Ransom sighed. "I'm afraid not. He's coming to the house. He probably just has some work to do."

"Ah, well . . ." Emily said wistfully. She straightened herself up and said, "Now, what do you think our next step should be?"

"*Our* next move," said Ransom with emphasis, "is for you to get some rest."

She blinked at him. "I haven't done anything all day."

"You've been overexercising those wheels and gears of yours," he replied more sternly than he ordinarily would have. "And you need your rest."

"Not quite so much, I should think, as Sara needs her peace of mind."

"Her peace of mind has waited two years. It can wait another day. Besides, this is supposed to be a vacation. If you don't allow for at least a little of that then I'll begin to think it was a mistake for me to agree to look into this case."

Emily eyed him shrewdly for a few moments, though her

smile never faded. "I'm not sure I think it gentlemanly of you to threaten an old woman."

He returned her gaze in kind, and replied, "Oh, Emily, I wouldn't dare."

Emily laughed, the renewed twinkle in her eyes a reminder to Ransom that she was on the mend (and that he had, indeed, been right to take on the case).

"So," he said with a return to his professional demeanor, "perhaps we can talk to Amy Shelton tomorrow morning. I think she's the next logical person."

"I agree," said Emily, not unlike a grandmother bestowing her blessing. Ransom couldn't help but smile.

"As for our holiday, tonight is the Nativity play that Millie told us about. I was wondering if you might like to go to that."

"That would be nice," said Emily. "If nothing else, it would be seasonal. And it might prove instructive."

"My dear Emily, I hardly think they'll put a new spin on the story."

Ransom left her resting in her usually unruffled fashion in the reading chair, a hand-knitted throw covering her lap and legs, and continuing her reading of *Lear*. He crossed the short expanse of living room to the kitchen and was surprised to find Sara alone at the table, quietly looking through a small wooden recipe card file.

"Oh," he said mildly, "I thought I saw Hansen Crane come in here."

Sara looked up from her search, and said, "He did. He just came in to borrow the car."

"The car?" Ransom echoed. He silently kicked himself for sounding so surprised, and once again chalked this uncharacteristic laxity up to being on holiday.

Sara looked up at him and blinked, obviously surprised by the reaction. "Yes."

"Does he borrow your car often?"

"Not really. He just wanted to run into town for some tobacco."

A smile spread across Ransom's face. "Did he, now?"

"Yes," said Sara, her expression becoming more quizzical by the minute. Since Ransom continued to stand there without saying anything more, apparently lost in thought, Sara finally asked, "Was there something I can do for you?"

"Oh, no," he replied, "you've done more than enough for me."

Ransom left Sara with a puzzled look on her face and went back up to the smoking room. It looked as if Emily had been right. Maybe their speculations weren't so far off.

8

Ransom and Emily invited Sara to accompany them to church, but she begged off, claiming to have a slight headache. Emily narrowed her eyes at the young woman, and said, "You know, my dear, I think it's best in situations such as this to face people squarely. Otherwise you simply add to it by making them think you have something to be ashamed of."

Sara looked down at the floor, and replied quietly, "I really do have a headache. But . . . thank you."

"Very well," said Emily kindly, "you must do what you think best."

The First Presbyterian Church of LeFavre would have been more aptly named the First and Last, since it was the only church actually located within the town's limits, although there were three others in nearby Mt. Morgan. The church had been built between the First and Second World Wars with a sudden influx of money from the more wealthy members of the congregation who seemed to think that a healthy monument to God would stave off any further international conflict. A wide, brightly lit stone staircase, rather ostentatious given that there were only seven steps, led up to two enormous oak doors, curved at the top, each of which was decorated with proportionate wreaths of holly. Inside was a broad narthex surrounded by arches opening into recesses that led nowhere, except for the one directly across from the doors, which served as the entrance into the nave. Ransom felt as if he were entering a Swiss convent.

The narthex was so crowded with people it was easy to see why Sara hadn't wanted to come. It seemed that the annual Nativity play was popular enough that people had come from miles around to see it. Either that or they really didn't have much to do around there, which was the explanation Ransom chose to adopt. There was a slight dip in the general buzz of conversation as he and Emily entered the church, which quickly regained momentum and was accompanied by furtive glances in their direction.

They ran into Millie Havers almost immediately. She was dressed in a deep green skirt and jacket, and a cotton blouse of a contrasting shade. The phrase "Sunday-go-to-meeting outfit" wryly sprang to Ransom's mind, and he tried to dismiss it quickly for fear that, in his newly acquired laxity, what he was thinking would transfer to his face.

"Nice to see you could make it," said Millie a little too loudly. It was apparent that if there was any scandal connected with their having come, Millie was more than prepared to brazen it out.

"Thank you," said Emily. "My, but there's a lot of people here."

Millie nodded. "Lots of folks look forward to this, though you wouldn't know why when you've seen it. It's pretty much the same every year."

"Well, then," said Emily brightly, "it's taken on the aura of tradition."

"Like as not," replied Millie with a brisk nod. A silence fell among the three of them. Millie looked from Emily to Ransom, then back again. "Sara didn't come, I take it."

"No," said Emily, shaking her head regretfully, "she said she had a headache."

Millie's face clouded over. "Damn people, anyway, though I shouldn't talk that way in church."

Her gaze wandered over Emily's shoulder, and her face brightened with recognition. " 'Scuse me, Miss Emily, I have to go say hello to Mrs. Parker. This is the first time she's been up and out since having her youngest." With this, Millie disappeared through the crowd, apparently parting it through sheer force of personality.

"Since having her youngest?" said Ransom, curling his lips. "Are we to assume that Mrs. Parker's eldest sprang out of her fully grown?"

"Jeremy . . ." Emily said warningly. The stern yet amused expression on her face made him laugh.

"Mr. Ransom!" called a familiar voice a little more loudly than Ransom would have preferred. He and Emily glanced around the crowd—a useless reflex on Emily's part since most of the churchgoers towered over her, making it almost impossible for her to see past the surrounding bodies. The voice called Ransom's name again, closer this time, and Ransom spun around to find Johnnie Larkin approaching from the outer door, smiling and waving his hand.

"Hi, there!" said Johnnie as he reached them.

"Hello," said Emily with cordial formality.

"Mr. Larkin," said Ransom.

"Wow! Big turnout," Johnnie went on with youthful exuberance. "Who'da thought they'd pack them in like this?"

Emily gazed at the young man with the kind of expression usually reserved by the elderly for when they suspect that our future generations might be unredeemably lost. She thought it best not to say anything.

"Where's Sara?"

"At home," Ransom replied.

Johnnie's face darkened. "Damn. I was hoping to sit with her."

"You're welcome to join us if you like," said Emily in a tone that caused Ransom to shoot a glance in her direction. Her eyes remained trained on the young man.

"Oh, thanks," he said amiably, "but I got a lot of friends here, and I'll probably hook up with one of them."

Emily smiled at him.

"You know most of the people around here, don't you?" Ransom asked.

"Sure I do. I been here long enough."

"Is Amy Shelton here?"

Johnnie's face went blank. "Amy? I . . . I thought I saw her. Why?"

"Miss Charters and I need to speak with her, and I thought perhaps you could point her out to us."

A smile spread across Johnnie's face. "Oh, yeah! Sara told me what you were doing. I hope you can help her."

Johnnie stopped speaking, and Ransom continued to look at him until the young man suddenly realized he hadn't answered Ransom's question.

"Oh! You wanted me to point her out." He laughed at himself, then craned his neck and rolled up on his toes to scan over the crowd. After a few moments, he said, "There she is! Come on! I'll introduce you."

Johnnie led the way through the crowd like a human cow-catcher parting the way for Ransom and Emily. Johnnie came to a stop by a timid young woman who stood with an older couple that Ransom took to be her parents. Amy hadn't noticed their approach.

"Hey, Amy! Hi!" Johnnie nodded a greeting to the couple but didn't speak to them.

Amy turned when she heard her name, but when she saw Johnnie her eyes darted away from him. She looked at her hands, then her shoes, then off to the side as if she'd just seen the last remnants of a vanishing spirit.

"Amy, I got to introduce you to somebody. This is Mr. Ransom and Miss Charters." He leaned in toward Amy, who leaned backward slightly. "Mr. Ransom is a detective, and he's looking into Nathan's murder."

Amy glanced at Ransom, her expression a mixture of curiosity and wariness, and a touch of something else Ransom thought he noticed in Sara when he'd first offered to investigate: hope.

Ransom's first impression of Amy Shelton was that Jeff Fields's assessment of her had been right. He couldn't imagine a young woman who seemed so diminutive and insignificant being able to wield a pitchfork with enough force to penetrate a man's heart. Then again, he couldn't imagine her generating enough force to penetrate a man's heart in any other way, either. He wondered if she had seemed this insignificant before the loss of her prospective fiancé.

"I'm Amy's mother," said the woman standing behind Amy. Mrs. Shelton was an excessively angular woman with high, jutting cheekbones, close-set eyes, and a pointed nose. She looked like a clay figure that had been pinched in the center of the face by its creator. She stepped forward, between Amy and Johnnie, in a way that cut him out physically if not emotionally. She waved a hand over her shoulder in the general direction of the man standing behind her who was so nondescript as to be almost invisible. "And that's Amy's father."

Ransom stared into the woman's eyes for a moment before transferring his gaze to Amy.

"Miss Shelton, would you mind if Miss Charters and I stopped by tomorrow morning and asked you a few questions?"

"We're very busy," said the mother. "It's almost Christmas, and we have a lot to do."

Ransom didn't even bother to glance at the woman. His eyes remained on Amy, who continued to look at the floor.

"Miss Shelton?" he said with kind insistence.

There was a pause of the type in which one imagines the earth is holding its breath in anxious anticipation of the answer. Without looking up, Amy replied very quietly, "I don't mind."

"Amy . . ." said Mrs. Shelton with overt disappointment. She then clucked her tongue loudly and glanced over her shoulder at her husband, who looked as if he wouldn't have dared to interfere, even at his wife's entreaty.

"Would ten o'clock be all right?"

"Yes," said Amy, barely audibly.

"Well, there you are!" said Johnnie brightly. Mr. and Mrs. Shelton both looked at him so coldly that even Johnnie couldn't ignore the drop in temperature. He cleared his throat and muttered something about going off to find his friends, which he did immediately without looking back.

Whether or not Mrs. Shelton would have gone further in protesting the intrusion of the detective, any more discussion was interrupted by the church organ beginning to boom a seasonal hymn from the sanctuary, which Ransom took to be the church equivalent of blinking the lights in the lobby. Mr. and Mrs. Shelton hurriedly led Amy away, with Mrs. Shelton furiously whispering in the poor girl's ear, as the crowd began to pour into the nave of the church.

Emily slipped her arm through Ransom's as they followed the crowd.

"You don't care for our Mr. Larkin, do you, Emily?"

"I don't dislike him," said Emily in a tone that implied she would never actively dislike anyone, "I just wonder about his upbringing. It's amazing how many people, despite what they may wish for themselves, end up like their parents. Look at Sara and Nathan. They were brought up by their mother who by all accounts was quite a responsible woman, and without the influence of their father, they turned out to be quite responsible themselves."

"Unlike Johnnie Larkin."

"I fear not. Still, he's young."

They entered the cavernous nave with the stifled reverence usually reserved for unfamiliar places of worship. Even to the casual observer the interior of the church would have been impressive: the ceiling was extremely high and curved with exposed rafters that gave Ransom the feeling of being in the belly of a whale. On each side, there were seven towering windows of intricately designed stained glass depicting the stations of the cross.

The chancel was festooned with a controlled riot of poinsettias arranged as a circular frame around a small wooden replica of a stable, the centerpiece of which was, of course, the manger.

As usual, Emily's eyes were alive to everything around her. She surveyed the scene with admiration, letting out an occasional "Hm" to signify her approval. Ransom, on the other hand, was more aware of the curious unity that seemed to form among the congregation, the type of unity common to any large group of people who gather together for a common purpose, whether it be to worship or to stone someone. But a gathering in a church was usually imbued with a positive energy that was hard to resist, and, added to that, the fact that they were there to celebrate the apex of the Christian religion the atmosphere was doubly charged.

As Ransom helped Emily into her seat, he glanced back to the entrance and saw Jeff Fields coming into the church alone. He was wearing a black suit with a white shirt and black tie, but his straight posture managed to make him look as if he were still in uniform. He took a seat on the aisle in the last pew.

Appropriate Christmas hymns were provided by a children's choir that filed into pews on either side of the chancel with childish solemnity suitable to the occasion. The Christmas story was then read by a young boy of about ten years who seemed undaunted by the task, and actually seemed to understand some of what he was saying. His words were acted out by children of various ages to the accompaniment of the usual ooohs and aaaahs and reminiscent chuckles of the adults of the congregation. The minister gave a brief sermon on the importance of each section of the Christmas story, after which the congregation joined in singing several of the more familiar carols. Emily sat quietly during the proceedings, an unreadable smile on her face and the trademark sparkle in her eyes.

When the service was over, the congregation filed out of the church. The organist provided a steady stream of carols as they left. If anyone had paid extra attention to the sleuthing duo on their arrival, nobody seemed to take notice of their exit. The members of the congregation were much too caught up in their delight over the success of the children's performance.

"You seemed to have enjoyed yourself quite a bit," said Ransom as he ushered Emily to the car.

"Oh, yes," said Emily, "it's always nice to see traditions being passed on to the next generation. And they acted it nicely, don't you think?"

"I suppose," said Ransom, his mind going back to when he'd first met Emily in a case involving what she would always refer to as "a rather unfortunate production of *Love's Labors Lost.*" She seemed to have a talent for adjusting her assessment of a production to the specific situation, making allowances for the children's performance that she never would have allowed for the more mature actors who had adulterated her Shakespeare.

"You know," Emily continued, "just being in a church reminded me of *King Lear.*"

Ransom couldn't help stopping in his tracks he was so surprised by this.

"*Lear?* You're joking!"

"Oh, not because of the service, but because of the horrible muddle of Nathan Bartlett's murder. I don't know . . . being in church made me think that—just perhaps, mind you—being a detective is a sacred duty, a duty to put things right."

"I'm sure I've never thought of it that way," said Ransom, his tone more sardonic than he normally would have allowed for Emily.

She patted his arm for emphasis. "No, I'm not putting it correctly. What I mean is that it brought to mind that line from *Lear:* 'We'll talk with them too—Who loses and who wins; who's in, who's out—And take upon's the mystery of things, As if we were God's spies.' "

Ransom stared at her incredulously. "You got that from the Nativity play?"

"My mind wandered a little."

"That quotation is hardly appropriate to the season."

"Perhaps," Emily replied lightly, "but entirely appropriate to the situation."

While the childish shepherds were watching their stuffed animal flocks by night in the sanctuary of the First Presbyterian Church, Hansen Crane lay on the narrow bed of his rough apartment watching nothing in particular on the small black-and-white television Sara had "loaned" him years ago, telling him at the same time that she didn't want it back.

The promise of snow Ransom had noticed earlier in the day had been realized in the form of a light flurry that had been falling for about an hour. The evening was very quiet and very dark, the only light being provided by the images flickering across the television screen that Crane had perched on the foot of his bed.

He was just beginning to doze off when he heard a loud rumble from the lower part of the barn. The sound started suddenly and stopped just as abruptly. Though Crane believed he knew what had caused the noise, he thought it best to go down and check it out, to make sure it wasn't anything more serious.

He hoisted himself out of bed with a grunt, retrieved his bulky wool coat from the back of the chair over which he'd slung it, and as he slipped it on he patted the pocket, feeling for the penlight he usually kept there. He then headed down the stairs on the side of the barn. He slid open the barn door and reached for the light switch and flicked it. But as with Nathan two years earlier, the action was not accompanied by the expected flood of light. He extracted the penlight from his pocket, and flicked on.

Though it didn't provide a lot of light, it was enough to see that it was just as he had thought—the woodpile had toppled over again.

Crane cursed at the sight and stepped closer for further inspection, all the while thinking of just what he was going to say to Johnnie tomorrow about his inability to perform even a simple task correctly.

He let out a satisfied "Humph" and straightened up, and it was at that moment he heard a step behind him.

He wheeled around but was so startled that he was unable to focus either the light or his attention on the assailant who had so quietly stolen up behind him. The only thing he saw in a quick flash was the block of wood just before it came in contact with his head.

The penlight fell from his hand with a soft clattering noise, and Crane was not far behind it in reaching the ground. For a few seconds after he sprawled out, immobilized by the blow, he was unsure whether the light had gone out or he'd suddenly been blinded. A flood of thoughts poured into his mind, the uppermost of which was the fact that he should have known this would happen. It was his last thought before the second blow fell.

9

Ransom and Emily set off for Amy Shelton's house at about nine-thirty the next morning. Sara gave them explicit directions that were easy enough to follow given that the Sheltons lived in town, and there wasn't exactly a maze of streets in which to get lost.

As Sara helped Emily on with her coat, she said, "Please be gentle with Amy. I haven't seen her since the murder, but I understand that it . . . well, that she took it very hard."

"Of course," said Emily with a questioning look on her face.

Sara smiled sheepishly. "I know you will be . . . but could you caution Mr. Ransom as well?"

"I can assure you that Jeremy will adopt whatever attitude he finds suitable." As this didn't appear to placate Sara, Emily laid a thin, pale hand on the young woman's arm, and said gently, "I know that he can seem abrupt at times, but I've never really known him to be unkind."

Sara's cheeks turned pink, and she looked away from Emily's penetrating eyes as she replied, "Thank you."

The Sheltons' house was located on one of the more residential streets in LeFavre. Butler Drive was approximately the length of three city blocks and lined on both sides with large wood-framed houses, each centered on its own generous plot of ground. A few of the houses had their windows shuttered for the winter, indicating that they were owned by summer dwellers, but most of the houses were still occupied, as testified to by the presence of plentiful but tasteful Christmas decorations. It crossed Ransom's mind that this was what Chicago had probably looked like at the turn of the century, before multigenerational family residences became too costly or too cumbersome to be maintained and were either divided into ill-shaped apartments or demolished altogether and hauled away along with the trees that had sheltered them to make way for modern apartment complexes.

The Sheltons' house was an ample two-story structure painted a muted tan with decorative shutters in brown. A wide veranda surrounded the front and left side of the building.

Ransom helped Emily out of the car then up the walk to the five steps that led to the veranda. Emily's right hand held the railing and her left tightened on Ransom's arm as they made their way up the steps, which were lightly dusted with snow. It appeared that someone had shoveled before it had completely stopped snowing and hadn't returned to remove the remainder. When they reached the door, Emily loosened her grip and Ransom pressed the lighted doorbell. The door was opened before the second tone of the bell had completely faded. They were confronted by the stony countenance of Mrs. Shelton, who looked as if she might have raced for the door to beat all comers. Her face was red and she was making an effort to breathe evenly. She'd opened the door just far enough to fit her body in it as a blockade, and stood with her left hand gripping the outer doorknob with enough strength that her knuckles whitened. Ransom half expected the knob to bend in her hand.

"I thought I made it clear to you last night that we were too busy for this sort of thing!" she said without preamble.

"You made your feelings quite clear," said Ransom with calculated calmness, "as did your daughter."

Mrs. Shelton set her jaw and grasped the doorknob even tighter. Unattractive red blotches appeared on her fingers. "We have company, you know. We can't have our holidays upset like this."

"We'll only take up a few minutes of her time."

There was just a beat before Mrs. Shelton spurted out, "It's bad enough we all had to go through it once without Sara Bartlett dragging us all through it again."

Throughout this brief exchange Emily stood with her arm through Ransom's looking at Mrs. Shelton as if she were an unfamiliar creature that Emily feared might not be entirely responsible for its actions. "Surely you don't blame Sara for wanting to know who killed her brother?"

Mrs. Shelton transferred her glare to Emily, and said, "I blame the Bartletts for bringing this whole mess down on our heads."

"Really?" Emily replied incredulously.

Ransom sighed and cocked his head at the woman. "Mrs. Shelton, I realize that my investigation is purely unofficial, but the matter might very easily become official again."

"What?" the woman said sharply.

Ransom smiled, clearly aware of the effect his next words would have on her. "I mean that the case is not closed. The sheriff can ask your daughter to come to the station at any time to be questioned."

"Questioned!" Mrs. Shelton replied venomously. She began to sputter, apparently so stunned that she was unable to find exactly the right words with which to tell the detective exactly what she thought of him. She sounded like a motor boat that couldn't quite get started. Ransom was just about to interrupt the performance to ask her point-blank whether or not she was going to let them see her daughter, when he was saved the trouble by the young woman herself.

"Momma," Amy's voice came from behind the door.

Mrs. Shelton started and ducked her head back behind the door, twisting the knob in her hand as if she had hold of Ransom's head and was trying to snap it off.

"Gladys wants to know what you want for dinner."

"Tell her I—"

With uncharacteristic assertiveness, Amy cut her off. "I think you should go talk to her yourself."

"You what?" the mother snapped.

Amy gently pulled the door open the rest of the way as she repeated calmly, "I think you should go talk to her yourself." There was a slight pause, then Amy added much more meekly, "I won't remember. I'll probably get it wrong. It would be much better if you did it."

Mrs. Shelton glanced from her daughter to Ransom, who she remembered to face with a scowl, then she heaved a world-weary sigh designed to let everyone within earshot know that she was always being sorely tried.

"Oh, all right!" she said as she marched down the hallway, her wooden heels thumping noisily. For all her ferocity, Ransom thought her exit made her look more like a petulant child than a protective mother.

"I'm sorry," said Amy, her eyes downcast so that she appeared to be apologizing to the floor. "Won't you come in?"

They followed her into the hallway, the floors of which were heavily varnished hardwood. The most prominent feature was a staircase, curved at the bottom, with an ornately carved mahogany banister. In the curve of the staircase stood an enormous Christmas tree decorated entirely in white lights and tiers of gold garland so carefully arranged that they might have been done by an interior designer. The tree stood very straight and erect, not as if it were proud to be displayed in such a stately home, but more as if it were afraid to droop. Ransom wouldn't have been surprised to find the branches trembling.

All of the visible wood had been polished to within an inch of its life, which elicited a muffled "Oh, my" from Emily. Just to the left of the door stood a big, sturdy coatrack with hooks that reached out threateningly—as if it would snatch the coats off the backs of the passing guests and not be terribly circumspect about whether or not the guests came with them. A spacious living room was visible through an archway on the right. It was antiseptic and the carpeting and furniture all looked as if they'd never been touched, let alone used. Ransom thought with an inward chuckle that there should be a red velvet rope stretched across the entrance.

Amy led them through the second doorway on the left, closing the door behind them and inviting them to sit on the leather couch under the window on the far wall. A glass display coffee table flanked the couch and two matching chairs were opposite it. Displayed beneath the glass of the table were a fishing reel and a variety of brightly colored lures.

Amy sat across from them in one of the chairs. She was wearing a dark blue knee-length skirt, a white blouse, and had a white angora sweater draped over her shoulders. To Ransom, the ensemble made her look like an overaged teeny-bopper. She folded her hands neatly in her lap and crossed her ankles in the most ladylike fashion.

"Your father is a fisherman, I take it," said Ransom.

"It's a quiet sport," Amy replied in a forlorn tone that suggested that she didn't think further explanation was necessary. "I really have to apologize for my mother."

Emily breathed a gentle tut-tut to let her know that she didn't need to do this.

"Oh, yes," Amy said, lifting her eyes to Emily's for the first time. "I'm afraid my mother . . . my mother is a bit sensitive when it comes to 'the family name.' " She apostrophized the phrase with some distaste. "Any hint of scandal sets her off. So you can imagine what bringing up Nathan's murder does to her."

"No," said Emily kindly, "I can only imagine what it does to you. And we're the ones who should apologize. I'm sorry if we've made things more difficult for you."

"No. No, you didn't," said Amy, looking down at her hands. Emily took this as a sign that Amy couldn't look her in the eye while telling a lie, no matter how politely that lie might be meant. "It doesn't matter. I only want you to find out who killed Nathan," Amy said more forcefully than she'd spoken before. Then she faltered. "It's just that . . ."

Her voice trailed off and Emily attempted to complete the thought for her. "It's just that you're afraid the killer may be someone of whom you are fond."

With tears welling up in her eyes, Amy responded with a nod of her head.

"I think you can rest easy on that point," said Emily. "We don't believe that Sara killed Nathan."

Amy looked up suddenly, the look in her eyes showing that she was grateful she hadn't had to say it. The tears had started to run down her cheeks.

"It's just that everyone seems to believe it."

"Well, we don't necessarily," said Ransom slowly, "but I'd be interested to know why *you* do."

Amy looked startled for a moment, her eyes darting back and forth from Ransom to Emily as if beseeching their forgiveness for something.

"Me? I don't believe she did it!" There was a slight hesitation before she continued. "But everyone seems so sure and . . ." Her voice trailed off again.

Emily smiled at her. "You like Sara Bartlett, don't you," she said, making it a statement rather than a question.

"I did," said Amy. A tear that had been sliding straight down her cheek had its course altered when it was caught in the small crease caused by the slight smile she exhibited. The tear disappeared in the corner of her mouth. "I do," she amended, "it's just . . ."

"I understand," said Emily. Ransom glanced at her and raised an eyebrow. Emily continued more for his benefit than for Amy's. "You *want* to still like Sara but you don't know what to think."

"Yes," said Amy, nodding her head eagerly as if greatly relieved that someone really *did* understand.

"Well," said Ransom, taking charge of the conversation from which he felt he'd been excluded long enough, "perhaps if we can clarify the matter things will be able to get back to normal."

Amy looked at Emily as if in mute appeal for further consolation. Emily noticed a curious similarity to the desperation that often appeared in Sara's eyes: a silent cry for help dulled by the belief that no help was to be found. She gave Amy a single nod, which seemed to signify that she could trust the detective.

"All right," said Amy.

Ransom cleared his throat. "Miss Shelton, I understand that you had a date with Nathan on the night he was killed."

"Yes, but it was canceled. The weather was so bad."

Ransom raised his right eyebrow. "You say that as if you don't quite believe it."

Amy lowered her head but not before Ransom noticed her rueful smile. "The weather *was* very bad. I suppose it's just . . . vanity. I guess I thought—at the time—that if he really cared he would have come over despite the snow, but that's just silly. I wouldn't have wanted him to risk his life or anything." She raised her head and blinked away a fresh onslaught of tears. "It's just I loved him so much."

"Had he ever broken a date before?"

Amy responded with a shake of her head.

"Did you think there was another reason for it, other than the storm?"

"Not really," she replied with a pronounced lack of conviction.

Ransom studied her for a moment. He crossed his legs, laid his right hand on his uppermost knee and began to silently drum his fingers across it.

"Did you notice anything different about Nathan just before he was killed?"

She looked up at him. "Different?"

"Yes. Was he acting differently at all?"

Amy had been looking at Ransom. She slowly turned her head toward Emily. Ransom sighed and his drumming fingers stiffened and slowed. "Miss Shelton, we've heard that Nathan was a bit preoccupied just before the murder."

Amy lowered her eyes to her lap. "Yes, he was."

She stopped and Ransom struggled to retain his rapidly diminishing patience. Emily shot him a concerned glance, then turned to Amy and said, "Do you have any idea what was on his mind?"

The peculiar half smile returned to Amy's face. "I thought it was because of me."

"I beg your pardon?"

Amy looked up. "I thought it was because of me. I thought he was working himself up to asking me to marry him."

The slight quaver in Amy's voice caused Emily's eyebrows to slide upward and Ransom's fingers to pause in their steady rhythm. "And were you proven wrong?" Emily asked. Despite the lightness of her tone, Emily's eyes had narrowed and were trained on the young woman as if she were trying to see into her mind.

"After a few days I thought it couldn't be what I'd been thinking. Nathan was usually very up-front. I'd never known him to be timid. And"—she paused and glanced from Emily to Ransom, her cheeks flushing red—"and I'd given him every reason to believe I'd accept." Amy stopped and pressed her fingers against her forehead as if admitting this had caused her physical pain. The three of them sat in silence for a few moments. When Amy finally moved her hand, it was to wipe away her freshly flowing tears. "But like I said, after a few days I realized it wasn't that he was worried about proposing."

"Did you ask him what was bothering him?" asked Ransom.

"Many times. Many times. At first jokingly, because . . . but he didn't tell me—he said it was nothing. Then I began to think maybe what was bothering him was that he didn't want to . . . that he wanted to stop seeing me. So I pressed him about it."

"What did he say?"

"I asked him if he was unhappy with me."

She stopped for a beat and smiled as the scene came back to her. "He put his arms around me and hugged me and told me I was just being silly."

"But you didn't let it go at that," said Emily, giving the young woman a benevolent, understanding smile.

For the first time, Amy gave a little laugh which was checked quickly by a demure cough into her hand. "Of course not. I kept pressing him to tell me what was wrong—once I knew it wasn't me I wasn't so afraid—and he finally . . . after a lot of . . . well, he finally told me."

She stopped again, and Ransom fought the desire to finally let go of his temper and yell "And?" He was spared this by Emily putting the word to Amy much more gently than Ransom could have managed at that point.

Amy gave another little cough, and said, "He said he thought he'd seen a ghost."

"A ghost?" said Emily with perfectly Victorian amazement.

Amy smiled. "I know. I thought he was putting me on because I'd been pestering him. But that's what he said."

Emily leaned forward slightly in her chair. "Did he say anything further?"

"Well, I asked him if he meant he'd seen it at Hawthorne House, because there's always stories about old houses, and that's when—" She paused again and looked at Emily and Ransom in turn. "That's when he said something even more strange."

"Stranger than that he'd seen a ghost?" said Ransom wryly.

"Yes. He said he'd seen it all around."

Both Emily and Ransom emitted a "Hmm" in unison, sounding so much alike one would have thought they really were related.

"He changed the subject after that, and I didn't pursue it. He tried for the rest of the evening to act perfectly normal . . . but I could tell there was still something wrong."

Ransom uncrossed his legs. "Did you tell all of this to the sheriff at the time?"

Amy shook her head blankly. "Why would I?"

"Because it might be important."

Amy mustered enough spirit to wrinkle her forehead and stare at the detective as if she thought he might be pulling her leg. She shook her head as she answered, "A ghost can't stab somebody, Mr. Ransom."

Ransom sat back in his chair and folded his arms, a smile spreading across his face.

"Some of them can."

Ransom and Emily didn't stay much longer after that. There wasn't much more Amy could tell them, and Ransom didn't feel the need to ask her about her own alibi for the time of the murder—that had already been checked by the sheriff.

Amy led them from the room, pausing by the door to glance down the hallway before proceeding, presumably to check for the presence of her mother, though Ransom didn't know what difference her mother's presence would've made to their exit. She showed them to the door and went with them out onto the veranda. Just as Ransom and Emily were about to descend the stairs, Ransom stopped and turned to Amy.

"Miss Shelton, one last thing. Last night I thought I noticed a certain . . . coolness on your part toward Johnnie Larkin. . . ."

Amy lowered her eyes to the ground, her face turning beet red, "Not really. Not . . ."

"I was wondering what the cause of that was."

Amy didn't answer. Though Emily had stopped along with Ransom, she hadn't looked back at Amy until Ransom asked this. Amy's reaction created a great deal of interest in the old woman.

"I don't mean to embarrass you," Ransom continued, "but the relationship between all the people who were here at the time of the murder is very important."

Amy lifted her head just enough for them to see her lower lip was trembling. "I didn't have a relationship with Johnnie then."

Emily's eye widened and she inclined her head just slightly. "*After* Nathan was murdered?"

A fresh flood of tears streamed down Amy's cheeks and for the first time she seemed in danger of breaking down completely.

"I was so lonely, you see . . . and I needed someone to talk to. And so did Johnnie. He and Nathan were . . . friends. And I guess Sara was so upset she couldn't talk to anyone. So Johnnie sought me out. And we spent most of the time talking about Nathan. Most of the time."

Emily had slipped an arm around the young woman. She patted her arm, and said, "There, now. There's nothing to be ashamed of. It was a very difficult time for you."

Ransom stood staring at Amy through thoughtfully narrowed eyes. "Did Johnnie break it off?"

Amy shook her head. "There was nothing . . . serious to break off. He just drifted away. But . . . I should've expected that, because I'm sure Sara needed him eventually, and he's always had a crush on her. I think I was just . . ."

Emily patted her arm again, but Amy broke away from her and ran into the house, shutting the door behind her. As Ransom led Emily down the steps he said, "It seems our little Johnnie isn't above 'comforting the widow.' "

Emily clucked her tongue, her eyes trained on the walk beneath them as she replied, "Oh, I hope Miss Shelton is right. I hope he wasn't just taking advantage of the situation." From the tone of voice in which she'd said this, Ransom gathered that this strand of hope was very tenuous.

Inside the house, Amy paused by the door and made an attempt to wipe away her tears with the tips of her fingers, succeeding in little more than smearing the salty streams across her face. She listened intently for a moment for any sound of her mother's approach. Though the interview had been short, it had been exhausting, and the last thing she wanted to do at that moment was face another interrogation from her mother.

Hearing nothing, she started for the staircase. She hesitated when she reached the tree, looking at it with no discernible expression. After a moment, she reached up and unhooked a part of a gold garland from one of the branches over which it was draped and released it, letting it droop down unattractively and leaving a gaping dark space on the side of the tree.

She smiled and went up the stairs.

❄

It was shortly after Ransom and Emily had left for their meeting with Amy Shelton that Sara made her circuit of the bathrooms, collecting soiled towels and replacing them with fresh. She loaded the used towels in a round laundry basket and headed downstairs.

"Have you seen Hansen this morning?" Sara asked as she came into the kitchen.

Millie looked up from the bowl in which she'd been mixing the ingredients for pumpkin pies. She'd already made the crusts and fitted them into four pie plates, which she had sitting on the counter. She swiped a loose strand of hair off her forehead with the back of her wrist and sighed. "Not hide nor hair," she said in answer to Sara's question.

"The front walk hasn't been shoveled yet from last night. I swept off the porch. I suppose I can do the walk. . . ."

"Nonsense," said Millie, "you let Hansen do it. Lord knows he should earn his keep."

Sara pursed her lips and looked down through the back-door window. "He usually does it without being asked."

Millie went back to mixing the pie filling. "He's probably out there sleeping it off."

"Oh, Millie! Hansen doesn't drink. At least, not that I know of."

"He's a man," said Millie with a shrug.

Sara laughed. "Does your Herbert drink?"

Millie shrugged again. "He's a man, too. But Herbert doesn't do anything to excess. Lord knows there's some things I wish he would!"

"Well, I'd better go check on him and tell him there's work to do," said Sara with a definite lack of enthusiasm.

She crossed the kitchen and reached for her coat, which was hanging on one of the pegs by the back door, pausing for a moment with her hand resting on the sleeve. If Millie had been facing her, she would have seen the black shadow that passed across Sara's face, a shadow caused by a sudden, sickening sense of déjà vu. She shook her head briskly as if physically attempting to cast off the cloud, plucked the coat from the peg, and slipped her arms into the sleeves. Then she went out the back door, letting it close behind her with a soft thud.

Millie continued to blend the pie ingredients in the bowl until they reached a consistency that met with her satisfaction. She popped the blades of the mixer into a bowl of water she'd left in the sink for just that purpose and pushed the mixer to the back of the counter out of her way. Then she took a long-handled wooden spoon, picked up the bowl, tilted it, and began to push the filling into the crust-lined pans with the spoon.

She had just finished filling the second and was about to start the third when the back door was flung open with such violence that it banged loudly against the wall, startling Millie so badly that she dropped the bowl onto the counter. She rushed over to the steps leading to the back door and looked down. There was Sara, half collapsed with her back against the door and her eyes closed. To Millie she looked like a deflated accordion.

"What is it? What's wrong?" she said anxiously.

Sara's eyes popped open and she turned her face to Millie. She looked at first as if she didn't quite recognize her, then suddenly her expression changed, as if a curtain had fallen from her eyes, revealing her surroundings as familiar.

"Oh, Millie!" she exclaimed, racing into her arms. She buried her face in Millie's shoulder and began to cry.

"What is it?" said Millie, who was becoming greatly alarmed.

Sara lifted her head and tried to focus her bleary eyes on Millie's face.

"What is it?" said Millie again, almost shaking her.

"Oh, Millie! It's happened again!"

Jeff Fields arrived soon after receiving the call. He went out to the barn to view the body. Even with the barn doors fully open there was not quite enough sunlight to take in the scene in detail. He flicked the switch to the right of the door and the work lights sprang on. He crouched by the inert form of the handyman and surveyed the damage, paying special attention to the head. When he rose, he was shaking his head. He didn't need a coroner to tell him what had happened, but he'd have to call him just the same.

Fields went back to the house and made the necessary calls, then had a brief talk with Millie, who seemed to be more aggravated than shocked by the situation. She told him what she knew, which amounted to little more than explaining that she was in the kitchen when Sara ran in as if she were being chased by the devil and said "It's happened again." Fields then asked her where Sara had gone.

"She's waiting in the library," said Millie, pursing her lips and rolling them sideways as if she were moving a particularly vexatious plug of tobacco around into her cheek.

"Thank you," said Fields as he started to leave the room.

"Wait," said Millie, catching him by the arm, "you listen here, Jeff. Sara's really shaken up by this, so you go easy with her."

Fields stared at her a moment, his expression unchanging. "I always have," he said with meaning, "you know that."

Millie wouldn't relent. "Then you be easier than easy."

Fields hesitated as if he would have liked to say something more, but without so much as a shake of his head he left the room.

Though Sara didn't usually like the closeness of the library, she was finding it oddly comforting at that particular moment, like a cat who retreats to a small space for an imagined sense of security. She glanced up as Fields entered the library. She closed a book that was lying open and unread in her lap and set it on the table by her chair. A blue-and-white cup of tea that Millie had provided to settle her nerves rattled in its saucer as the book reached the table. She absently smoothed back her hair, then dropped her hands to the arms of the chair and turned away from him.

"He *is* dead, isn't he?" she asked quietly.

"Yes."

"Was it an accident?"

There was a barely perceptible beat before Fields said, "No, he was murdered."

Sara's head snapped up, her expression full of dull shock. "Murdered? But the woodpile . . . I thought . . . he was warned . . ."

Fields shook his head. "Someone tried to make it look like an accident, but it wasn't."

"Murder . . ." said Sara in disbelief.

There was another pause during which Fields stared at her as if he were studying her face for a sign of something, while at the same time worried that he might find it. Finally he asked with quiet firmness, "Sara, what did you mean when you said 'It's happened again'?"

"What?" she replied, her face screwed up with confusion.

"After you discovered the body you came running back into the house and said to Millie, 'It's happened again.' What did you mean?"

She answered falteringly. "I meant . . . only that . . . I guess that I'd found another body. That's all."

"You're sure."

She nodded.

"You're sure you didn't mean there'd been another murder?"

She looked up at him. "Well . . . I might have assumed . . . I don't know, it was such a shock to find him like that . . . what difference does it make?"

Fields continued to stare at her as ideas ran through her head, until suddenly the difference became clear. Instead of looking shocked or angry, all strength and emotion seemed to drain out of her at once. Her limbs went slack and her head drooped as if she simply no longer had the power to hold it up. Rather than defeat or sadness, her expression seemed to be one of complete and utter hopelessness.

"Oh, I see," she said vacantly. "That would've been a slip. It would've meant I knew he'd been murdered."

For the first time there seemed to be a chink in Fields's armor.

"Sara, I don't want to have to question you, but you know I've got to."

"I know."

"When was the last time you saw Crane alive?"

"Just before Mr. Ransom and Miss Charters left for the play last night. About six-thirty, I guess. I saw him closing up the barn."

"The play. You didn't see him after that?"

"No."

There was a long pause, then Fields asked, "Was there anyone out here with you last night?"

She turned her dulled eyes up to him and shook her head. "No. Nobody was here but me. And no, I didn't see or hear any cars or anyone come to visit Hansen. I spent the evening watching *White Christmas* on the television up in my room, and then the news, and after that my guests came home. I didn't hear anybody or see anybody or talk to anybody in all the time they were gone. And yes, I know how that looks. I know it looks like I was the only one out here again when somebody got murdered, and I know what everyone will say. They'll say the same thing you're thinking. But I didn't kill Hansen, and I didn't kill my brother." She buried her face in her hands and wept audibly.

Fields slowly moved to her side in fits and starts, his tentative approach at odds with his granitelike expression. Once he was by her side he reached out a hand toward her shoulder, but withdrew it just before making contact. A few seconds went by, then he tried again, successfully bringing himself to lay a sturdy, comforting hand on her shoulder.

Sara bristled slightly at his touch, then seemed to relax a bit, though she continued to cry quietly.

With hand in place, Fields crouched down beside her, and said, "Sara, I don't believe you killed Hansen, and I never believed you killed Nathan, either."

She turned her face, wet and distorted with crying, toward him and said, "Yes, you did."

Fields closed his eyes and exhaled. "I had to proceed . . . I had to go on what evidence there was. I had to go on the facts. That doesn't mean I believed them."

"Of course you did," she said sadly. "Don't you think I can tell?"

His normally impassive face looked pained. He had worked for years to cultivate an unreadable countenance, and was now distressed to find that the one time he'd needed most to remain a blank page, when Nathan was killed, he'd somehow betrayed himself.

He sighed. "Sara, I've been trained to look at the facts and only the facts—it's the most important part of my job—to look at the facts and no matter what, not let my emotions get all tangled up in what I can see, because that's the easiest way to screw up a case."

She shook herself loose from him, stood, and crossed to the window, keeping her back to him. "I could see it in your face, you know—back when Nathan was killed—I could see it in your face that you thought somehow I'd done it."

Fields had remained crouched by the chair. He rose slowly. "All you saw in my face was frustration. I couldn't believe you would kill anyone, let alone Nathan, and I couldn't prove you hadn't done it."

Sara stared out the window, tears hovering on the rims of her lower lids as if they'd been arrested there by his words. There was a glimmer of understanding in her mind that she knew hadn't been there before, and she couldn't quite bring herself to focus on it. But in her mind she could see Jeff as he was when he'd come there in response to the call about Nathan's murder. He'd seemed gruff and cold, and as the investigation wore on he grew even colder and more irritable, to the point where she knew that he thought she was guilty. For the first time she began to have an inkling that his actions may have had a completely different meaning, one she'd misunderstood. But if she was mistaken, it was now too deeply rooted to be swept away in only a minute.

"And what do the facts tell you now? That I'm guilty again?"

"Circumstances don't look good," he said, "I know how it looks."

"So do I," Sara said dully.

Fields crossed to her, this time without hesitation, and stood close behind her, his hands on her upper arms.

"Sara, just because I've taught myself not to listen to my emotions, that doesn't mean that my heart's stopped talking to me. I know you wouldn't kill anyone."

There was a long silence. At last Sara reached up and covered his right hand with her left. "I was right. It's happened again. Only this time it's worse."

10

After their interview with Amy Shelton, Ransom walked Emily back to the car in silence. He saw to it that she was safely buckled into the seat belt on the passenger side, then rounded the car and climbed in behind the wheel. Emily stared at him as he stuck the key in the ignition, held his hand there for a moment without turning it, then released the key and sat back in the seat, his eyes gazing all the while through the front windshield.

"Jeremy, what is it?"

"Hm? Nothing," he replied. He made an abortive reach for the ignition then sat back again.

"It must be something," said Emily.

He sucked in his cheeks for a moment, then exhaled and turned to her. "It's this unbridled speculation we've been indulging in."

Emily hesitated for a second, then said, "Well, I said before—"

"No, it's not that," he said, gently cutting her off as he turned his gaze back to the windshield. "Emily, I've just had the most peculiar idea, and I don't know if I finally have let my imagination run wild with me."

Emily looked at the side of his face, her eyes playful. "And are you going to tell me what it is?"

Ransom could feel his face flush. Once again he'd forgotten that Emily was not his partner, Gerald, and unlike him would be far less inclined to accept the role of Boswell. He cleared his throat, and said, "Sorry. If I hesitate it's because the idea seems crazy . . . and yet, it fits what we've learned so far." He turned to her and explained more forthrightly, "It's everyone's insistence that Sara must've killed Nathan, and money being the only possible motive."

"Yes?"

"Well, what if they're right?"

"Jeremy, I refuse to believe—"

He raised his palm, signaling her to wait. "I don't mean about Sara, I mean about the money."

There was a pause during which Emily's eyebrows knit very close together. "You mean that someone else killed Nathan for the money? But who?"

He sighed very deeply. "It was what Nathan said about seeing a ghost. First of all, from what we've learned of Nathan Bartlett, does he strike you as the type who would imagine things?"

Emily considered this for a moment, then said matter-of-factly, "No. He kept the books for Hawthorne House, and I'm inclined to believe that you won't find a fanciful bookkeeper outside of your Mr. Dickens."

"*Hardly* fanciful," said Ransom, with slight annoyance.

Emily smiled. "But what is your point?"

"Just this: When he said he saw a ghost, he meant it *almost* literally."

"Almost?"

"I think what he was saying was that he saw someone either that he didn't expect to see *here,* or that he didn't expect to see at all." He paused for a moment, turning a significant glance toward Emily as he said, "Perhaps someone he didn't even know was still alive."

Emily gazed at him for a few moments, her lips pursed and her eyebrows arched. Suddenly her eyes widened and the furrows over her brow deepened so much it almost made her look cross. "Their *father?*" she said, her voice rising so high at the end that it practically disappeared.

"Um hm."

"But Jeremy, even supposing you're right about what Nathan meant when he said he'd seen a ghost, it could've been anyone. He could've seen someone from school, someone from Chicago, an old friend. Even an old enemy. What makes you think it was his father?'

Ransom shook his head ruefully. "I admit it's purely conjecture. Very thin conjecture. And you're right, it very well could've been anyone. But it's also an educated guess based on some rather uneducated gossip."

"Yes?"

"Well, assuming that the 'ghost' he saw was someone from his past, whoever it was caused him some distress—two different people noticed he was preoccupied."

"That still could've been anyone," Emily interjected.

"Except for one thing. A few days after he said it, he was dead. And we keep coming back to the money. If Nathan was murdered for his money, and Sara didn't do it, it had to be someone else who stood to inherit."

"But Sara was the only one to inherit, wasn't she?"

"That's right. But their father has been estranged from them for years. He couldn't know how their money would fall out."

Emily thought for a moment. "Assuming their father could possibly be the murderer, how could he inherit? He divorced their mother ages ago."

Ransom sighed. "I can tell you, but you're not going to like it. The only way he could inherit is if neither Nathan nor Sara had made wills, and they both died. At least, I believe their money would go to their father, divorced or not, if they had no other immediate family."

Emily blinked. "You're quite correct. I don't like it at all. If that's true, then Sara's life is in danger."

"Well, if it'll ease your mind any, this conjecture of mine is probably just a bunch of rot. It's been two years since Nathan was killed and Sara's still alive. It's just as likely that Jeff Fields really is the murderer and his plans to marry Sara just fell through."

"That's true . . . there's only one problem with that: Nathan had seen Jeff Fields for three years before being killed. Why would Fields *suddenly* have needed to kill him?"

"Maybe he learned something about Fields that wasn't to his advantage."

Emily clucked her tongue. "That still wouldn't explain why Nathan said he'd seen a ghost so late in the game. Oh, Jeremy," said Emily with frustration, "the timing is all wrong. It doesn't work with Fields, and if what you're thinking is true, then Sara would've been killed long ago. But she's still alive. Why all the waiting? Why all this time in between events? It's all most irritating. And I can't see why their father . . ."

"You're right," said Ransom with a degree of self-disgust as he sat up and turned the key in the ignition, "it's a perfectly ludicrous idea." He drove to 130th Street and headed back toward Hawthorne House.

Emily clenched her right hand into a frail fist and rubbed it into the open palm of her left, all the while gazing out the window as she mulled over all they'd said. Suddenly her face brightened.

"Oh, how perfectly stupid of me! *King Lear!*"

Far from expecting this response, Ransom was completely bewildered. "What?"

Emily shook her head and clucked her tongue with disappointment. "How unbelievably stupid I've been! I should have seen it before. And what makes it worse is that I've been rereading it, and never once made the connection."

"Emily, what are you talking about?"

Emily turned to him, and explained. "*King Lear*, the father who was cast off by his daughters and then turns to them for help. And all that tragedy happens after he has been spurned." Emily suddenly turned away from him, looking out the windshield as if a fresh idea had just sprung up in front of the car. "Oh, dear! I wonder if that really happened?"

"What?" said Ransom, his exasperation increasing. It was the first inkling he'd ever had of what it was like for Gerald to be his partner.

"Of course," she continued as if turning her thoughts over aloud, heedless of Ransom's presence, "I don't suppose he really would've had to contact her. Then again, one would think he would have tried that first before resorting to murder. . . ."

Ransom's expression had changed from exasperation to concern. "Emily, I think I've been running you around too much. I brought you up here for rest, and I've been the one that's keeping from it."

This broke in upon her reverie. She shook her head, and said, "No, Jeremy. I think I've had quite enough rest already. That's the only reason I can see for my muddled thinking." She shifted very purposefully toward him in her seat. "Now, there are some things we need to know: First of all, we need to know whether or not Nathan and Sara made out wills, and we need to find out if it's possible for their father to be here without their recognizing him."

"Well, we can assume that Nathan *did* recognize him."

"But not readily," Emily said correctively, "or else he would've acted on it."

"Maybe he did. That could be what got him killed."

Emily folded her hands in her lap. "I suppose that could be true . . . but still . . . that wouldn't explain why Sara didn't recognize him as well."

"How old were they when their father and mother divorced?"

"I don't know," Emily replied, elevating her shoulders in a slight shrug. "All Sara said was that her mother and father divorced when she was a child, and that the divorce was acrimonious. I wonder just how acrimonious it was." She paused for a moment, then posed a question more to herself than to Ransom, in a tone of utter disbelief. "*Could* Sara's father be around here without her recognizing him?"

Ransom narrowed his eyes and began to drum his fingers on the top of the steering wheel. "You would think that even if she didn't recognize him outright, there would be something familiar about him."

"Yes, but that's just it," said Emily with renewed vigor, "you'd also think that if Nathan had known their father was in the area, he would've said something to her. And yet she's never said a word about her father, except when she told me of the divorce. I can't believe she would've held that back if she knew. So the most important thing we need to do is locate Sara's father!"

"Well," said Ransom with a heavy sigh, "I have another bit of conjecture for you that you're going to like even less. If their father really is here, I have an idea who he might be."

"Hansen Crane," said Emily vacantly, almost as if she hadn't been listening to him.

"I give up," said Ransom, laughing, "I might as well turn my badge over to you and retire to Sussex and keep bees. Or do whatever Dr. Watson did when he retired."

Emily smiled appreciatively, but replied with a simple tut.

"And how did you arrive at Mr. Crane for the role of Mr. Bartlett?"

"The same way you did, Jeremy, simply arithmetic. He's the only one we know of who's involved in this case who's old enough to have been Nathan and Sara's father. Of course, I *suppose* it doesn't have to be somebody connected with Hawthorne House . . . and in that case, it could be anyone in the area."

"Except it would have to be someone who came here in the past five years, since Nathan and Sara came here."

"Not necessarily. You have to remember, Jeremy, that we have no idea where this father has got to since he left their mother. He could've settled here long ago."

"I suppose so," said Ransom with a heavy sigh, "but I really do like Hansen Crane in the role."

"Why?"

"Because he's hiding something. I'm sure of it."

Emily sighed with frustration. "But even if it were true, and Hansen Crane was their father, it still leaves us with more questions than it answers."

"Yes," Ransom interjected, "the first and foremost being why did it take Nathan so long to recognize him? Crane was here for quite a while before Nathan was killed. Which would mean that Nathan didn't recognize him at first . . . or . . ." His voice trailed off as he mentally went through the possibilities. Emily picked up the thread.

"Or . . . somehow Nathan discovered who Hansen Crane really was. Remember, Millie told me that Nathan asked a lot of questions about Crane when he first showed up."

"Yes, but that could have been nothing more than natural worry on his part."

They fell silent for a few moments, each lost in their own thoughts as they sped on toward Hawthorne House. Finally Ransom shook his head. "I still have trouble believing that they wouldn't have recognized their father somehow."

"Hmm," said Emily, giving this due consideration. "Mr. Crane seems to be a very credible character . . . very much of a type. Maybe it's simply a very credible disguise."

Ransom looked at her, returning the playful smile she'd given him earlier. "A lost relative showing up in disguise? How perfectly Shakespearean."

Emily could not help but laugh at the struggle he seemed to be having to keep the smugness out of his tone. She refolded her hands, and said, "Well, Jeremy, I believe you would say touché, wouldn't you?"

Hawthorne House had just come into view when Emily uttered an involuntary "Oh, my!" Ransom saw immediately what had drawn her attention. In the drive alongside the house were several cars, two of which were readily identifiable as belonging to the County Sheriff's Department, along with Johnnie Larkin's beat-up hatchback.

Emily's hand went up to the side of her face as she said, "Jeremy, you don't think . . ."

"It could be anything," Ransom replied with an assurance he didn't really feel.

Ransom applied additional pressure to the gas pedal so that they covered the short distance that remained to the house in record time. He turned the wheel, slowing down just enough to keep Emily from flying into the passenger door, and sped up the driveway sending a shower of snowy gravel onto the road. Emily seemed completely unperturbed by this, her attention set on the house as if she could pierce its mysteries through the sheer intensity of her gaze.

Johnnie was standing in the parlor window, his hands resting on either side of the frame as if he were holding himself back from diving through the pane. His face was ashen and blank, and even at this distance Emily could tell he'd been crying. His body jerked in a sudden spasm, apparently startled by their arrival. Emily noted with interest that it had taken him an inordinate amount of time to notice their approach, given that the road was visible from the parlor window. She feared that his distracted state didn't bode well.

Ransom pulled the car up on the left side of the sheriff's cars and switched off the ignition.

"You wait here," he said peremptorily as he pulled the keys from the ignition and popped open his door.

"I'll do nothing of the sort!" Emily said so firmly that Ransom was checked in the act of climbing from the car.

"Emily, we don't know what's happened."

"And do you think for a moment that I'm going to wait out here, nibbling my fingernails and waiting for you to come back and break the news to me? I'm not as frail as all that!"

Ransom paused just long enough to shoot her a half smile,

then jumped from the car and went around to her side and helped her out.

"You've never nibbled your fingernails," he intoned.

They crossed the paving stones, from which someone had cleared the snow, and entered the house through the front door.

Johnnie was on them before Ransom had even managed to close the door. "Thank God you're back! That damn sheriff is gonna screw this up, just like he did the last time! I *told* him," he whined, tears welling up in his eyes, "I *told* him!"

Ransom looked at the young man sternly. "You told who?"

"I told him it was dangerous! You can ask anybody! Oh, God! I can't believe it!"

"I don't know what you're talking about," Ransom said, his voice hardening in an attempt to quell Johnnie's rush of emotion and bring him into focus.

"Is Sara all right?" Emily said.

"Sara?" said Johnnie, his face going blank again. "Of course." He turned back to Ransom and said, "I came out here— just like I do most days—to see if there was any work for me to do and I found all this! He waved his arms in the direction of the kitchen as if the movement were somehow sufficient explanation.

At that moment Jeff Fields came into the living room and saw them. "Larkin, I told you to wait in the parlor."

"I've told you everything I know," said Johnnie with no hint of the bravado with which he usually addressed Fields. "Just ask Millie and Sara . . . I warned him."

Fields's expression remained closed, his jaw set solidly. "Wait in the parlor."

Larkin stared at him doe-eyed for a beat, then turned and went back into the parlor like a dog that hates its master but is afraid to disobey.

"Well," said Fields, turning his stony gaze on Ransom, "I must say you sure know how to stir things up. We haven't had a murder out here for two years, then you show up and poke your nose in and first thing you know we got another body."

Emily stiffened her spine until she seemed to tower in her tiny frame and demanded in her harshest tone, "Is Sara all right?"

Fields barked a single "Huh" at her, and said, "She's fine."

"Then who's been killed?" Ransom asked.

"Hansen Crane."

"Hansen Crane?" said Emily, her voice hollow with disbelief, "Hansen Crane?"

"Yeah," said Fields. He turned back to Ransom, and said, "And I want to talk to you."

Emily shook her head as if the action was necessary to get her brain back into working order. She looked at Fields, and said, "Where *is* Sara?"

"She's waiting in the library, and nobody's going to see her until I'm finished with her." He jerked a thumb at the door to the library, in front of which stood a young deputy whose arms were folded across his chest. He seemed to stand just a little straighter when attention was directed at him.

"You need to guard her?" Emily asked disapprovingly.

"I was talking to her and we got interrupted when everybody else showed up. The coroner's out back now. I want to keep her from talking to other people until I'm done questioning her. She preferred waiting in the library." He paused and folded his arms. "And there isn't a guard on the door to keep her from coming out, it's to keep others from going in. This is an investigation and I'm not going to be accused of not carrying it out right." He stopped just short of adding, "Not this time," but all three felt it was implicit. Fields looked at Ransom, and said, "You, in the kitchen."

Ransom gave Fields one of his most infuriating smiles, and said, "Yes, Officer."

Fields marched into the kitchen and Ransom followed him at a more leisurely pace, pausing in the doorway just long enough to shoot a glance at Emily. He raised an eyebrow and gave a slight nod, then turned away and disappeared into the kitchen. If Emily could have managed a smile in these circumstances, she would have done it for Ransom's uncanny talent for terse, expressive nonverbal communication.

She headed for her bedroom door, a certain frailty being added to her gait as it had been when she'd approached the clerk in the drugstore.

"Where're you going, ma'am?" asked the deputy with all the severity of a youth in authority.

"I'm going to my room . . . Sergeant," said Emily, faltering noticeably over his rank and giving a little nod in the direction of the door to her room.

He flashed a superior smile and corrected her. "That's Deputy, ma'am."

"Oh, yes, of course," said Emily. "I have to lie down. I've been ill, you know, and this has all been very upsetting. You see, I have a heart condition. . . ."

The deputy's eyes showed signs of beginning to glaze over. He cut her off with a "Yes, ma'am," and carelessly waved a hand in the direction of the door she'd indicated.

"Thank you," Emily said meekly.

Emily went into her room, closing the door behind her. She crossed to the communicating door to the library and paused with her hand on the knob, putting her ear close to the door and listening for the sound of voices. Satisfied that Sara wasn't being questioned, as quietly as she could Emily turned the knob and opened the door just a crack and peered through the space to make sure Sara was alone, then stepped into the room.

"Emily!" Sara exclaimed.

Emily quickly put her finger to her lips. "Quietly, Sara. I'm not supposed to be in here."

The admonition was almost unnecessary, since the hundreds of books that lined the shelves of the little room seemed to swallow sound the moment it was emitted, but Emily wasn't taking any chances.

Sara had risen to her feet and rushed to Emily. Her eyes were read and swollen and her face looked puffy and wet. There were damp stains on her white blouse from where her tears had fallen. She said in an anxious whisper, "I didn't do it! But it's like Nathan all over again. My God, what am I going to do?"

Emily took Sara's trembling hands in her own and gave them an encouraging squeeze. "First, you're going to have to calm yourself. I have some questions to ask you and I don't know how long we have."

Sara stared at Emily through eyes bleary with tears. Something about the matter-of-factness in Emily's tone seemed to stem the young woman's rising panic. She squeezed Emily's hands in return and took a deep breath, which she released slowly.

"Could we sit down, please?" said Emily.

As they took their seats, Sara explained, "I found Hansen, dead, in the barn. Just like . . . just like before. Only I thought it was an accident. The woodpile fell over. I'm sure it was an accident. I don't know why Jeff thinks otherwise."

"I'm sure he has his reasons," said Emily, adjusting the hem of her dress. "But I need to ask you about something quite different, and it may be a bit difficult for you."

"What?" Sara said after a slight pause, looking exactly as if the last thing she wanted was for things to get more difficult.

Emily cleared her throat. "First of all, how old were you when your parents divorced?"

"My parents?" Sara said, her complete surprise diverting her from the problems at hand. She cast a glance at the door, half-afraid that she had spoken too loudly.

"Yes."

"Well . . ." Sara continued slowly. "I was a little less than two, I think. Nathan would have been about four. Why?"

"You *think?*" Emily said, her eyes narrowing. "You don't know?"

Sara shook her head.

"Less than two . . ." Emily said vacantly, "yes, that's very curious."

"I don't understand."

"Well, if you were that young at the time of the divorce, how do you know that it was, as you said, acrimonious?"

"From my mother. She didn't . . . exactly put him down all the time, but she didn't make any bones about him being . . . unreliable. From what I could gather over the years, he didn't do a day's work from the minute they married. How he'd been struggling along before that, I don't know. But according to my mother, once they were married he was in and out of jobs all the time, never holding one for very long and it was never his fault that he was fired, if you know what I mean. Mother just thought he was a deadbeat."

Emily gave a single nod, meant to convey both that she understood and that she wanted Sara to continue. "And what did you think of him?"

"My father?" said Sara, drawing back as if she wanted to physically withdraw from the subject. Her right hand went up to her hair, one strand of which she fiddled with absently as she continued. "I was so young . . . I don't remember anything about him. I do know that he never made any effort to see us after the divorce, so I have no reason to . . . so I think my mother must've been right." This was said in a tone mixed with regret and bitterness, and Sara averted her eyes as if despite the abandonment she'd suffered, she was ashamed to speak ill of her absent parent.

Emily considered this for a moment, then leaned forward in her chair and said, "Did you hear from your father recently?"

Sara's eyes opened wide with astonishment. "How did you know that?"

"It was just a guess on my part," said Emily with a shrug, "but I thought it likely."

"But why?"

"I'll explain that when we have more time. Now, when did you hear from your father?"

"It wasn't exactly recently. It was . . ." Her voice trailed off. She looked down at her hands. A flood of memories brought the blood to her cheeks in red splotches, as if it couldn't decide which emotion it wanted to convey.

Emily looked at the young woman, her eyes filled with compassion. She tried to help her along by offering a possible answer. "Was it after your mother died?"

Sara moved her hand from the button with which she'd been playing to her forehead and a choked sob escaped her lips.

"Mother was right, you know," she said haltingly, her voice catching after each word.

"About what?" Emily asked gently.

Sara looked up at her. "About my father. When she was sick she said if anything happened to her, he would come out of the woodwork. And that's what happened."

"He contacted you."

Sara nodded, sending a tear flying onto the front of her blouse. "About six months after she died—that would've been about six years ago—he wrote to me."

"Do you remember where the letter came from?"

Sara sniffed, then wiped the tears away with her fingers and cleared her throat in an attempt to regain her composure. "San Francisco. It was . . . he started by saying how sorry he was about my mother, and how sorry he was about the divorce, and how much he wanted a relationship with me and how much he regretted not having been there when we were growing up. But it ended with an appeal for money."

Emily let out a mild "Tsk."

"Not overtly, you understand, just telling me all about how he'd fallen on hard times and how his health wasn't as good as it used to be, and how he'd heard that I was doing well, and was very glad of it. He didn't come right out and ask for money, but I think it was there between the lines."

Sara stopped and Emily didn't reply, her attention apparently being taken up by the middle-most shelf of books directly across from her. Sara was confused, thinking perhaps that Emily's lack of response was in fact a form of silent condemnation. She said quickly, "I don't think I was imagining it . . . I mean, because mother had warned me about him ahead of time. I was actually surprised at how right she was."

Emily turned to her, and said, "Oh, I'm sure you were right. I'm sorry, my dear, I didn't mean to let my mind wander, it's just you set me to thinking about how difficult it is to change one's nature. I assume that each time your father went out and got a job, he was trying to change his nature, and each time he failed. It would seem that your mother knew him *very* well."

"Yes," Sara replied quietly.

"Now," said Emily, shifting in her seat as if preparing to get on with business, "how did you reply to your father's letter?"

"I didn't."

"Oh?" For the first time Emily registered genuine surprise. Her eyebrows slid upward and her eyes widened. "Not at all?"

The red blotches, which had begun to dissipate during the previous exchange, began to deepen and spread until Sara's cheeks were in full flush.

"I didn't know what to say. Part of me wanted to lash out at him for not being there, and for hurting my mother, but part of me . . . well, he was my father, and part of me wanted to know him . . . or at least, not to hurt him. As much as my mother had come to dislike him, I couldn't help thinking . . . how sad it was."

"The divorce?"

Sara shook her head. "No. To be so irresponsible."

An approving smile spread across Emily's face. "You're quite wise for your age."

Sara looked away from her. "I wasn't wise enough to know what to say to my father. I kept putting it off and putting it off until . . . it wasn't forgotten, but I didn't think of it any more."

Emily's gaze had gone back to the books. " 'I cannot heave my heart into my mouth,' " she quoted vacantly.

"What?"

Emily shook her head and smiled. "Just a little quote from *King Lear*. Something that somehow seemed pertinent. Did you never hear from him again, or see him?"

"See him?" Sara seemed horrified at the thought. "No, of course not. I don't think I'd recognize him if I did see him. I wasn't even two years old when he left, remember. And mother was bitter enough that she didn't keep any pictures of him."

"Would Nathan have known him?"

"I . . . I don't know. He might. He was a little older. I don't know. Why?"

"We're just trying to look at every possibility."

"Every possibility . . ." Sara repeated slowly. Suddenly the color left her cheeks. "You mean you think that my father might have had something to do with all this?"

Emily gave a single nod.

"But that's impossible."

"Oh, no, my dear. It's simply difficult to believe. But we think that Nathan saw somebody here in town just before he died— someone who he didn't expect to see. Did he say anything about this to you?"

Sara shook her head vigorously. "Nothing. No. And he would have."

Emily paused before saying, "Unless he was trying to protect you."

Sara stared at her for a moment, then said, "Yes, that could be true. It would be like him."

Emily shifted in her seat, and said, "Sara, is it possible . . . is it at all possible that Hansen Crane could have been your father?"

"Hansen?" Sara said loudly, recoiling slightly. "No! Of course not! I would have known!"

"But you said you wouldn't have recognized him."

"I . . . I wouldn't. But I think that somehow I would've known. Besides, Hansen's been here a long time. If Nathan had recognized him, wouldn't he have done it a long time before he was killed?"

"Possibly," said Emily, "that's what we thought. But you knew that Nathan asked a lot of questions about him."

"Oh, that," Sara said with a smile, "that was just because Nathan was so suspicious. He didn't understand how anyone just drifting around like that could be up to any good. He felt the same way about street people back in Chicago. He didn't understand how a grown man could be rootless like that. It reminded him of—" She broke off and looked away from Emily.

"It reminded him of your father?" said Emily gently.

Sara shook her head.

"Is that why you let him stay?"

Tears streamed down her cheeks. "I felt sorry for him. I couldn't believe he could be happy living the way he did."

"Of course you couldn't," said Emily kindly, "his kind of life was too foreign to you."

Sara made an attempt to recover herself. "But I know he wasn't my father. The only contact I've had with my father since the divorce was that one letter."

Emily thought for a moment, then said, "That does strike me as strange. Given the fact that you didn't respond to your father's letter, I'm surprised that he didn't try again."

Sara looked down at her hands. "I suppose I really should've answered him one way or the other."

"Yes . . . yes . . . I suppose that might have made a difference. . . ." Emily spoke so abstractly that Sara thought her mind might be wandering in more ways than one. "I suppose it might have *forestalled* what happened, but I can't imagine the outcome wouldn't have been the same." She stopped. Her eyebrows knit together and she stared off at nothing.

"Emily?" Sara said with concern.

"Now, there are a couple more things I need to know," said Emily, suddenly reanimating. "Did you and Nathan make out wills?"

"Oh, yes, even before mother became ill, she insisted on it. She was very concerned that her money not end up in my father's hands. She worked very hard, you see, making a living after he left. She saved every penny she could. And she inherited a little from her parents. She couldn't bear the thought that my father might somehow end up with it. So Nathan had a will leaving everything to me, and I did the same for him. Of course, that would've changed if either of us had gotten married, but . . ." Her face clouded over and there was a catch in her throat, but she went on. "But as it turned out, that never happened. There was a provision in both our wills that all of our money would go to charity if we died at the same time."

"Ah," said Emily, moving forward in her chair so that she was sitting almost on the edge, "and when Nathan died, did you make out a new will?"

Sara rose from her seat, smoothed her green skirt, which had wrinkled rather markedly from so much sitting, and walked to the bookcase, resting her arm on one of the ledges. "Almost immediately. I know it sounds . . . it may sound awful, but I had this overwhelming feeling that something might happen to me."

Emily smiled at the young woman's back. "That is not an unusual reaction in someone who has just experienced a tragedy, as you had." She took a deep breath, and added, "At the risk of seeming impertinent, may I ask about the contents of the will?"

Sara emitted a short, rueful laugh. "You mean because I had nobody left?"

"Oh, no, because the contents of your will may be very important."

Sara sighed and dropped back into the chair. "I guess because I'd just lost Nathan I was thinking . . . I thought a lot about my friends . . . all the people I'd been close to throughout my life. . . ."

"And?"

Sara heaved a heavier sigh and ran the fingers of her right hand through her long, wavy hair. "And I finally decided to leave everything to the best friend I'd ever had—Lynn. Lynn Francis."

"Really?" said Emily in undisguised amazement.

Sara was somewhat taken aback by the overt surprise on Emily's face. She said, "Was that such a strange thing to do?"

"Not at all," said Emily, laying a hand on Sara's wrist, "it was a very thoughtful thing to do. And very wise. Did you tell anyone about your will?"

"I . . . well, Millie witnessed it, so she knew about it." Here

Sara smiled and her cheeks turned pink, rather than the blotchy red they'd exhibited before. "And if she knows, then everyone else does, too. I love Millie, but she's not . . . necessarily . . . discreet."

"Oh, I wouldn't speak a word against her," said Emily firmly, "she may have saved your life."

Sara blinked. "Saved my life? What do you mean?"

"I'm not exactly sure, because there are still so many questions. But you've managed to throw some light on some very important matters."

Sara sat back in her chair and stared at Emily, looking exactly as if she didn't think she'd been any help at all. Emily didn't return her gaze. Instead, she stared straight ahead as if she were looking at an optical puzzle the solution to which, with some uninterrupted conversation, she might be able to divine. They had sat in silence so long that Sara was just about to ask if there was anything else Emily wanted to know when Emily suddenly said, "I wonder how he knew?"

"What?" was Sara's startled reply.

Emily turned to her. "I wonder how your father knew that your mother had died."

Sara smiled ruefully. "Oh, that's easy. . . ."

While Emily and Sara were having their quiet talk in the library, a much more electrified discussion was taking place in the kitchen. Ransom sat with his chair pushed back from the table, his legs crossed and his hands folded on his uppermost knee, an attitude so casual and unconcerned one would have thought it was designed to further rankle the sheriff. Jeff Fields sat with his forearm resting on the table. It seemed to be costing him an effort not to drum his fingers on its top. His face was as set and expressionless as always, save for the pulsating vein on his temple that bore witness to his agitation. Despite these minor flaws, which would have escaped the notice of a less practiced eye, Fields was doing well at maintaining his unreadable facade. Ransom thought with an inward smile that the only thing Fields lacked was a pair of mirrored sunglasses to complete the picture.

"I want to know what you've learned," said Fields without preamble.

"I haven't learned a single thing that's new," Ransom replied.

"Look, I told you that if you were going to go poking around in this business that I expected you to report back to me. I don't hear anything from you, and the next thing I know, Hansen Crane's murdered."

"When did it happen?"

"So far as we know, last night. That'd be the *logical* time, don't you think?" He hadn't modulated his voice much when he said this, just enough to let Ransom know he was being sneered at. "Sara found him a little while ago, out in the barn, half-buried by the woodpile."

"You're sure it wasn't an accident?"

Fields produced an unamused smile. "We were meant to think so is my guess. But from the looks of his head, I can tell you no log would've gashed him that bad just by falling. Somebody cracked his head open pretty good—more than once from the looks of him."

"Hm."

"Sara says she saw Crane not long before you and Emily left for the play. Of course, we only have her word for that."

"There's no reason for her to lie. Surely she wouldn't want to account for his being alive right up to the time she was left alone with him if it wasn't true."

Fields slapped a palm on the table, then held it there a moment, apparently trying to regain his composure before speaking.

"So we know he was alive just before everyone went to that damn Nativity play. I wish to God Sara had gone, too! She was the only one here *again!* Before the play you were here, and I suppose you came back right after. So that'd make the best time to kill him while the play was going on."

Ransom nodded. "I agree."

Fields shot him a glance designed to let him know that his agreement was not only unnecessary but unwanted. "And everybody in the whole damn territory was *at* the play, including the people connected with this house. That leaves Sara."

Ransom shrugged. "The service went on for quite some time. Anyone could've slipped out, come out here and killed Crane, then slipped back into the crowd at the church." Ransom paused for a moment, then added significantly, "Anyone."

Fields stared at him, the expression on his face showing that he didn't at all like the emphasis Ransom had placed on the word. His voice was hollow when he said, "Someone could've slipped out of the church without being seen?"

Ransom elevated his right eyebrow. "Would you have noticed someone leaving?"

"I would think so," Fields said doubtfully after a long pause, "but there were three aisles and I was watching the play. I suppose somebody could've gotten out without being seen. It would've been an awfully big risk, though."

"Unless whoever it was sat way in the back," said Ransom with a smile.

There was a very long pause during which Fields sat glaring at Ransom, his breathing becoming heavier. Finally he said, "You seem to be going out of your way to let me know you suspect me of something."

"It's not out of the way at all," said Ransom coolly, "but with everyone so ready to accuse Sara, I felt it was important to point out other possibilities."

"Including me."

Ransom shrugged. "You're as good as anyone else."

For a moment it looked as if Fields might actually smile. He leaned in slightly, and said, "Then it's too bad I'm the one doing the *official* investigation, isn't it?" He sat back and after a pause added, "Now, what we got is that Sara was left out here alone when somebody got killed. I don't do something about it this time and there's gonna be more than just *talk* about her in town."

Ransom waited a beat before saying, "I thought you did something about it last time."

It looked to Ransom as if the effort it was taking Fields to hold his temper might just make the top of his head blow off. "I *did,*" he said loudly. "There was no *evidence.*"

Ransom smiled. "There's none this time, either. Is there?"

Fields took a deep, silent breath that he never visibly released. "Look, I brought you in here to ask you questions, not the other way around. You still haven't answered the first thing I asked you."

"Which was?"

"I want to know what you learned. No matter what you might think, I'm not stupid, Mr. Ransom. You must've dug something up, or I think Hansen Crane would still be alive."

Ransom stared at Fields for a moment. He didn't like being questioned, and he didn't particularly like Fields, though he could feel for him. Ransom had to admit that he wouldn't like it if someone interfered in one of his cases, let alone if there was the possibility that that interference had caused another death. Under such circumstances, it was tempting for Ransom to take pity on his fellow officer and go against his usual closed-handed nature by sharing with Fields all the speculations in which he and Emily had indulged. But Ransom reminded himself that no matter what professional empathy he might feel for Fields, the sheriff actually could still be considered a suspect.

"I assure you," said Ransom civilly, "that I have learned nothing more concrete than you did. Everyone I've questioned has told me the same stories they did two years ago. Including Crane."

"So why the hell do you think Crane's been murdered?"

Ransom shrugged. "Coincidence?"

"You don't believe that!" Fields spat back with something approaching venom.

"No, I don't," said Ransom, narrowing his eyes meaningfully, "but it wasn't because of anything he told me, either." He paused, allowing his features to soften, then said in his most conciliatory manner, "He didn't say anything more to me than he had to you."

Fields seemed somewhat mollified by this affirmation of his judgment. "I tried to tell you you'd be wasting your time."

Ransom smiled. "Oh, but it hasn't been wasted."

"What?" For the first time in their brief acquaintance, Fields looked unsure of himself.

Ransom leaned in toward him. "I'm sure that you must've thought—just as I did—that since Nathan was murdered two years ago and nothing has happened since then, that the murderer had either left the area, or was still here but had some reason for killing Nathan that we could never discover and was fairly certain of his safety."

"Yes . . ." said Fields warily.

"Well, since you believe—and I'm in complete agreement with you on this point—that Nathan's and Crane's murders are related, then it would appear that the case is more active than either of us thought, wouldn't it?"

"Obviously," said Fields, folding his muscular arms across his chest and sitting back in his chair. "So?"

"So," Ransom continued with measured patience, "if you're correct, and my looking into the case has caused Crane to be murdered, then it would also appear that the murderer has something to fear. And if he—or she—is fearful enough of discovery at this point to risk another murder, then there *must* be something that can be discovered, wouldn't you say?"

With this, Ransom folded his own arms across his chest in a conscious mirroring of Fields's posture. They stared at each other for a while in this rather countrified version of a Mexican stand-off, when Ransom had an idea. He thought it just possible that he could manage to get Fields to do a bit of work for him, while at the same time convincing him that he was willing to share. Ransom sighed, trying to convey that he was giving in to the superior will of the sheriff. "Maybe you're right. Maybe my investigation has caused Crane's death. I'll tell you something that may help verify that. Right after I had my talk with Crane, he made an unexpected trip into town—at least that's where he said he was going—supposedly to buy tobacco. If my talking to him actually caused his death, then it might be worth finding out where he really went yesterday."

Fields eyed him suspiciously. "Why couldn't he have just gone into town for tobacco? What would be so strange about that?"

"Only that he had a full tin of it when I talked to him not five minutes before he left to buy some."

Fields grunted. "I suppose I can check to see if he really did," he said reluctantly, "it should be easy enough. The only place to get tobacco in town is at the drugstore. But I don't see what difference it makes if he went someplace else."

"It could make all the difference in the world," said Ransom with a coy smile. "Where Hansen Crane went yesterday after I talked to him might be the answer to all of our questions."

11

Before going to join Emily, Ransom went to the parlor to see if Johnnie Larkin was still there. Johnnie had gone back to his place by the window, though his hands were no longer resting on the frame.

"Mr. Larkin," said Ransom, "I would like a word with you."

Johnnie wheeled around. His long dark hair was unkempt and his eyes were bloodshot and open wide. "Jesus! You scared me!"

Ransom fought the urge to retort with "And well he might one day."

"That old fool!" Johnnie continued, "I told him that damn woodpile was too high! But he had to have it his own way. He made me repile it, you know. Halfway up to the damn roof!"

Ransom considered the boy for a moment. Before this he had only seen Johnnie in passing, but now that he was face-to-face with him, what had seemed at first to be youthful exuberance or excess energy now seemed like barely masked anxiety. The problem was that under the circumstances, anxiety would be understandable, so Ransom was left wondering if Larkin's went any deeper than the norm.

"You can set your mind at ease on that one," said Ransom

without inflection. "The woodpile didn't just fall on Crane, he was murdered."

Johnnie's mouth dropped open in a picture of surprise. He looked as if he half suspected that Ransom was playing a trick on him.

"Murdered?" he said breathily. "How do they know that? Are they sure?"

"Yes. Now, tell me, you said you *told him*. What did you mean?"

"Hansen," Johnnie replied vacantly. "I told him it was dangerous to pile the wood so high. I . . ." He faltered and looked to the floor, then back up. "He yelled at me the other day. He accused me of knocking over the pile when Sara sent me out for more wood. I mean, I *did* do it, but it wasn't my fault. The thing was just too high. And that's when I told him that. And he made me pile it back up, just like he had it."

"Was anyone else present when this conversation took place?"

Johnnie face went blank for a moment, as if recalling this was difficult. At last he said, "No. We were out in the driveway. Nobody else was there."

"Did you tell anybody about it afterward?"

"I—" Johnnie stopped as quickly as he'd started. The blood drained from his face and he stared openmouthed at Ransom. "I told Sara, 'cause she asked me why it took me so long to bring in the groceries."

"Anyone else?" Ransom asked, his expression unchanging.

"Your friend was there. Miss Charters."

"I mean anyone else . . . outside the immediate household."

There was a sudden rush of color back into the young man's cheeks. "I told a couple of my friends the other night. We went out for some beers, and I was telling them about the old—" He stopped suddenly, apparently realizing that it was not considered proper to speak ill of the dead, then continued meekly, "Yeah, so I told a few people."

"Hm," said Ransom, looking at Johnnie through narrowed

eyes, "So, basically anyone in town might have known about the 'woodpile incident.' "

"I suppose," said Johnnie sullenly. "What's it matter?"

"It could matter very much if you made it common knowledge."

Johnnie frowned as if he didn't quite know whether this was meant as encouragement or an insult. Then his face suddenly brightened with understanding. He said excitedly, "Oh, I get it! Yeah, I did tell people about that old crock and the damn woodpile! I told lots of people."

"Good," said Ransom with a perfectly opaque smile. "Thank you."

Ransom started to walk from the room, but paused in the archway and turned back to Johnnie. "Oh, by the way, we had a chat with your girlfriend yesterday."

"My what?" Johnnie exclaimed, looking so alarmed that it took an effort for Ransom to refrain from raising an eyebrow. "I don't have a girlfriend."

"You don't?" Ransom said lightly, then with elaborate signs of recalling something, he added, "Oh, that's right. I should've said your ex-girlfriend. Amy Shelton."

"Amy?" Johnnie said vacantly, his previously raised spirits now noticeably deflating. "Oh, Amy. She wasn't . . . she never really was my girlfriend. She was just . . ." His voice trailed off. He was silent for a brief interval, then looked up at Ransom and crossed to him. He whispered haltingly, "She was just . . . everything was so bad here when Nathan was killed. I needed someone to talk to. . . ."

"Talk?"

Johnnie stopped for a moment, then continued with additional embarrassment. "I was lonely. And so was she. And almost everyone else . . . Sara . . . was so screwed up at the time." He raised his eyes to Ransom and said somewhat more defiantly, "Amy needed someone as much as I did."

"I see."

Johnnie looked down at the floor again, and said quietly,

"But Sara has always been my—she's always been special to me. And after a while things got back to—well, not normal, but . . . you know what I mean. And me and Amy drifted apart." There was another pause, after which Johnnie looked into Ransom's eyes and pleaded quietly, "*Please* don't tell Sara about it. Please. She really is special and I wouldn't want to do anything to hurt her. Please."

Ransom eyed the young man for a moment, resting his chin in one hand and tapping his lips with his index finger.

"It shouldn't be necessary," he said as he turned from Johnnie and left the parlor.

Johnnie stood for several minutes, staring after the detective, wondering exactly what he'd meant by that.

Next, Ransom checked on Emily and found her lying on her bed, her eyes firmly closed and her breathing even. Her expression was a mixture of contentment and calculation, as if she were happily doing sums in her sleep. He smiled, then quietly closed the door and retreated to the smoking room with his pack of cigars and his well-worn copy of *The Haunted Man*.

As he settled back into the Christmas story, reading as he filled the room with a cloud of heavy smoke, his own measure of contentment fell just short of that being enjoyed by Emily, due primarily to the fact that he was longing for the additional pleasure of indulging in his favorite pastimes while soaking in a hot tub. He sighed at the thought, but dispelled any further dissatisfaction (however little) by immersing himself in the book.

He had reached the point in *The Haunted Man* where Mr. Redlaw, robbed of all compassion by the loss of his painful memories, seeks solace in the company of a feral child. The child had remained in his greedy, animal-like state from a life in which he'd never been touched by kindness or compassion. This part of the story always reminded Ransom of the admonition given to Ebenezer Scrooge by the Ghost of Christmas Present: "This boy is Ignorance. This girl is Want. Beware them both . . . but most of all beware this boy. . . ." It was another one of the very few passages that would, on occasion, cause Ransom a moment of doubt as to the infallibility of his beloved author. In his many years as a homicide detective, Ransom had seen a lot of people who could be termed ignorant, most of them truly happy. He'd also seen a lot of want and it almost always had the same effect that it had on the feral child—it caused insatiable greed. Ransom knew that many people, no matter how intelligent, had destroyed their own lives and the lives of other through their greed. This all led Ransom to believe that Want was the child of which one really had to beware.

He closed the book, his mind too consumed by these thoughts to concentrate on the story. He gazed out the window and lit another cigar.

Ransom and Emily met shortly after four o'clock to compare notes. By that time Emily had had a long nap and Ransom had finished four of his small cigars. Both of them had achieved a sense of rejuvenation from their solitary pursuits. They met in Emily's room for privacy, and Ransom related the results of his interview with Jeff Fields.

"Do you think it was wise to tell Mr. Fields about Hansen Crane's hasty departure after you questioned him?" Emily asked.

Ransom lifted his shoulders. "It probably made Fields feel that I'm not entirely holding out on him, and from a purely practical standpoint, he can surely find out where Crane went a lot more quickly than I can." He paused, then added ruefully, "Assuming, of course, that Fields didn't kill Crane himself."

Emily then reported on her conversation with Sara. After that they fell silent for a while, each digesting the new information.

"Well, this is most vexing," said Emily at last, bouncing her folded hands in her lap to emphasize each word. She said this with such delicate vehemence that it almost made Ransom laugh.

"Emily, I did warn you that trying to solve a two-year-old murder would have its difficulties."

She looked at him and pursed her lips. "Jeremy, you failed to mention that one of those difficulties might be another murder." She dropped her hands with finality and sighed. "Oh, well, I suppose when you stir up a hornet's nest—even an old one—you should expect to find hornets. But one doesn't expect to lose the chief suspect directly after selecting him. Oh!" She shook her head as vigorously as she was able, her eyebrows knit and her frown so deep it made the lines around her mouth droop. She looked almost as if she thought Hansen Crane had proven rather ill mannered to get himself murdered so inconveniently. After this temporary, and quite mild, loss of control on the part of Ransom's adoptive grandmother, she laid her hands calmly in her lap and gathered herself together with renewed resolve.

"Now, it seems to me that Sara has provided us with at least one important piece of the puzzle."

"Hm?"

"She accounted for the lapse of time—the reason that no further calamity happened after her brother was killed."

"How's that?" said Ransom, raising his right eyebrow.

"She changed her will immediately. If her father had been planning to kill both Nathan and Sara in hopes that all their money would revert to him, then Sara foiled that plan by making out a new will so quickly. It was an act that probably saved her life. The murderer has most likely been lying in wait, trying to figure out how to get his hands on the money."

Ransom was sitting in the reading chair, resting his head on his right hand. His legs were crossed and he was drumming the fingers of his free hand on his knee.

"Emily . . . if that's the case there's another problem. Sara has been implicated in both murders. If her father hopes to inherit, why implicate Sara? Wills aside, if she was jailed for murder he still wouldn't get the money."

From her perch on the corner of the bed, Emily allowed her gaze to travel out the window to the barn, which had twice been the scene of violence. Even in the late afternoon light, its roof framed by gathering clouds, it was hard to imagine such sinister goings-on in such a placid setting.

"That's true. . . ." Emily replied at length in answer to Ransom's objection. "But I think I can account for that."

Ransom smiled fondly at her. "Somehow I knew you could."

Emily returned the smile in kind, and replied, "Jeremy, you're making fun of me."

"Never!" said Ransom, laughing. "What's your idea?"

"Well, it's supposition, of course, but it's based in part on what Sara told me and what you yourself have supposed. *If*"— she laid great stress on the word as if it were a reminder that this was all conjecture— "if I am correct and the murderer was forced by Sara making a new will to wait to make his next move, then it would explain why Hansen Crane stayed on here instead of drifting along his way."

"It would?" said Ransom. He sat up and leaned forward.

"Yes. Again, *if* you were right in your belief that Hansen had actually seen or heard something the night Nathan Bartlett was killed."

Ransom stared at her for a moment, the wheels and gears in his mind turning so rapidly as to be almost audible. At last he shook his head, and said, "I'm sorry, Emily, I don't follow."

Emily shifted in her seat. "Well, you remember when you were talking about how Sara's father might be the killer, you referred to this idea as 'pure speculation.' That term struck a chord with me, only I couldn't quite put my finger on why. But now I do. It's because the term has two meanings: the way you meant it, and then . . ." her voice trailed off suggestively.

Ransom's face brightened. "Gambling on something."

"Exactly!" said Emily, sitting back triumphantly. "You see, if Crane's object was to blackmail the murderer, and the murderer doesn't yet have the money, then he would have to hang on, waiting for the day when the murderer *gained* the fortune, which he couldn't do immediately because of Sara's will." Emily spread her palms expansively. "Pure speculation!"

"Rather impure," said Ransom wryly. "Which means that whatever we thought before, Crane couldn't have been Sara's father."

"It doesn't appear so now that he's dead," said Emily, her head tilting slightly upward as she punctuated her reply with a single stroke of her index finger.

They fell silent again for a few moments, Emily looking on intently as Ransom continued to ruminate on all of this. Ransom stared into the air in front of him with an intensity that made it look as if the very air might split from the force and reveal all the mysteries of the universe to him. Finally he took a deep breath, and said, "None of this would explain why Crane was killed now, after all this time."

"Who knows?" said Emily with a shrug. "Perhaps he grew tired of waiting." Her eyes grew more incisive. "Perhaps he grew afraid. Perhaps the renewed interest in the case, after an interval that would have led him to believe all was safe, made him think he should put whatever pressure he could on the murderer to move forward."

Ransom frowned and shook his head slowly. "I don't know, Emily, that's an awful lot of supposition."

"Well," said Emily with a smile, "as long as I've gone this far, let me take my little hypothesis one step further. What I have proposed to you would also explain how the murderer came to implicate Sara in the murder, even though it might keep him from the money he wants to inherit."

Ransom couldn't help but smile. "I can't wait to hear it."

There was a sly twinkle in Emily's eyes as she said, "He didn't mean to."

"What?"

"He didn't mean to. You said it yourself to Jeff Fields. The murder of Hansen Crane means that the murderer has something to fear. That being the case he probably killed out of necessity and implicating Sara was probably the furthest thing from his mind."

Ransom gazed at her in wonder for a moment, then said,

"I've changed my mind, Emily. You shouldn't be on the force, you should be a prosecuting attorney."

"Thank you," said Emily primly. She refolded her hands and cleared her throat. "Of course, the real difficulty is how exactly Sara's father—if, indeed, the mysterious father has anything to do with it—plans to get hold of the money." She thought about this for a moment, then looked up at Ransom, and said, "Now, Jeremy, it is vitally, *vitally* important that we discover the true identity of Nathan and Sara's father."

"I agree," said Ransom with a weary sigh, "but that's going to be no small task if he really did disappear almost thirty years ago."

Emily cocked her head and raised her eyebrows as she flashed him a mischievous smile.

Ransom looked at her quizzically for a moment, trying to read the meaning in her expression. At last a smile spread across his face. "Of course," he said, folding his arms, "if Sara's father knew that her mother had died, and if he knew that she and her brother had moved here . . . somebody's been in communication with him."

Emily beamed at him like a proud parent. "Exactly."

"And you know who that is."

Emily leaned forward, and said, "I asked Emily how her father could've known these things, and she said two words: Myrtle Girdler."

"Myrtle Girdler?" said Ransom with a laugh. "That sounds like the female commandant at a concentration camp."

"Nothing as overtly sinister as all that, I'm sure," said Emily.

"And how do we reach this woman?"

"Very easily. We can go and see her. She lives in Mt. Morgan."

Sara stood at the kitchen counter making an attempt to calmly drink a cup of tea. But no matter how hard she tried, she couldn't steady her trembling hand as she lifted the cup to her lips. She watched through the side window as the van into which Hansen Crane's body had been loaded was driven away, leaving ruts in the snow out to the barn, which Sara knew would serve as a signpost to the scene of the crime until the next storm came and swept them away. The van was followed out by Jeff Fields. As his car pulled out of the driveway, Sara could feel her emotions draining away as if they were being pulled out of her in his wake and dispersed into the air with his exhaust.

This was the first time since Nathan's murder that Sara felt she just might have been too hard on Jeff, that she'd completely misunderstood his own position and his own frustration. But instead of finding some measure of solace in this newfound understanding, she was feeling even emptier than before. She pondered this for a few moments, standing at the sink with the cup poised halfway between its saucer and her mouth, her hand continuing to tremble. At last she realized that the deepening void she was experiencing stemmed from the fact that if Jeff, on whom she'd pinned her hopes at one time, felt so powerless over the situation, then what hope was there for her?

"Are you okay?" Johnnie's voice suddenly broke into her thoughts.

Sara started, letting the cup clatter down into the saucer, splashing tea onto the counter.

"Oh!!" she exclaimed. "I didn't know you were still here!" She grabbed a towel from the sink and quickly wiped up the spilled liquid.

"I'm sorry," he said quickly as he advanced into the room, "I didn't mean to startle you—but I wasn't gonna leave as long as Jeff and his goons were still here. I wanted to wait and make sure you were all right."

"I'm fine," she said as she wrung out the towel and draped it over the center divider of the sink.

Johnnie watched with a concerned look on his face as Sara refilled her cup with her still-shaking hands and then moved to the table.

"You don't seem fine," said Johnnie as he took a seat opposite her.

"All right," Sara said with weary resignation, "I'm not fine."

"I didn't mean . . . I just meant I'm worried about you."

Sara finished taking a sip of tea, then slowly lowered the cup back into the saucer, never lifting her eyes from it. "I know," she said quietly, "I'm sorry. I know you are. And I appreciate it. And I appreciate you waiting to check on me."

Johnnie looked at her eagerly. "You do?"

She nodded. "But really, I'm all right. Or as all right as I could be under the circumstances."

"I was never worried about *that*," Johnnie said pointedly, "I always knew you'd do fine as far as . . . mentally, I mean, 'cause you're strong. That's one of the things I admire about you. I meant I'm worried about your safety."

"I'm not," Sara replied softly, still not looking up.

"Huh?"

"I'm not."

There was a pause, then Johnnie said, "What do you mean?"

"Just what I said. I don't care what happens to me any more." There was no self-pity in her tone as she said this, only sadness.

"Well . . ." said Johnnie with a slight tremor in his voice, "some of us care what happens to you."

"Thank you."

"And with two murders out here, I'm worried about you being out here alone."

"I'm not alone," said Sara, "Mr. Ransom and Miss Charters are here for the next few days."

"What about after that?"

"After that . . ." said Sara absently, her voice trailing off as she realized she hadn't thought past the present moment at all.

"Because," Johnnie continued hesitantly, "I was wondering how you'd feel about . . . maybe having me move out here."

"What?" Sara said, her expression clouding over as she looked up at him for the first time.

"I don't mean into the house, I mean I could even just move over the barn—"

"Oh, no!" Sara said, horrified at the thought of anyone going near the barn again.

"Oh, come on, Sara," Johnnie said earnestly, "I don't mind that stuff's happened out there near as much as I mind the thought of you being way out here all alone."

Sara faltered. "I'll be sure I'm all right. Jeff's going to find out who did it this time, and then everything—"

"Jeff!" Johnnie spat, cutting her off. "Jeff's gonna screw this up just like he did the last time. Jeff couldn't find his own ass if his hands were glued to it!"

"That's not fair. You've just never liked—"

He cut her off again. "Liked him? Of course I don't like him, not the way he's treated you! How could I like him? How could *you?*"

Sara suddenly buried her face in her hands and began to cry. Johnnie shot out of his chair and crossed to her.

"I'm sorry, I'm sorry," he said, rubbing her back gently, "I didn't mean to upset you. That's the last thing I meant to do. But you got to face the facts. Jeff Fields aside, you're not safe. And I want to stay out here and . . . I want to protect you."

He knelt beside her and laid a comforting hand on her right leg. "Sara, I've never made it any secret how I feel about you. You know that. And I've always tried to respect your feelings. You know that, too. But . . . this thing with Jeff Fields . . . I mean, you got to stop putting your faith in the people who don't trust you, and start putting your faith in the people who *do.*"

Sara slowly lowered her hands from her face, turning her watery eyes on him. He managed a half smile in her direction.

"Oh, Johnnie!" she said plaintively as she slipped her arms around his neck. He returned the embrace, slipping his arms around her waist and drawing her as close as he could given their relative positions. Sara buried her face in his shoulder and wept for a few minutes. When finally her tears began to subside and her breathing became easier, she released him, but he kept his arms wrapped tightly around her. She gently took his forearms and pushed them away.

"Johnnie, that's so sweet. You're a very sweet boy . . ."

" 'Boy'?" he echoed, obviously not pleased with her choice of words.

". . . but I've just made a decision. I'm going to take Miss Charters's advice."

"Miss Charters? What's she got to do with anything?"

Sara sniffed deeply and cleared her throat, trying to more fully regain her composure. "She asked me if I might be better off selling the place and starting over somewhere else. I think she was right. This place is just poison to me. Nothing will ever be right for me here. If I didn't know it before, I know it now. When Emily and Mr. Ransom leave, I'm going to ask them if I can go back to Chicago with them. I have friends there I can stay with. I'm going to sell Hawthorne House and never look back."

Johnnie, still on his knees beside her, fell back on his heels. He looked absolutely stricken. "You're kidding!"

"No," she said, shaking her head sadly. "There's nothing for me here now."

"But where will you go?"

"I don't care as long as it's away from here."

"But Sara," he pleaded, taking her hand in his, "don't you understand what I've been trying to say? I'm in love with you."

She tried to withdraw her hand, but he held it tightly. "Johnnie, I'm sorry. There's just too many bad memories. I couldn't stay here now if I wanted to."

"Then we could go together. It doesn't matter to me."

"Johnnie, please!" She tried hard to pull her hand away, but his grip continued to tighten.

"Excuse me. I hope I'm not interrupting," said Emily from the doorway.

Johnnie let go of Sara's hand and stood up. Sara heaved a sigh of relief.

"Well, you are, kinda," said Johnnie anxiously.

"But it was all over, wasn't it, Johnnie?" Sara said pointedly.

He looked down at her, his expression as poignant as if he'd lost his best friend, and said, "Yeah, I guess it was. 'Scuse me."

He walked out of the kitchen, almost knocking into Emily as he passed through the doorway. After a few seconds they heard the front door slam.

Emily turned to Sara apologetically. "I seem to have turned up at an embarrassing moment."

"Yes, it was," Sara said. Emily thought she detected a slight shudder. "But it needed to be interrupted."

Emily raised her eyebrows coaxingly. "Indeed? Is there anything I can do?"

"Yes . . ." said Sara slowly, the courage of her convictions beginning to gel. "When you leave, when you go back to Chicago, could I ride with you?"

"Well, of course you can," Emily replied, wide-eyed.

"I've decided to take your advice and sell up and move on."

Emily nodded sadly. "I seldom advocate retreat, but in this situation it might be the best."

"That's what that little scene was about. I was just telling Johnnie about my decision, and he's . . . well, I guess he's become attached to me. He was distressed when I told him."

"To say the least," said Emily disapprovingly. "He looked as if he wanted to become attached to you permanently."

Sara shrugged. "He's always had a crush on me. I didn't realize it had gotten so serious. I suppose I'll have to do something about it. But I don't want to hurt his feelings. He's really a nice boy and I suppose I could have been interested in him if it wasn't . . ."

"If it wasn't for the fact that you're in love with somebody else."

Sara's cheeks reddened attractively. "I'm that obvious?"

"Oh, no," said Emily kindly, "but your anxiety over Mr. Fields is rather pointed. I don't think you could be quite so anxious about someone for whom you didn't care."

"It's ridiculous, isn't it?" said Sara with a rueful laugh.

"You'd think I'd hate him. How could I love someone who's actually suspected me of murder?"

"The heart is a very difficult thing to govern," Emily replied with gently twinkling eyes.

Sara was struck by the similarity between this and what Jeff had said to her in his more gruff way, but she made no comment. "I think it would be . . . best . . . there's many things I should leave behind."

Emily looked at her a moment, then said, "You know, Sara, I doubt very much that he's ever truly suspected you of murder."

"But he—" Sara began, but Emily cut her off.

"He did his job. And it would have caused much more comment in the community if he hadn't."

Sara shook her head. "I suppose that's true. But he's been so awkward and cool to me since then."

"Has he? I wouldn't think that would be from suspecting you of anything," said Emily vacantly. "Perhaps you should consider what kind of man he is."

Sara blinked. "I'm sorry, I don't understand."

Emily folded her hands neatly on the table and leaned forward as if to give her words more emphasis. "I don't think he's the type of man who would take defeat easily."

Sara's eyebrows knit closely together, and she half thought of pressing Emily for further explanation, but the expression on the old woman's face told her that she'd said all she was going to say on the subject and was content to leave Sara to put the puzzle together for herself.

"Now," said Emily brightly, "if you'll forgive my changing the subject, there's a little call I'd like you to make for me."

12

Sara phoned Myrtle
Girdler that evening, as Emily had requested, and asked if it
would be all right for Emily and Ransom to visit the next morning to pursue their investigation. Sara was very timid and apologetic about the fact that the next day was Christmas Eve, and she
was sure that Mrs. Girdler must be very busy. But rather than
acting overcome with the responsibilities of the season, which is
what Sara had expected, Mrs. Girdler barely allowed a decent
pause to elapse before expressing her overly avid interest in helping in any way she could. Her eagerness, in fact, left Sara with a
sense of uneasy distaste that remained with her until she retired
for the night.

Ransom phoned Jeff Fields the next morning and Fields told
him that they'd verified that Hansen Crane actually had gone in
to town and bought tobacco, and so far there was no evidence
that he'd driven anywhere else. The sheriff delivered this news
with enough of a sense of superiority to fill the detective with a
strong urge to show him up. Ransom had to remind himself that
his and the sheriff's aims were both the same.

It was shortly after breakfast that Ransom and Emily set off
for Mt. Morgan. The sky was so thick with dense, dark clouds
that the morning of Christmas Eve had barely dawned at all.

Emily sat in the passenger seat comfortably swathed in her heavy coat, and gazed out the windshield at the sky. The crowded clouds shifted into and around each other as if engaged in a silent, celestial wrestling match. They weaved patterns whose outlines became clear for a moment, only to fade quickly, leaving nothing but indeterminate masses. Emily thought she knew just how they felt. She clucked her tongue.

"What is it?" Ransom asked.

"I can't help feeling that we're always a day late in this matter."

"Not a day late," said Ransom, curling his lips, "we're two years late."

"You were quite correct in what you said about investigating a case when the trail has gone cold. It's most frustrating."

Ransom smiled inwardly. Although Emily might profess to be frustrated, it didn't take a detective to see just how much she'd returned to herself. Ransom glanced at her as she continued to stare out the window. He could tell from the look in her eyes and the bend of her brow that her mind was keenly and actively engaged in putting the pieces of their present puzzle together. She was still too frail to appear anything like robust, but the color had returned to her cheeks in a way that made her look healthier than she had for months. *All in all,* thought Ransom, *I was right. This little holiday has done her a world of good.* It was with only a slight touch of embarrassment that he remembered that it was her own insistence on becoming involved in this case that was responsible for her return to normalcy.

For her part, even though Emily's mind was occupied with the problems at hand, she was aware that whatever tension Ransom had brought with him to the quiet countryside had dissipated as he'd become interested in the case. *Almost like a bored child whose mind could be fully diverted with a puzzle book,* she thought with grandmotherly amusement. But she amended this thought almost immediately with silent admonishment directed toward herself. She knew that Ransom's desire to solve crime did not stem from a Holmesian need for mental diversion, but out of a deep-seated desire to see justice done. The pleasure he took in bringing criminals to book was merely a happy by-product.

"What exactly did Sara tell you about this Girdler woman?" Ransom asked, putting an end to both their reveries.

"Only that she was a long-time friend of the family. She knew Sara's parents before they were married and kept in touch with them both after the divorce."

"How very nonpartisan of her."

"Yes . . . yes . . ." said Emily slowly, adopting the vagueness of tone that usually indicated she was trying not to think ill of someone. "Let's hope that's all it is." She stopped for a moment, then continued in a much lighter tone. "Anyway, the Girdlers are from Chicago. They had a second home here to which they have retired. It was the Girdlers, in fact, who introduced the Bartletts to this area of Michigan."

"Hm," was Ransom's only reply.

They reached Mt. Morgan, passing Macklin's Supermarket, which was located just inside the town limits, where the main highway became Main Street. They followed Sara's instructions, continuing down Main through the downtown area, or what the locals simply called "town." Though Mt. Morgan was by no means large, compared to LeFavre it was a budding metropolis. Main Street was lined with stores that had none of the unpolished quaintness of the shops of LeFavre. These were glass store-fronts of a much more commercial nature that included a dry cleaners, a laundromat, and two different hardware chains. A JCPenney stood like a flagship at the center of the first block.

They had soon passed through the center of town and reached Sycamore, the first cross street after the commercial district. Ransom turned left as indicated in Sara's directions and they found themselves on a street very much like one of the older neighborhoods of Chicago. The left side was lined with houses that were a bit closer together than he would have expected to find in such a rural setting, but the right side was devoted to a sprawling park, studded with leafless trees and scattered snow-covered benches. The importance that the community placed on children was evidenced by the amount of playground equipment that stood inert at one end of the park. There were slides, swings, monkey bars, and even one of the horseless merry-go-rounds that children propel with their feet. Ransom smiled, realizing that he hadn't seen one of those since he was a very small child.

With the address Sara had given him in his hand, Ransom quickly located the Girdlers' house at the end of the second block. He switched off the engine, then he and Emily sat for a moment looking at the house. It was a sprawling two-story building, which had received a fresh coat of bright white paint in the not-too-distant past. There was no veranda, but there was a wide columned porch, the roof of which served as a balcony for the front bedroom on the second floor. The property was hemmed in by a short white picket fence that tilted outward at the top as if it were a belt straining against an expanding waistline.

Ransom helped Emily out of the car, up the walk, and then up the five steps to the porch. The front door contained a large window that looked into a wide, open hall. To the right of the door, just above the bell, was a brass plaque on which *Girdler* was embossed in tight, almost illegible script.

Ransom rang the bell, and he and Emily watched as a thin, pleasant-looking woman of about fifty, clad in an industrial gray dress and a small white apron, appeared through the door at the back of the hall and approached them.

She smiled as she opened the door, which seemed to be so heavy that it took most of the woman's strength to get it to budge.

"Mrs. Girdler?" said Ransom.

"Oh, no," said the woman with a sudden rush of color to her cheeks, "I'm Sophie, the cook. I assume you're Mr. Ransom and Ms. Charters. Mrs. Girdler's waiting for you in the living room."

She said this all with the accomplished grace of someone who's spent a lifetime in domestic service, an image that was slightly tarnished when she led them into the room directly to the left and said simply, "They're here," then disappeared back to the kitchen.

The living room was a study in oppressive opulence. The furniture was all plush and overstuffed to the point that it looked like the couch and chairs were growing and might soon engulf the room. In the front window was a tree at least eight feet tall, its branches so choked with lights and ornaments that they sagged under the weight. The air was so heavily scented with cinnamon that Ransom found it difficult to breathe.

The lady of the house was seated at one end of a huge white sofa facing the Christmas tree. She was, to put it nicely, a large woman. Her hair had been dyed white, and she was wearing a bright red dress that was divided in the middle by a ridiculously thin silver belt. Though she was sitting, the belt gave the only indication of where her waist might be, not to mention her lap. Ransom thought with distaste that she looked like a grossly overfed version of the caterpillar from *Alice in Wonderland*. Several boxes of chocolates lay open on the coffee table in front of her, and in the crook of her arm she held a pomeranian that looked absolutely terror stricken. Though Ransom didn't really like small dogs, he had to feel sorry for this one. If its mistress happened to hold her too tightly to her bosom, the poor dog would never be seen again.

"I think I'll let you handle this one," Ransom said to Emily in a furtive whisper.

"Come in, come in. Forgive me if I don't get up." Her voice was much too light for her girth, and it had a giggly quality to it that would have been more suitable to a woman two thirds younger.

"Please, have a seat," she said with a sweep of her arm in the direction of two chairs grouped together by the side of the couch on which she was seated. The motion set the skin on the underside of her arm wobbling.

Emily looked doubtfully at the excessively fluffy chair that Mrs. Girdler had indicated for her. It was covered in pastel pink with curved arms that put Emily in mind of an overflowing orchid. She hesitantly lowered herself onto it and sank with dismay into the much-too-soft cushion. As Ransom took his seat next to her he shot her a reassuring glance to let her know he was aware of her predicament.

"It's very kind of you to see us on such short notice," said Emily with a little cough, "and at such a busy time."

"It isn't any trouble at all," Mrs. Girdler replied eagerly, "the family doesn't start arriving until after noon, and Sophie has everything under control. Would you like a chocolate?" She waggled her stubby fingers in the direction of the candy.

"No, thank you," said Emily. Ransom shook his head.

Mrs. Girdler leaned forward without appearing to bend in the middle and extracted a piece from the nearest box. The dog gave a little yelp.

"Frou-Frou! Shhh!" she said lovingly as she sat back and popped the candy into her mouth. "All of my friends back in Chicago send these to me for Christmas. Fannie Mays, you know. They're my favorites."

Emily smiled and nodded.

"I was shocked," Girdler continued, scrunching her face up as if she'd discovered something in the chocolate's center that she didn't quite like, "*shocked* to hear about Hansen Crane. Of course, he wasn't from around here, but that doesn't mean he should die. Honestly, just when you're beginning to think you're safe in your home, something like this happens *again*. LeFavre is becoming more and more like Chicago every day!"

Hardly, thought Ransom, trying very hard not to let the disdain he was feeling become evident on his face. The woman reminded him of a fluttering elephant. Just as this thought entered his mind, Mrs. Girdler swallowed the bit of chocolate with an apparent effort. Ransom noted that her neck didn't move when she swallowed.

"But I couldn't imagine—when Sara called me, I mean—I couldn't *imagine* whatever you'd want to see me about. Good heavens! I couldn't possibly know anything about Nathan's murder, and even less about Hansen Crane's. I don't think I ever even saw Hansen, although, of course, my friends have told me about him because you know this is a rather small place and people will talk."

"Hmm," said Ransom, wondering how it had been possible for her to expend so much oxygen without collapsing.

"But," she said, raising her index finger as if she thought someone might have been about to interrupt her, "*but*, I would do anything—*anything*—to help Sara. I've known her and I knew her brother since they were babies. *Babies.*" She repeated the word as if she were inexplicably proud of it.

"So we understood," said Emily with her usual quiet grace, "that is why we came to you. We understood that you knew their parents, and we were hoping you could give us a little information about them."

"*Their parents?*" said Mrs. Girdler, italicizing the words with a mixture of surprise and pleasure. "Whyever would you want to know about them?"

"Just for background," Ransom quickly interjected. "When I'm working on a case, I like to know as much about the participants as possible."

"Oh," Mrs. Girdler said with such palpable disappointment that it was clear to Ransom and Emily that whatever she might have said before, she had hoped that she was to be an important player in the mystery and it was quite a let-down to find that she was merely meant to paint the scenery. She heaved a bored sigh and continued, "Well, I knew David and Gina—those were their names—way back in high school, before they'd even met each other. David was a wonderful man! I was quite in love with him myself, you know." She averted her eyes and managed a coquettish blush that Ransom found perfectly revolting.

"Really?" said Emily with enough gusto to convince Mrs. Girdler of her interest.

"Oh, yes! He was very handsome and charming. What they used to call a ladies' man. But, of course, once he met Gina there was simply nobody else for him. I was, in fact, the one who introduced them, and it was the biggest—" Her face turned red again, but this time it was not out of coquettishness. "Well, in light of what happened I suppose I'm justified in thinking it was a mistake to introduce them. I'll never, never forgive myself for it. I could have told David it wouldn't work out, because Gina was simply *not* the type of woman who could understand him. A man like David required a special kind of understanding. He was a true visionary! That was something that Gina never understood. She was always sooo . . . *practical.*" She curled her lips as if the sound of the word left a bad taste in her mouth. "She was always after him to get a job, get a job, get a job. She didn't realize that a man of David's nature needed nurturing, not *nagging.*"

"Yes, well, perhaps she was worried about the welfare of their children," said Emily so lightly that Mrs. Girdler completely missed the implication.

And perhaps she thought two children were enough to nurture, thought Ransom, each passing minute convincing him that he'd been right to pass the reins to Emily on this occasion.

"Oh, but David loved the children. He absolutely doted on them!"

"He did?" said Emily, careful to give the word the proper inflection.

"Oh, yes! He doted on them!"

"But we understood that he never made an effort to see them again, after the divorce."

Mrs. Girdler suddenly lurched forward and selected another chocolate, which she popped into her mouth. The dog used the opportunity to escape her grasp. He ran yapping in the direction of the kitchen as if to complain to the cook about his treatment. Mrs. Girdler didn't seem to notice his departure.

"That was because of Gina. Gina did nothing but poison Nathan's and Sara's minds against poor David once he was gone. What could he do? How could he fight?"

"But surely he could've seen them if he wanted to," said Emily coaxingly.

Girdler shook her head slowly and sadly. "No, it was not to be. He moved out West—to San Francisco—to find his way—he had so many ideas for business, you know, but like so many great men, none of them ever panned out. It wasn't his fault, it was just the way the fates played it. David told me so himself. But he never saw the children again."

"He could've written to them," Emily said with a noncommittal shrug designed to make it clear that she wasn't being judgmental. Ransom shot her an approving glance.

Mrs. Girdler shook her head again, her frown deepening so much that it looked as if it were being branded into her moonlike face. "No, not with Gina around. That would never have done."

Emily cocked her head slightly to the side. "But *you* kept in touch with him, didn't you?"

Mrs. Girdler looked from Emily to Ransom and back again. From her expression she appeared to feel that she had inadvertently painted herself into a corner. "How did you know about that? Oh, I suppose Sara told you."

"She did mention it, yes," Emily replied.

The woman swallowed again and her eyes became watery. "He wrote to me from time to time, maybe once a year, asking about them. I thought it was very touching, and very sad that he should want so badly to keep in touch with his children, and have to do it through an intermediary, although I was more than happy to be the one to do it. I thought it was only right that their father be kept apprised of how his children were doing. I tried at first to talk to Sara about him, but she wouldn't have any of it, so I stopped trying. That's why I was so pleased when Nathan came around and asked about him."

"He did?" said Ransom so suddenly that he startled Mrs. Girdler. Her head snapped in his direction, which sent a corresponding ripple through the exterior of her body. Ransom felt that he now had an idea of how an avalanche could be started by a loud noise.

"Oh!" she exclaimed, putting her hand to her heart.

"I beg your pardon," said Ransom, "I was just so surprised that after so many years Nathan had suddenly become interested in his father."

"Yes . . . well . . ." Mrs. Girdler continued a bit hesitantly, as if she feared Ransom might be prone to outburst. "Well, so was I."

"When did this happen?" Emily asked.

Mrs. Girdler looked pleased to redirect her attention to her older, more subdued, visitor. "Let me see . . . you know, oddly enough, I believe it was just before he was killed."

Emily leaned in toward the woman, her eyes narrowing insightfully. "Did he tell you why he wanted to know about his father?"

Mrs. Girdler rolled forward and picked out another chocolate. "Yes. I asked him. He told me he just felt badly about never having known him—and I know that's true because you read about that sort of thing all the time, I mean about children wishing later in life that they'd known their parents and such. He was very concerned that his father had had a good life and was happy. He was very, very particular about his father's happiness. It was quite touching, really."

"Yes," said Emily, her tone designed to keep drawing the woman out without appearing to do so. "That's very admirable."

"If a little late," Mrs. Girdler replied with a nod. She turned the chocolate back and forth between two fingers. "I suppose it was guilt, mostly."

"Guilt?" Ransom prompted.

She nodded. "For having deserted him. I mean for not having allowed his father any contact for all those years. It was really, *really* very sad. I like to think that after his mother had been dead for a while, her influence began to weaken and Nathan realized how wrong he'd been to ignore his father. He said he couldn't bear to think of his father being all alone. He asked if he'd ever found anyone else."

Emily leaned in a bit more, her eyes becoming even more narrow. "He asked if his father remarried?"

"Um hm."

"And had he?"

"Oh, yes. More than once, I believe. But that was always the way with David. He could never find the right woman." Her expression became infused with meaning. "But then, of course, people like David usually have their heads in the clouds. They rarely notice what's right under their noses." She gave a little sniff, the implication of which was obvious. "But David was one of those men destined to be unlucky in love, even if he was lucky in other ways."

"What do you mean?"

"Whenever he was particularly low he would meet someone—some woman who he felt could take care of him."

"You mean financially?"

Mrs. Girdler blinked at her. "I mean in *every* way. Being low financially is bound to make you feel low in other ways. I've been very fortunate myself. Mr. Girdler has quite a bit of money."

"Mrs. Girdler," Ransom said, "we were hoping, since you kept in touch with him, that you could tell us where he is now."

She blinked at him, her thick lashes making her look like a mountainous Betty Boop.

"Who?"

Ransom checked himself in the act of a frustrated sigh. "David Bartlett."

"Well, I knew where he *was,* but I haven't heard from him in years. I don't expect I ever will again, assuming he's still alive." She gave another little sniff that clearly signified how deeply she felt slighted.

"Why do you say that?" Emily asked.

"Because the last letter I sent to him was returned with one of those yellow stickers on it that say the forwarding whatsits has expired. Honestly, you'd think they would send it on anyway, since the address is always right there on the sticker!"

"Do you remember the address?" Ransom asked nonchalantly, not wanting to give the woman the satisfaction of knowing that she held any important information.

Mrs. Girdler rolled her eyes up to the ceiling and stuck her pudgy index finger into her cheek, for a moment lost in trying to recall it. Just when Ransom was about to repeat the question, she looked back at him and said, "No, I'm afraid I don't. But I remember the name of the place. It was the Crestview Nursing Home, San Francisco. I sent the letter there, but I never received a reply."

There was little left for Ransom and Emily to do then but to extricate themselves from Mrs. Girdler's company as quickly as they could without appearing to be rude, a social nicety that Ransom would easily have forgone were it not for the presence of Emily. When they had exhausted such topics as mutual acquaintances in Chicago and holiday menus, when Ransom felt he had reached the last thread of his patience, Emily said brightly, "Well, I think we'd better be going and leave you to your preparations."

"I hope I've been of some help," Mrs. Girdler said languidly as she made an abortive attempt to get to her feet.

"Don't get up," said Ransom without inflection. He helped Emily from the chair, the cushions of which had so swallowed her that he was almost forced to lift her bodily from its clutches.

"Oh, yes, you've been most helpful," said Emily as she slipped her arm through Ransom's.

He led her to the entrance to the living room where she applied a gentle pressure to his arm, signaling her desire to stop for a moment.

"By the way," she said, turning back to Mrs. Girdler, "who was it that put David Bartlett into the nursing home? His wife?"

"His wife?" Mrs. Girdler echoed, blinking her large eyes. "Oh, no, she's long gone. I assume it was his son."

Ransom's interest was arrested by this revelation, and Emily's eyebrows rose half an inch as she cocked her head. "Nathan? I didn't think Nathan knew anything about his father."

"Oh, no! Not Nathan," Mrs. Girdler returned with her underaged giggle, "David's other son. The one he had by his second wife. Or was it his third? I don't remember which. It's hard to remember family ties any more."

"Yes . . . " said Emily slowly, "and yet some remember them very well."

As they stepped outside onto the porch Ransom turned up his collar. The promise of snow was being realized in the form of a light shower that looked as if it might become a blizzard with little provocation.

"What a perfectly odious woman," said Ransom as he walked Emily back to the car.

"I *suppose* she's managed to delude herself into believing that all of her motives have been altruistic, but she is foolish enough to have been used by David Bartlett."

"You think that's what it was?"

"One way or another. Sara's father strikes me as the type of man who wouldn't stick at keeping contact with this woman for the express purpose of keeping track of the family money. And she's credulous enough about him that his true motives would never occur to her."

"Hm . . ." said Ransom abstractly. He grew pensive as he helped Emily into the car, then climbed behind the wheel. He sat for a moment, staring out the window without saying a word.

"Is anything the matter?" Emily asked.

Ransom sighed disgustedly. "I've been guilty of the fuzziest thinking, which has succeeded in doing nothing more than leading us around in circles."

Emily's forehead creased in reply.

"This is what comes of unbridled speculation. And I'm not happy to think I'd indulge in it after all the times I've warned others against it." He paused, sighed again, and his lips curled as he added, "I don't suppose I'll ever be able to look my partner in the face again."

"Jeremy, I wish you would speak more plainly."

"We've wasted all this time on the Bartletts' father—who couldn't possibly have anything to do with these murders—on what now look to me to be the flimsiest sort of notions I've entertained in the whole of my professional career," he said in a burst of temper that he rarely—if ever—had displayed in front of Emily. "I suppose I could blame it on the fact that I'm on vacation and my brain isn't functioning properly, but it's impossible to excuse any way you look at it, especially in light of the fact that my stumbling around has apparently cost Hansen Crane his life."

Emily gave him her most benignant smile. "Certainly you can't believe that. Hansen Crane's death was caused by whatever Hansen Crane was doing, not by your investigation of it."

"That doesn't alter the rest of it. I've approached this case as a fishing expedition—something I was forced to do because the murder happened so long ago—as if I was on some sort of busman's Christmas. And all I've proved is that you should never *play* at solving murder."

"Well," said Emily somewhat grandly, "you'd do as well to put the blame on me. I was in full agreement with you on what you call your 'unbridled speculation,' and it was I who got you involved in this business to begin with." She said this lightly, not from any desire to second his opinion of their investigation, but to get him to snap out of it. To a certain extent, it had its desired effect.

Two red patches appeared on either side of Ransom's jaw, as if this was as close to his cheeks as he would allow the blood to rush. It nettled him that as usual Emily had caught him out. He wouldn't allow her to take the blame for something for which he truly felt responsible, any more than he would ever be willing to admit that he'd allowed her to influence him into handling the case in the first place.

"I will, of course, call the nursing home to see if David Bartlett is still there, but I hardly think that he left a nursing home and came halfway across the country to kill his nearest relations. Assuming he's even still alive."

"Well, what about this other son of his, the one who put him in the home?"

"What about him?"

"If Sara is killed, and her father is dead, wouldn't that make this other son the next in line to inherit?'

"It won't wash, Emily!" Ransom exclaimed with exasperation. "Even if this nameless son had anything to do with this, he couldn't inherit if his father was still alive—and if he's still alive and in a nursing home all the money would probably end up transferring to the state for his care, so neither of them would get the money. And if the father's dead, the son *would* be the next in line, but what's he going to do? Go back to San Francisco and suddenly put in a claim for the inheritance? That might have worked in *The Hound of the Baskervilles,* but it would never work in this day and age. With an inheritance based on three deaths, Jeff Fields would be on a plane to San Francisco in a minute to see this guy, and if he didn't then I would, and the game would be up. And all of this money passing from mother to son to daughter to father to half brother? I'm sorry, I just don't buy it. The chain of inheritance is too long and far too complicated, and too many things could go wrong. And then there's still the matter of Sara's will. Neither the father nor his son would inherit, anyway!"

He fell silent again and stared out the window. Though he had not yet turned the car on, he seemed to be generating enough heat on his own to keep them both warm. Emily sat with her gaze transfixed on a huge oak tree in the park on her right. Something Ransom said had caused something else to click in her mind.

"The chain of inheritance . . ." she said very slowly and very quietly. "The chain of inheritance . . . yes, it is too long and too complicated. Yes . . . yes, you're right about that, I suppose. . . ."

"What?" said Ransom, her words only half breaking through his own confused meditation.

He looked over at Emily and was alarmed at the look of utter astonishment on her face. Her jaw had dropped open and her eyes were as wide as they would go. But the most alarming aspect of her expression was that all the blood had drained from her face, leaving her as pale as a ghost.

"Emily! What is it?"

She shook her head slowly, which at least had the effect of bringing a little of the color back into her cheeks. "Oh, Jeremy, I've been such an utter and complete fool! It's been there all along, and I never saw it!"

"What?"

She faced him. *"King Lear.* 'Let me, if not by birth, have lands by wit. . . .' "

"Emily, I don't understand."

"Oh, dear Lord," she continued, turning away from him, "how could I have been so foolish! Jeremy, if ever I speak with authority on the usual viability of gossip, I give you my full permission to remind me of this moment. We've been blinded by gossip, by everyone telling us that the object of Nathan's murder was inheritance. Oh, good heavens!"

"Emily, would you please tell me what you're talking about!" Ransom demanded in the severest tone he'd ever taken with her.

She turned back to him and adopted the schoolmarmish attitude she exhibited whenever explaining something. "The object of the murders was not the inheritance, at least not directly. You're right, that was far too complicated. The object was safety. The safety of the murderer, that is." She stopped and her expression became more vacant as a new idea occurred to her. "Of course, the problem is we don't know how Nathan discovered what was going on. Although it doesn't really matter, I suppose."

"Safety?"

"Yes. And Sara's life was never in danger. At least, not before. I fear that it is now, because I think the murderer is getting desperate. Oh, Jeremy! We must do something about this immediately!"

"Emily," Ransom said firmly, "we're not going anywhere until you explain to me what you're talking about!"

Emily took a deep breath to order her thoughts, then calmly told Ransom what she was thinking. When she'd finished, Ransom drew back against his seat. He extracted a cigar from his coat pocket, lit it, and took a long drag at it. Though Emily was so lost in her thoughts she seemed largely unaware of what he was doing, she did take a moment from her preoccupations to roll down her window.

"That's fantastic," said Ransom at last.

"But it does fit."

"Yes, it does. Especially with what you said earlier, about children turning out so much like their parents." He sighed and wrinkled his nose. "If you're right, I don't think I'll ever get over that gargantuan woman holding the key to the mystery." There was another pause, after which he added, "Except . . . you do realize that he doesn't have to be David Bartlett's son."

Emily replied, "Perhaps not, but it would account for why Nathan was murdered."

Ransom stubbed the cigar into the ashtray, and suddenly realized what he was doing and turned to Emily. "Oh, I'm sorry! I didn't mean to smoke."

"That's quite all right," said Emily magnanimously, "you needed it."

"Now I think we'd better go and decide what to do about this business. It's not going to be easy," said Ransom as he turned the key in the ignition.

Emily laid a thin hand on his arm. "Jeremy, I think we should go to Jeff Fields."

Ransom sat back in his seat and looked at her. From his expression he was obviously displeased. "Why?"

"Because it's Christmas Eve," she replied with a mischievous smile, "and I think we should give our first Christmas present."

13

The snowfall continued to grow steadily heavier into the late evening. By nightfall the prospect had ceased to be picturesque and had instead become worrisome. Still, it wasn't bad enough for Ransom and Emily to abort their plans and stay home from the carol service.

They arrived at the First Presbyterian Church of LeFavre shortly before ten o'clock when the service was scheduled to begin. The narthex was once again full of people shaking the snow off their hats and coats, but generally the atmosphere was more quiet and subdued than it had been for the Nativity play. Though Emily knew that this was most likely due to worries about the snow and the more somber nature of the occasion, she couldn't help feeling that the church and all its members were holding their breath to see if her little plan would work.

The crowd was making its way into the nave to find seats, and Ransom and Emily were being swept along with it when Ransom heard someone call his name. He turned to find Johnnie Larkin just pushing his way through the couple nearest them. His trademark smile beamed in their direction.

"Hi, Mr. Ransom, Ms. Charters. Merry Christmas."

"Thank you," said Emily.

"I see Sara didn't make it again."

"Did you expect her to?" said Ransom, raising his right eyebrow.

Johnnie glanced at the floor sheepishly. "God, I guess not. 'Specially not with another murder." He glanced to the left and to the right. "You seen Amy?"

"No," Ransom replied after a beat.

"Well, I suppose I'll go look for her. I should say hi to her if she's here. It's only right."

"Um hm."

"Enjoy the show," said Johnnie as he started to make his way back through the crowd, "I mean, enjoy the service."

"Oh, dear," said Emily in her most disapproving tone, "are we now to suppose that he could turn to Miss Shelton again?"

"Now that Sara has made her position clear?" said Ransom with a curious smile in the direction in which Johnnie had disappeared. "Any port in a storm, I guess."

Emily held Ransom's arm as he ushered her halfway up the aisle and into a pew. She pulled a hymnal from the rack in front of her and placed it on her lap, then opened her program on top of it and proceeded to read.

While she was doing this Ransom scanned the crowd, looking for familiar faces. He didn't find any.

Emily looked up from the program, and said, "It looks like it will be an interesting evening."

Ransom sighed. "Yes, it does."

The murderer stood obscured from view by the barn, taking an occasional stealthy peek around its corner to reassure himself that the coast was clear. He was filled with a sense of déjà vu, though this storm was not quite so bad as it had been the night he'd committed his first murder. The house was still visible, though the only light coming from it was the glow from the parlor window dimly lighting the driveway. Sara's car was there, but the guests' car was gone, just as he knew it would be. He started for the house.

Sara sat reading in the parlor, or at least trying to read. She found it impossible to concentrate. The words seemed to float off the pages and spin around her head like an alphabetic tornado. She shook her head and the words and letters would scatter as if caught in the eddies on a brook, then flow back onto the page, only to spring up around her again the moment she tried to focus on them. She sighed heavily and looked up at the tree, whose lights seemed curiously lifeless. She hoped once everything was settled she'd be able to find some joy again . . . somewhere.

She gazed at the tree for a moment, hoping that it might manage to lift her spirits, but in spite of the glistening glass ornaments and the small white lights, it looked to her to be little more than a lifeless monstrosity.

The silence was oppressive. Although the snow was falling heavily, this storm was not as violent as the one on the night that Nathan had been killed: there was no rushing, howling wind and no sound of snow pelting against the window as it was swept against the house, all of which made the silence so acute that Sara felt she could hear the snowflakes as they landed on one another.

It was because of this undue quiet that Sara could hear the creak of the back door as it opened, though it was obvious that whoever had entered was trying not to be heard. It required all of her restraint for Sara to keep herself from calling out to the intruder, or to keep from crying out. She knew it didn't matter. She was the one he had come for and she was sure he would have no trouble finding her. But that didn't stop her from being startled when he spoke her name.

"Sara."

She looked to the archway and there stood Johnnie Larkin. He was wet with snow and had a length of rope coiled into a loop and draped over his shoulder.

"Johnnie," she said in a surprised tone, "I didn't hear you drive up."

"I used the access road. Back by the vineyard."

"The access road . . ." Sara repeated weakly. She had to fight the urge to ask him to explain why he'd done that. She already knew. She swallowed, then said, "I thought you would be at the carol service."

"I am," he replied with a smile that Sara no longer found ingratiating. "I think what they say is 'I put in an appearance.' "

"What . . . what do you want?" she asked after a pause.

Johnnie's smile disappeared. "I can't have what I want. I just wanted you and that would've solved everything. Nobody would've gotten hurt. It's not like I don't care about you."

There was so much sadness in his tone that Sara, though she knew she had to keep to the subject, couldn't help but respond.

"I never did anything to lead you on."

A trace of Johnnie's smile returned, but it faded quickly. "It would've been easier if you had. But you couldn't give me a second look, you were too stuck on the cornfed moron, Jeff Fields, even after he thought you murdered your brother! Jesus!"

"But why did you have to murder Nathan?" Sara asked, tears welling up in her eyes. "Why, if you didn't want to hurt anybody? Why did you do it? You were the one who killed him, weren't you?"

"He found out who I was. By mistake. By a stupid mistake. My wallet . . . my wallet fell out of my pocket when I was helping Nathan out, just like it did the other day in the kitchen . . . and he saw inside."

"What?"

Johnnie reached into his back pocket and withdrew his wallet, then flipped it open and shoved a picture at her. It was slightly yellowed with age, but the image was still quite clear. It was of a man who looked to be in his midforties, his hair slicked back and just beginning to gray. There was something vaguely familiar about the face. Sara felt almost compelled to reach out and touch it, but when she did, Johnnie snatched it away and shoved it back into his pocket.

"Who is that?" Sara asked tentatively.

Johnnie's eyes narrowed, his expression becoming infused with contempt. "Our father, Sara."

"*Our* father . . ." Sara faltered, then as the full weight of his words began to hit her, her eyes glazed over as if they'd been covered by an invisible barrier to protect her from what she was seeing.

"Our father, who you've never cared about but who's lying in a goddamn, filthy nursing home, the best that public aid can buy. And would someone like you help him?"

"I didn't know . . . if I'd known how bad things were . . ."

"You would've helped him?" Johnnie snapped.

"I . . . don't . . . know . . ."

"He wrote to you and you didn't help him!"

Sara received this like a slap in the face. She couldn't deny it, and couldn't explain to the angry young man the confusion of her feelings at the time, and how time had slipped away from her.

"I didn't know," she said slowly. "I didn't know things were that bad. He didn't tell me in the letter."

Johnnie paused as if this had brought him up short. His jaw slackened and he looked down at the floor sadly. "He didn't know at the time. Neither did I. He started to develop Alzheimer's disease and by the time we realized what was wrong . . . it doesn't matter . . . but now there's nobody to take care of me."

Sara took a step toward him. "Johnnie, I . . ."

He looked up at her quickly, tears coursing down his cheeks. "I didn't want to hurt anybody. Especially you. I just wanted to marry you. That would have solved everything."

"*Marry me!*" Now knowing their relationship, the disgust she felt at this prospect broke through the barrier she'd erected.

Johnnie's face hardened. "But it's too late for that now."

"What are you going to do?"

"First you're going to show me where your will is."

"Then what? Are you going to kill me, too?"

The right side of his mouth slid upward. He tapped the rope. "No, you're going to kill yourself. 'Cause you're so despondent. Everybody knows how you've been since Nathan died. Nobody'll be surprised."

Sara hesitated a moment, wondering whether or not she

should challenge him and ask him why she should bother giving him what he wanted if he was going to kill her anyway. But she decided against it. It wouldn't really serve any purpose.

She crossed the parlor and passed him. He followed her through the living room and up the stairs to the bedroom that had once belonged to her brother: her *real* brother, she thought with pride. Johnnie continued to follow close on her heels as she crossed the bedroom to Nathan's desk, where they'd always kept all of the business papers and their important personal papers. She opened the lower right-hand file drawer, rifled through it for a moment, and pulled out a single sheet. As she stood back up, Johnnie slipped the rope around her throat, twisted it behind her neck, and pulled it tight.

Sara's hands instinctively flew up to her neck and grappled with the rope as she choked and tried to gasp out a scream. Johnnie pulled backward on the rope, stepping back to elude her grasp, and causing her back to arch in a way that made it difficult if not impossible for her to reach her arms backward and hurt him, or to kick back at him without losing her balance and toppling over.

There was a sudden jerk backward, and for a flash Sara thought he was going to make very quick work of her, when suddenly the rope was released and Sara flew forward, sprawling out onto the floor. She wheeled around and saw what had caused the last pull of the rope. Jeff Fields had caught Johnnie by his long, dark hair and jerked him backward. Johnnie let out a low, guttural scream, like a cornered animal, as Jeff spun him around and plunged his massive fist into Johnnie's stomach. Johnnie doubled over and Jeff swiftly brought his knee up into contact with the young man's jaw. Johnnie's head snapped back, banging against the footboard of the bed. He crumpled to the ground, unconscious.

Jeff flipped Johnnie over, pulled his arms behind his back, and handcuffed him.

"Are you all right?" he demanded of Sara as he turned Johnnie over on his back.

Sara sat on the floor rubbing her neck, dazed both by the blood resuming its flow to her head and the suddenness of the attack and her rescue.

"Yes . . . yes . . . I think so." Tears were already welling in her eyes.

"You didn't think you left me behind, did you?" said Jeff as he helped her to her feet. "I followed right along with you, but I had to be careful coming up the stairs. Those damn things creak."

Sara's eyes were fixed on the limp form of the man she now knew to be her half brother. She slowly turned her eyes to Jeff, who looked down at her with a mixture of relief and love. Suddenly Sara could feel the door to the void in which she'd lived for the past years had been flung open, and the emptiness that had been there rushing away like a gust of wind.

"Oh, Jeff!" she cried, burying her face in his shoulder. "It's over! It's finally over!"

14

"**Y**ou don't know how much excitement this is going to cause," said Millie as she poured out tea, first for Emily, then for Ransom. Millie had been just returning home from the carol service when Ransom called her at Emily's insistence. Emily felt quite strongly that Sara would be in need of a familiar female presence after her ordeal, and Millie was, if anything, a completely comfortable choice. As she fixed two more cups of tea on a tray she added, "To think that after all this time, Jeff goes and nabs the killer!"

Ransom paused for barely a second in the process of lifting the cup to his lips. Without a word he took a sip.

"And I can't tell you how glad people are gonna be that it was an outsider!"

"Indeed," said Ransom flatly.

Oblivious to his tone, Millie lifted the tray and hurried out of the kitchen. "Be right back!"

"Now, Jeremy," said Emily with such overt amusement that Ransom had to fight to keep his cheeks from turning red, "you said yourself that it doesn't matter who is responsible for catching a murderer as long as the murderer is caught. And we all know who's responsible for solving this case."

"Yes, we do," he replied, eyeing her significantly, "and I can't take any of the credit. You were ahead of me all the way. You were the one who put it together."

"Well," said Emily, blushing with Victorian modesty, "I can't really take the credit, either. Most of that goes to Myrtle Girdler."

"What?" Ransom exclaimed, dropping his cup onto its saucer with such a clatter that he was moved to quickly inspect it for damage. "I hope you're joking. Just because she told us there was another son? We could've found that out easily enough."

"Perhaps. But she was also the one who told us of David Bartlett's propensity for marrying himself out of financial difficulties. It was like I said before, children have a tendency to turn out like their parents, for better or for worse. Nathan and Sara were raised by their mother, who was a practical woman most likely made even more practical by the experience of being married to their father, who was her polar opposite. I daresay that Gina Bartlett's anxiety over the fate of her and her children's money was not just for their benefit, but for their father's as well. I'm sure she believed that the only thing that would ever straighten him out was for him to have to make his own way. Johnnie Larkin, or Johnnie Bartlett as I presume we'll have to think of him from now on, was raised by their father, and so became like him. I suppose, in a way, Johnnie was even lazier than his father. Instead of relying on trial and error for finding a woman with money to marry, he went to a woman he knew to have some, ignoring the social implications involved in marrying his half sister." Emily gave a little shudder and took a sip of tea. "I'm afraid Johnnie doesn't have much in the way of moral sense."

Ransom had to smile at her gift for understatement. It was so like Emily to look at the lesser transgression as a true sign of a murderer's mettle, not that she would ever discount the seriousness of murder.

"Anyway," Emily continued, "the knowledge of their father's character, coupled with the show Johnnie made of being devoted to Sara and the little scene I witnessed in the kitchen earlier is what put the idea into my head."

Millie bustled back into the kitchen carrying the now-empty tray and smiling broadly. "What a Christmas this is gonna be!" she said as she ran some water over the tray. She gave it a light scrub with the dishrag, then grabbed up a towel and proceeded to dry it. "I just wish I knew how anyone knew that Johnnie would try to kill Sara tonight!"

"We didn't, really," Emily explained, "we were just taking a chance that he might. Sara made her feelings quite plain to Johnnie yesterday where he was concerned, so it must've been obvious to him that his plan had failed. And you must remember he'd put a great deal of time and energy into his little plan— probably more energy than he'd ever expended on anything before. And here was Sara telling him not only that she was not interested in him, but that she planned to return to Chicago with Jeremy and myself. That didn't leave him a lot of opportunity. He could, I suppose, have followed her to Chicago and either tried to pursue her there, or murder her, but that would have been far too risky a proposition. It's more than likely that following her there he would be noticed. Here was a last golden opportunity to finish what he'd started before she had a chance to get away, and we provided further opportunity by leaving her 'alone' in the house."

"But she had a will and everything!" Millie protested. "What good would killing her have done?"

Emily replied, "I'm afraid that Johnnie Bartlett is a very, very foolish young man. I don't think he had any concrete plan in mind when he came here. He knew that Nathan and Sara had money, but not how it was entailed. He soon found that they had wills . . . I don't know how. . . ." Emily turned her twinkling eyes on Millie.

Millie wasn't embarrassed enough to blush, but she did choose that moment to turn away to put the tray in a cupboard. "Well, people will talk," she said lightly.

"So Johnnie came up with what he thought was a better plan, to follow in his father's footsteps and simply marry someone who was financially stable. He saw only two obstacles to that. One was that Sara was already interested in Jeff Fields, and, if reports are to be believed, was on the road to marrying him. The other was more serious, and that was that Nathan, quite by accident, had discovered Johnnie's identity. He'd seen a picture of his own father in Johnnie's wallet. Unlike Sara, Nathan had a dim recollection of what his father looked like. So out of curiosity he went to visit Myrtle Girdler, who unfortunately told him not only about his father's subsequent marriages, but also of the existence of another son. Apparently Nathan confronted him about it, and Johnnie killed him. This turned out to be a fortunate move on Johnnie's part, because not only did it give Sara even more money, it all but destroyed the relationship between Sara and Jeff Fields, his rival for her affections."

"But why did he kill Hansen Crane?" Millie asked.

"Well, of course this is only speculation," she said with a mischievous glance at Ransom, "but we think that Nathan was killed shortly after nine o'clock. Crane was adamant about having been asleep at eleven, when Sara came to his door, but he couldn't account for nine. We suspect that he either heard a sound from the barn below or perhaps heard Nathan cry out, and then looked out the window, where he would have seen Johnnie leaving the barn."

"Pure speculation," said Ransom.

Emily nodded. "The double meaning of the word. Crane was blackmailing Johnnie, but could only do so against his future prospects."

"So that's why he stayed around here!" Millie said with satisfaction, as if this had been the bigger mystery troubling her. "And that's why Hansen used to ride Johnnie so badly and Johnnie just took it."

"I assume so," said Emily.

"But why kill him now? So long after the fact?"

Emily turned to Ransom. "I think that was a testament more to your prepossessing demeanor than anything else. Like most basically foolish people, Johnnie had a rather inflated ego, fed in this case by the fact that he had, for all intents and purposes, gotten away with the first murder. That certainly made him feel superior to Jeff Fields. But you were an unknown quantity, and you were asking questions. After you questioned Crane, he went into town ostensibly to buy tobacco."

"He chose to buy tobacco that he didn't need," Ransom explained to Millie, "because the only place to get it nearby was the drugstore, and Johnnie lived above the drugstore, so Hansen could park there and see Johnnie without anyone being any the wiser."

"I suspect that he started pressuring Johnnie to get on with his plan, and Johnnie either didn't like the pressure or was afraid that Crane would somehow give him away. Or it could be that he simply didn't relish the idea of being blackmailed. Few people do, you know. Least of all people who have murdered."

"But why do you call him foolish?" said Millie. "Seems to me Johnnie's been pretty clever."

Emily glanced at Ransom, who returned her smile.

He said, "Well, putting aside the fact that it was stupid of him to think he could get away with murder in the first place, the second murder was very badly planned. In his haste to make sure Crane was dead, he struck too hard, more than once, and didn't know that a trained eye would be able to see the difference between an attack and an accident. But his most foolish act was tonight."

"Though we must remember that he was getting desperate as he saw his plan slipping away."

Ransom gave her a nod of concession as he proceeded, "He was foolish in thinking he could kill Sara and destroy her will. I don't know how he could possibly have thought there would only be one copy."

"He's young," said Emily as she took another sip of tea.

"Well," said Millie, grabbing her coat from the peg by the door, "I'm gonna go home and try to get some sleep, but I don't know how I'm gonna do it! I'm just too keyed up!"

"You're not going to stay here with Sara?" said Emily, raising her eyebrows.

Millie smiled broadly as she slipped her arms into the sleeves of her winter coat. "Oh, no! I think she's in good hands. You just go and see!" She headed out the back door as she added, "I just can't wait to tell people what's happened! They'll be so tickled to know it was an outsider!"

The door closed behind her and Ransom heaved a heavy sigh. "She seems to forget that Sara is an outsider, too."

"Oh, I don't think she will be any more."

"Really?" said Ransom, allowing his right eyebrow to arch.

She nodded. "Now that the truth is known, I think it most likely the locals will feel somewhat ashamed of the way they acted, and will now welcome her as one of their own."

"Trial by fire," said Ransom with disdain.

"Exactly," said Emily, "and now that Sara has the answers she's needed, perhaps she won't hold it against them. Sara is most likely a practical enough young woman to accept their suspicions as a matter of course."

"Hm," said Ransom doubtfully. He wasn't sure he thought that was a good thing.

"The one thing I don't understand . . ."

"There *is* something?" he interjected in a mildly sarcastic tone.

She smiled at him. ". . . is why Johnnie had his affair with Amy Shelton. Since his object was always Sara, I would think the last thing he would've done is risk that."

Ransom looked at her for a moment, unsure of whether or not she was simply tossing him a bone to assuage his pride, but the gaze she returned was so genuine that he proceeded. "Simply a matter of ensuring his safety. Amy was right when she said Johnnie needed to talk after Nathan's murder, but she assumed he could have talked to anyone. What he *really* needed was to talk to her and make sure that Nathan hadn't told her anything of his suspicions.

"Of course!" said Emily brightly. "Of course!"

They finished their tea in silence and then Ransom helped her up from her chair.

"It's after one in the morning," he said. "It's well past time you were getting to bed."

"Jeremy, I can honestly say I haven't felt this good for years. You were quite right, you know, this rest has done me a world of good."

Ransom narrowed his eyes at her. "Emily, I suspect you're having a joke at my expense."

As he led her to the staircase, they noticed a faint light coming from the parlor. Emily held Ransom's arm as they went to the archway, where they stopped and looked in.

Jeff Fields and Sara Bartlett were standing in front of the tree. Jeff had returned to the house after seeing Johnnie safely into a cell at the sheriff's station. They stood with their arms around each other, admiring the tree. To Sara, the lights that had so recently seemed to her little more than a reminder of death now seemed to dance with life on the branches. She rested her head on Jeff's shoulder and sighed as he tightened his arm around her waist.

"I thought you said a sad tale was best for winter," Ransom whispered to Emily.

"Ah, yes," she replied with a benignant smile, "but a happy ending is best for Christmas."